0

THE FURROWS OF INJUSTICE

Part One:
The Benefactor

"It'll be a chance to start over, a chance at redemption," Dorothy said as she waved a small paintbrush to help illustrate her point. "Besides, from what you've told me, you need to get out of town."

"No one is after me," he said. "I'm not that important. Besides, that was a while ago."

"Maybe," Dorothy complied, "but that's not what I meant anyway." She walked behind the counter and opened the cash register. "I don't keep a lot of money on hand," she said as she took out a fist full of bills. "But I could go to the bank and give you whatever you need."

"I know you could, Dottie, but why would you want to do that? Why would you want to do that for me?"

"Because he could use your help, and I would feel so much better if I knew that you were there with him."

"He's always done fine on his own," he declared somewhat defensively. "He's always been very independent." He put his hand on top of hers and gently pushed the money back into the tray. "Besides, have you talked to him about this?" He shrugged his shoulders and gestured with open palms. "Maybe he won't want me along at all."

Dorothy smiled as she closed the cash register. "He knows the situation; he knows the score. He also knows about everything that happened to you and how unfair it was."

"Then he must be aware of how poorly I've handled the whole thing."

"He is," Dorothy responded quickly, "but he hasn't lost that respect he had for you." She clasped his hand and lifted it slowly. "Either have I."

His expression changed from solemn to confused but only for a moment as he looked directly at Dorothy and smiled weakly. "Is this more about me than him?"

"It's about the both of you," she stated with alacrity. "It's the perfect setup. I can help two of my favorite boys." She clasped one hand around the other as if she were holding something precious. "I have been a little over protective. I'll admit that. He should have started this already; and if he doesn't start soon, it will be too late."

"You still haven't answered my question – why are you doing this for me?"

3

"Look around you," Dorothy said calmly. "This isn't a work place, it's a hobby. This place just gives me something to do as I pass the time. Since my husband's death I've always had more money than I knew what to do with, and now – for the first time – I know what to do with it."

"I see," he concluded. "So it's about you."

"Some of it is," she agreed, "and what's wrong with that. I can finally put my money to good use." She hesitated as she searched for the appropriate facial expression to accompany her testimony. "Helping my son and an old friend." She took a deep breath and chose her next words carefully. "He could commute locally and then stay here with me for the rest of his life, but what kind of life would that be. This gives him the chance to strike out on his own."

"Talk to your son, Dottie, and let me know how he feels about it."

"I have," Dorothy said with assertion, "and he's all for it."

He took a deep sigh to convey his compliance, but it was actually relief, which he should have conveyed, because he knew this was something he really wanted – something he desperately needed. "Do we need to sign a contract?"

"Get lost!" she shouted as she threw the paintbrush at his head.

"Still throw like a girl," he quipped as he moved slightly to avoid the projectile.

"Perhaps I should get a gun," she said before laughing uproariously. "A hand shake would be sufficient to seal the deal, but a hug would be better." Their embrace resembled a mother and son or an aunt and a nephew as they held each other for a long time. "Of all the art supply stores you could have walked into, you walked into this one."

"Sounds like a line from *Casablanca*," he said as he gently pushed her away.

"Believe me," Dorothy said, "it wasn't luck; it was destiny."

"Now you're just being silly," he whispered loudly enough for her to hear.

"Maybe just a little, but let's talk more over some dinner."

"Can you leave before six?" he asked almost rhetorically.

"I can do whatever I want," Dorothy said insolently. "I own the place,"

Part 2
The Reporter

He had awoken earlier than usual, or at least he thought he did. That spot in the ceiling looked so familiar that he knew he was home in his own bed and not on some street corner where he was looking up at a piece of hollow sky, trying to collect the broken bits, which always followed one of his drunken stupors.

For a change he knew where he was, not that it made much difference. The walls were bare – almost a symbol of himself – and the carpet was torn and dirty, the bed rumpled, the sheets soiled. As he slithered out of this self-induced mess and drifted toward the kitchen where he would make himself a cup of coffee, he felt a strange pain in his back. He wondered if he had been in a fight the night before, but he couldn't remember. It must have been the lumpy mattress on which he slept. The texture never quite satisfied his bibulous nature, and now each ache had a signature on it. When the water boiled, he prepared the instant brew with the bitter taste, in hopes that it might cure what must surely be a hangover.

The apartment was cold, and he was angry at the lack of heat; but there was little he could do about it since the rent was cheap, and

6

inconveniences like these were to be expected. His one consistent friend meowed and jumped onto the stove where the warmth from the freshly lit burner came as a pleasant relief to the nip in the air.

The weatherman said that it might snow later in the day. His first winter in the North in quite some time, and it might snow. As a child, the thought of snow was always an exciting thing; but now he dreaded the feeling that he would have to travel through the white mess, which should be reserved for skiers in Colorado and not for lonely reporters in New York City.

He finished his coffee and returned to bed where he lay listening to the radio, not sure if he wanted to get up again. The cat crawled on his stomach but quickly rolled off to find a more comfortable place on the bed. He kept staring at that spot in the ceiling, hoping that through some sort of miracle it would change to a place from better times and fonder memories. The ringing of the phone broke his hypnotic state, and he jumped to answer it.

"Hello," he said in a gravelly voice that indicated weariness.

"Hey, Sugar, this is your wake up call. Rise and shine!" An expression from his childhood. He hated it then, and he hated it now. The fatuitous voice on the other end was a reminder that a full day's work was still ahead of him. "Thanks, Lorraine," he answered, not masking his lack of enthusiasm in the slightest. At least his memory was jogged about his previous night. "What time did you leave?" he asked, not really concerned

"Right after you fell asleep. Man were you wasted!"

"Yea, well, I'm paying for it now," he retorted while putting his hand on his forehead.

"So, how about tonight," Lorraine inquired. "Same time," she whimpered, "same price?"

"I doubt it," he said indolently. "I think I'm tapped out in more ways than one, but thanks for the offer." After a terse, impolite comment, the phone went dead.

At least the shower was hot, and the stinging needles of spray felt soothing as they hit his aching muscles; but as he stepped out of the tub, he could feel the cold again. He immediately wrapped himself in a Roman towel and shivered as he tried to brush his teeth. Shaving was even more of a chore since the lighting in the bathroom was very poor, yet somehow he managed to make himself presentable for his job at the newspaper – the world's worst newspaper – in his opinion anyway.

First, there was the long walk to the subway station, and on this windy day he could feel the icy draft clear through to his bones. Then there was the twenty-minute ride on a crowded subway car, to which he never got accustomed. People were always staring – at him, at each other, or at nothing, but the zombie-like expressions never varied; they always remained on something, even if it wasn't there. Occasionally a face with a paranoid grimace would give a furtive stare at reality, hoping that no one else was watching. There was always the frumpish bag lady who offered the world a piece of candy taken from a handout just received an hour earlier and the counterfeit businessman, who tried to take it all in, well aware that no other passengers were paying attention.

The reporter always noticed the newspapers, morning editions, evening editions; it didn't matter. Some had just been purchased; and others had been left on the train the night before, so a morning commuter could fritter away his idle time by reading yesterday's news. *The News*, *The Times*, *The Post*, or *The Journal* – they all printed the same thing; only the arrangement of the words was different.

He arrived at work his usual five minutes late and rushed towards his desk. His boss expected the tardiness but never hesitated to comment on it. "Well, I see that we're prompt as usual," he said with acrimony.

"I'm sorry," the reporter answered, not sorry at all.

"Don't hand me, 'I'm sorry'; this is an everyday thing with you, and I want it stopped!" he yelled despairingly.

"I can't be responsible for the weather and for slow trains." He began to walk away, ignoring his adversary totally but hesitated and then gazed at him with an almost salacious smile.

"Knock it off!" the boss said. "The weather has nothing to do with it. It's the same thing that it always is – booze. Do you think that people around here are stupid, that they don't know what you do the second you leave this office?"

The reporter always took offense when someone criticized his convivial spirit. Like a body that had performed this job for decades instead of months, he blurted, "My work is always done, on time, and properly." The boss began to tremble; but the reporter looked at him, realized how red in the face he had become, and made a pacifying gesture. Forced deadlines and outside pressures had given him the gray hair and facial wrinkles of a person in his sixties, a good twenty years more than his actual age. "Don't get too excited," the reporter said as he moved his hand to the boss's shoulder. "You might have a stroke. And besides, what I do when I leave here is my business."

"That's right," the boss declared while knocking the reporter's hand from his shoulder. "But when you come to work late, even if it's only one second late, then it is my business." He put his finger right in the reporter's face. "Do you understand?" There was no answer. "I said, 'Do you understand?'" he repeated more loudly.

"Yea, I understand," the reporter replied suppressing his own petulance.

"Now, listen up, hot shot. I've got a special assignment for you – a real schmuck job."

"That figures," the reporter warbled with disgust.

"You're damn right it figures. Now you listen, and listen good. I want you to take a cab to that private airport and wait for a special plane to arrive. When it does, I want you to get all the information you can on Jimmy Valentine and some crazy business that he now owns."

11

The reporter laughed. "That's no job for a sports writer. Why can't I do some background for Sunday's game with the Bills?"

"Because nobody knows you, and if they did, they probably wouldn't like you very much."

"No one cares about that stuff," the reporter interrupted. "We have the reigning champs for football and baseball, a team that's on the verge of making the playoffs, and a basketball team that's got the whole city hopping. There's so much out there to cover, and you stick me with high school sports or some nonsense that doesn't even register as human interest pap."

"You were hired by this paper because you came recommended by an old friend of somebody, but teaching kids how to put one foot in front of another doesn't qualify you to be a sports writer." He used his hand and signaled the reporter to be quiet. "And I don't want to hear about all those writing courses you took in college. It takes more than writing skills and more than a good head for sports."

"If you don't give me any decent assignments," the reporter pled shamelessly, "how can you possibly know what I'm capable of doing?"

"Just consider yourself lucky to have a job at all," the boss retorted. He started to walk away but stopped, faced the reporter, and handed him a piece of paper. "Here's the information we have already. Now, get out to the airport and earn your pay."

"I'm sure that there's no immediate deadline for this," the reporter said with condescension, "since it's unlikely that something this trivial will ever make the front page."

"Go," the boss demanded as he walked away and never looked back again.

"I think it sucks the way he treats you," a young voice said, just loud enough to get the reporter's attention.

"Don't worry about it, Tommy," the reporter said to someone who was just a few years younger than he was. "This isn't my first career choice, so I have some adjusting to do; and maybe the booze helps me get through it."

"It still doesn't give him the right to act the way he does."

"He's probably right," the reporter lamented. "I do drink too much." He smiled. "The college sent you over here because this *is* your career choice, so pay attention to everything: the good and the bad and you'll leave a better person. You might even land a job at this establishment."

"With college loans and all that other crap, I'll take whatever job I can get," Tommy said with compliance.

"I hear ya," the reporter said. "Keep going the way you are, and you'll be fine." He picked up a few things from his desk. "If I can ever throw a bone in your direction, I will."

"That would be appreciated," Tommy said.

The reporter nodded, then ran out the exit and returned to the frigid atmosphere from which he had just come; and on his third attempt he was able to flag a cab. The stop and go ride made it hard to read, but he was able to decipher the almost illegible scrawl and figure out the necessary information from the faded piece of notepaper that sat upon his lap. "Can't even give me a typed written statement," he muttered to himself. The information was simple but not the least bit interesting. A former boxer was coming home, a heavyweight whose greatest accomplishment was going the distance with the champion and then losing several unanimous decisions in the years that followed to a number of less than worthy opponents –

a boxer who had lost most of his money and his urge to fight as he grew older.

He was coming home but not a defeated shell of a person who spoke with a heavy tongue and wore layers of scar tissue and bumps on the scalp but a man who was wealthy. The purchase of some stock in a company believed to be worthless had somehow become profitable and turned the pugnacious mauler into an instant millionaire. He was the majority stockholder of a new industry that seemingly produced many a girl's best friend. A wife from Thailand, who was a former beauty queen, and his own private plane now made him something special – but not to the reporter. He just crumpled the paper and threw it out the window as the cab stopped for a red light and a parade of jaywalkers. His attempt to hit the litter basket had failed, so he watched as the paper bounced along the gutter where it mixed with the other garbage that accumulated by the sewer drains and street corners. "You can get fined for that," the driver said as he too noticed the discarded litter.

"Take it up with Mayor Lindsay," the reporter fired back as he repositioned and attempted to make himself more comfortable. The rest of the trip was even less eventful.

He arrived at his destination in under an hour where he waited for almost two more before the plane finally arrived. Valentine's newfound wealth had obviously gone to his head since flying on anything other than a private jet just didn't make it anymore. For years, this somewhat exclusive airport had been the landing stop for cargo planes, but businesses had taken their wares across the river, leaving a huge empty space. However, rather than allowing it to become a parking lot or an urban renewal project, a group of well-to-do dignitaries – who hated the hustle and bustle of a common airport – purchased the property in order to insure their privacy and convenience. The old buildings that seemed to hover in the background acted as a constant reminder that at one time, machine parts and crated goods were unloaded here rather than egotistical V.I.P.'s.

All the other reporters who had been given this dull assignment trudged out to the passenger ramp and fired off some meaningless questions at the plane's prestigious passenger. They asked him how long he would be in New York and who sold him the stock and even if he wanted to get into the ring again. Valentine put his hands in the air as if he were quieting a mob and stated, "No comment."

No comment indeed, thought the reporter. On what was there to comment? No one really cared about Valentine's purchase or anything else to do with his history – in or out of the ring. The only pleasant feature of the entire escapade was Valentine's wife, who clung by his side and looked as radiant as she did the night of the Miss Universe pageant.

The day was going just as the reporter had expected when suddenly his train of thought was broken by a loud bang. A shot had been fired, and the bullet hit the passenger rail. Alertly, Valentine pushed his wife down while three men from the prizefighter's exaggerated entourage ran and covered him from another possible shot. Valentine and his wife were hurried back into the plane, and the three apparent bodyguards blocked anyone else's entrance.

The reporter could not understand why anybody would want to "assassinate" a Palooka like Valentine; but a story, which originally generated less interest than a local flower show, now had some legs to it. The reporter looked in the direction where he thought the shot might have been fired and saw a few policemen, who had been on the scene, scurrying toward an old warehouse that stood just outside the far end of the runway. Rather than wonder why there had been

17

any policemen on the site at all, the reporter managed to slip through the modest crowd and run towards the main gate at the far end of the field. When he reached it, he noticed one cop who had spent an evening or two tilting shot glasses in the same tavern as he. "What the hell is going on?" the reporter yelled to the patrolman.

The officer turned his head and smiled. He could only disguise his over-the-hill status so well. A hat concealed his baldness, but the rotund body simply forced its way through a uniform that may have fit ten years or twenty pounds earlier in his life. "Who knows? I see they assigned you to cover this bullshit too. "Did you tick off your editor again?"

"Naturally," the reporter answered. "Otherwise, I'd be out interviewing the Broadway man about Sunday's game."

"Yea right," the officer said sarcastically. "How'd you manage to get over here?"

"I slipped away," the reporter acknowledged. "You know how good I am at that."

"Sure," the patrolman responded, "but aren't bedrooms or bar tabs more your style?"

"Cute," the reporter said without changing his expression. "Say, Jack, how about doing an old drinking buddy a favor."

"That depends on what it is," Jack said cautiously. "You want to borrow some money?"

"No, I'm serious," the reporter said somewhat querulously. "How about letting me go with you and the other cop to that warehouse over there."

Jack put his hand to his chin, "I don't know. You'll probably get in the way, and you might get hurt.

"Jack," the reporter pleaded, "this may not be the story of the century, but it's better than anything I'll ever get to do." The reporter put his arms out to enhance his plea and then started to make drinking motions with a cupped hand. "The first round'll be on me the next time we get together; for nothing more than letting me get a little insight as to why somebody played Lee Harvey Oswald to Jimmy-boy's President Kennedy."

Jack laughed. "Bribery is a crime; but you make it the first two rounds, and you got a deal."

"A deal it is," the reporter responded as he hustled through the gate and joined the two cops as they headed for the abandoned building. The warehouse had been deserted for years and was left standing for no apparent reason, except perhaps to act as some sort of shrine to the airport's elite, now that ghettoes were not that far away. All its windows were broken, and the plaster on the inside walls was chipping off. There were puddles of stagnant water, too polluted to freeze in the sub-thirty weather, and the only color that seemed to exist was a tired buff.

"Kinda looks like your apartment; doesn't it," Jack said priggishly.

The reporter didn't answer, and the two kept walking until they heard a shout from the floor above. It came from the other officer who had gone ahead. "We've got a gun!" he yelled.

"Let's go to the next floor," the reporter deadpanned, "and take a look." They both hurried to the higher flight, the reporter with alacrity in his step and Jack with fatigue in his. There they saw Jack's younger partner examining a high-powered rifle. He was handling it very carefully so no fingerprints would be smeared and seemed to pay no attention to Jack's unauthorized guest.

"Whatcha think, college boy?" Jack was sure to direct his question to the young peace officer, whom he obviously resented for

20

having gotten a higher education that he had. The reporter was tempted to answer as a reminder that he too had attended a university, but remained quiet to keep things simple. "I don't know, Jack," the young officer responded. "I've already sent word for them to send a fingerprint man out here. There might be prints around the area as well as on the gun."

"Do you really think it will be worth the bother?" Jack asked noncommittally.

"Yes," the reporter interjected quickly. "There may be more to this than you think."

"Who are you?" the young officer asked, now aware that he and his partner had company.

"He's a friend of mine," Jack responded quickly. "He's okay."

"I doubt this was a professional job," Jack's partner surmised while looking out the window. From this distance, a real pro would have put Valentine down with no problem. Especially with a gun like this." He pointed to the scope on the rifle. "No, gentlemen," he said with a slight cockiness, "this was done by an amateur."

"Why didn't he take the gun with him?" the reporter asked with skepticism directed towards the patrolman's conclusion.

"It's obvious," the patrolman returned. "The serial number's been filed off, and I'll bet we don't find any fingerprints on it when our guy gets here with the kit." He gently lifted the weapon and displayed it carefully. "The sniper was probably wearing gloves rather than taking the time to wipe it clean after the shot. To me, it looks like a case of panic. That's why I'm so sure that the guy wasn't a pro." He placed the rifle in an upright position against a broken down wall. "Who knows; maybe he was afraid that someone would spot him with the gun later on. Who the hell knows with these idiots?"

"So tell us, Sherlock. How'd he get away so fast?" Jack's question indicated more disgust with his overachieving accomplice than a desire for information.

"I'll bet we find some tracks leading to a service road where he had a car waiting," the officer replied, unaware that neither Jack nor the reporter had any real interest.

"Do you think he worked alone," the reporter inquired, getting in on the act now as well.

"Could have," the cop answered, still not aware that he was being played, "but it's not real difficult to get into a car and get back on the main road from here. Besides," he added, "from where most of us were standing, you can't see a person leaving down that road."

"Then why didn't he take the gun if no one could see him?" the reporter asked waggishly. "Those things are pretty damn expensive."

"Maybe he's trying to throw us off. Besides, it's probably stolen." the young peace officer said with sincere optimism.

"I think this guy's onto something," the reporter said in a thinly disguised attempt to make this a bigger story than it actually was. "Jack, you should be proud of this boy."

"Fuck the both of you," Jack spat out. "Let's see what the suits have to say."

As expected, there were no prints on the gun; but there were a few tracks that led to the service road. The only thing of interest was a watch with the initials R.G. engraved on the back. It wasn't determined whether this was a useful clue or not, but it was agreed that this detail should be left out of the papers. "No problem," the reporter said as he shrugged his shoulders in compliance.

As they left the building and started for their respective forms of transportation, the reporter pulled Jack aside. "The kid was right about a lot of stuff, but it could still be a professional hit."

"He doesn't know," Jack said trying to stifle a yawn. "He likes to blow smoke. Makes him look important to the suits."

"Could be a pro trying to make it look like an amateur," the reporter declared.

"That's what I thought," Jack agreed. "I just don't know what's behind it. You can be damn sure that it has something to do with Jimbo's new opulence."

"Opulence," the reporter said with false admiration. "How'd you come up with that word?"

"I looked up *wealth* in my thesaurus," Jack replied, well aware of the reporter's mockery.

"It doesn't take a detective to figure that this had something to do with opulence," the reporter quipped somewhat frivolously.

"I know," Jack said with a deep sigh. "Maybe that's why I'm still a patrolman."

They both laughed as they walked away.

***

The reporter made it back to his office just in time to type up his story for the earlier edition. As he removed the piece out of the typewriter, the boss walked over, politely took it from him, and read carefully. "Not bad, ace," he growled, practically chewing his cigarette.

"Not a single person in this city could give a damn about Valentine," the reporter stated bluntly, "but somebody takes a shot at him, and he becomes newsworthy."

"Well, it's not front page news, but it's still interesting. Why don't you follow it up? You never can tell what you might uncover.

"Sure thing," the reporter said with mock enthusiasm, "I'll get right on it. He left the office and spent the rest of the afternoon at his favorite pub where he could run up a tab and play darts. His shoes clicked with each lift from the tacky floor as he set himself to prepare for a bull's-eye, and his hand took up residence in a large bowl of pretzels until it satiated his hunger. When darts became boring, he traded stories and matched beers with the other local bar flies, who knew every quarterback's statistics and the winning score for each successful franchise from the Sunday before. By the time he left; Jimmy Valentine, the newspaper he worked for, and all of New York itself were just a blur.

Somehow, he managed to get home where he nodded out until eight o'clock. When he finally woke up, he was hungry, but there was no food in the house except for instant coffee and cat chow, so he walked across the street to a deli and ordered a roast beef sandwich. While biting down on his evening meal, a rather bizarre idea came to him. Since he had nothing else to do, he decided to act like the diligent reporter he had no desire to become. His previous background work showed Valentine's current residence at the penthouse suite at the Clermont. Naturally, the reporter thought, only the best for the Nuevo rich. Security – Valentine's personal security – would definitely be beefed up, which made entrance to the boxer's new headquarters a big problem. However, if a certain patrolman – who had even less ambition than he did – was spending time at home on his night off, there could be a solution to this problem.

"Hello, Jack," the reporter said with banalities, which camouflaged his delight that the off duty cop had not gone out for the evening. "I owe you two rounds, remember?" The reporter was trying to stop a case of the hiccoughs he had picked up by eating too fast. "How about meeting me down at Tony's so I can pay off?"

"Wait a minute," Jack said with skepticism in his voice. "When you call and remind me that you owe me a round or two, you want something else." He hesitated and then swallowed. "What is it?"

The reporter laughed. "Just get down to Tony's, and we can discuss it over a few tonics and gin.

"Ten minutes," Jack snarled before he abruptly hung up.

The reporter's one friend on the force of New York's finest rolled his corpulent figure into the tavern sooner than expected and planted his slightly overused frame in a booth just big enough for the two of them. The first round was ordered and then the second. After four rounds, the reporter was ready to explain his proposition in hopes of putting his plan into operation. "Who's working the chopper port tonight?" he inquired with a sudden outburst.

His drinking buddy looked up from the spirits he had been so graciously engulfing, and with more than a somnolent look in his eyes asked, "Whataya doing now – weather reports? What the fuck do you want with the chopper?" His words were almost a slur.

"I thought that maybe I could get a lift," the reported answered nonchalantly. He waited for a response, but Jack just kept gawking at him, bewildered more than angry.

"A lift!" he finally screamed. He pushed a dollar bill toward the reporter. "Here's a buck; take the fucking subway."

"Jack, listen to me," the reporter said as he pointed to the ceiling. "There's only one way to get to Valentine's penthouse suite, and that's to drop in on him from the sky." Jack was laughing out loud now, so much that he began to cough. He put his finger on the top of the reporter's glass and pulled it forward to examine the contents.

"What'd they put in your drink?" he asked as he craned his neck and studied the bottom of the container.

The reporter took it back, pushed it to the side and placed his hands flat on the table. "Come on," he said with his hands now resting on their sides. "After this morning, you know that a bodyguard or two will be blocking all entrances. Besides, you have to have a special key or something to get the elevator to go that far."

"Why are you trying to make a big deal about this stupid thing anyway? No one really gives a shit that somebody tried to drill

Valentine. You're no better than that young detective who thought he was Sherlock Holmes."

"Guilty as charged," the reporter conceded, "but this will give me something to do if nothing else. Besides, my boss wants me to follow up on this."

"He's a bigger asshole than you," Jack blurted with contempt. "You're hoping to make something out of this and cash in on it – you and your boss."

"So what if I am," the reporter concurred. "You'd be doing the same thing if you were in my position."

"You know, there's a better than average chance that you might be the only reporter who even tries to see this bum. You might be able to just walk right in – unmolested."

"Sure, Jack," the reporter said sarcastically. "I'm the only reporter in the city down on his luck looking for a story with a boss looking for a decent copy."

"Not everybody works for that rag you work for, and I don't know anybody who even reads the fucking thing."

"Touché," the reporter said humbly. "All the more reason that I need to get a story."

"Why don't you just lie your way in," Jack asked sardonically. "Tell them you're the mayor or maybe even the President."

"From the top, Jack. It's the only way."

"I think you have a huge flair for the dramatic," Jack countered. "That's what I really think."

The reporter paid no attention to Jack's remark and repeated, "From the top, Jack, from the top."

Jack just shook his head in disbelief. "I let a guy follow me to some old warehouse," he said while looking down into the table. "That's bad enough, and now he wants me to steal a helicopter."

"Not steal," the reporter corrected him.

"Not steal," Jack mimicked, using a different voice, "I know, just borrow." He lifted his glass and looked beyond the reporter till he spotted the waitress and signaled for another drink. "Two," he ordered when she acknowledged his request, "and one for my friend here." He searched his thoughts for a moment and tapped his fist on the table to clear his head. "Let's have our other drinks and talk about this. About how long are we looking at?" he asked with defeatism.

"As long as it takes to get me there," the reporter responded immediately, hoping to assuage his companion's fears. "You only have to get me in, not out."

Jack looked up. "Of all the reporters in town, I gotta be friends with one who wants to drop from the sky."

Fresh drinks arrived, and both men continued imbibing. "There's a guy who does a surveillance run in about two hours," Jack said reluctantly, "and he gets pretty close to that stupid penthouse. He might be able to give you a drop."

"Two hours makes it close to midnight," the reporter said with slight concern.

"It's the best we can do," Jack said, hardly apologizing. "And don't be surprised if he just throws you out of the chopper."

"Okay. Do you think this guy will do this for us?" the reporter asked eagerly.

"Well, it certainly is up to him," Jack responded.

"I realize that," the reporter apperceived, "but will he do it if you ask him?"

"If I ask him, he'll probably tell me to go to hell." Then Jack smiled, took a sip from his drink, and increased his grin. "But if I con him, bribe him, blackmail him, or make a deal with him…" He lifted his glass, "If we succeed, you owe me a month's worth of drinks."

"The way you fucking drink," whined the reporter, "no fucking way."

Jack laughed, well aware that his demand was unreasonable even by *his* standards. "How about we make it dinner for a week?"

"The way …"

"If you say the way I fucking eat," interrupted Jack, "I'll brain you."

"I doubt that Valentine is worth a week's worth of dinners…"

"At a decent restaurant," Jack again interrupted, "at a decent restaurant – not some sleazy dive."

"Fine," the reporter consented. "I'm so desperate for a story – it's a deal."

"But let me tell you something, all kidding aside," Jack said seriously. "Valentine may have goons sitting on the roof. Shoot your ass."

"That's a chance I'm willing to take," the reporter said with complete lack of apprehension. "I don't think that even Valentine would go to those extremes."

"You better hope not," Jack said while revealing a sly grin. "But if anything does happen, I'll toast you at the wake." He then proceeded to lift his glass higher than before.

"I think I'll be all right," the reporter declared with confidence.

"Yea, you're probably right," Jack agreed. "He'd never expect a nut like you to drop from the sky."

"To success," the reporter stated in a mock toast.

"Are you sober enough?" Jack asked as he pointed to the reporter's empty glass.

"The reporter shook his head and laughed loudly. "The question should be, 'am I drunk enough?'" he said. "Am I drunk enough?"

"Okay," Jack said, having difficulty with his speech now. "It's your funeral, but we'll give it a shot." He finished his drink and staggered to the door with the reporter by his side, both believing that the outrageous plan could actually be put into operation.

***

Jack suffered from vertigo when he got too high up, so helicopter trips were not his idea of a good time; but he went along for the ride out of curiosity and to keep the reporter company. The pilot of the chopper had not succumbed to conniving, bribes, or deals; but threats were more than he could handle. As he and Jack both watched the reporter shimmy down the fragile rope ladder, narrowly missing the lightning rods, which extended from the upper wall surrounding the artificially turfed patio of the penthouse; he was assured that his wife would never know of his whereabouts two Friday nights ago.

As the reporter suspected, no one was watching or paying attention to the outside; therefore, he was able to sneak inside untouched. He walked very slowly until he came to a huge den where he spotted Valentine sitting in a large comfortable chair. When Valentine became aware of the reporter's presence, he immediately moved his hulkish body out of the seat and jumped up to confront him. "How the hell did you get in here!" he yelled as he balled up his fists.

"There's no need to get excited," the reporter said calmly. He noticed a copy of the paper sitting on the coffee table, so cautiously he picked it up and made certain that Valentine could see it. "I'm a reporter," he said after taking a deep swallow. "I work for this newspaper, and I'm the one who wrote today's article about you."

Valentine's expression didn't change. "That doesn't answer my question. How did you get in here?" His voice suddenly grew louder and displayed more anger. "I had the whole area surrounded!"

"Not quite," the reporter said somewhat belligerently.

"I'll ask you again," Valentine said very slowly and deliberately. "How did you get in?"

"I recommend that you station some guards on the patio," the reporter stated with conviction.
"I have friends in high places, and there might be others with the same connection."

"Oh, that's cute!" Valentine bellowed. "You're really cute!" He reached out and grabbed the reporter by the collar of his coat. "Well, maybe you got in here unharmed, but you're not leaving in one piece unless I get some answers and I get them fast!" Suddenly two armed men came running into the room. Each one had his gun out, prepared to fire, but Valentine waved them off. "He's not armed fellas. I can handle this myself. One of you go out front and the other out on the patio." They both gave each other puzzled looks. "That's what I said. On the patio." They both nodded and each went to his selected position.

"You can let me go, Mr. Valentine. I'm no threat to your security. I really am a reporter." He worked his hand to his pants pocket and produced his wallet. "In here you'll find my press card and some corresponding identification."

Valentine released his grip and took the wallet. He found what he needed to see and handed everything back to reporter. "So you really are the guy who wrote the story in today's paper," he said affably. "I still don't like the way you snuck in here, but I'll give you credit for having guts." He tugged at the lapels of his sports jacket, and picked up a copy of the newspaper. He flipped through the pages till he reached the article concerning his arrival and the accompanying incident at the airport. "Ten years ago this would have been a fucking headline," he grunted as he threw the paper down in disgust.

"I have nothing to do with what page my articles appear on," the reporter said apologetically.

"I know that," Valentine said. "Besides, it was a pretty good article."

"Especially for a sports writer," the reporter said with a cynical tone.

"What was that?" Valentine snapped.

"Nothing," the reporter sighed. "I don't usually do that kind of work is all." He paused. "I'm on – let's say – special assignment."

"Well, it's a good article, kid. There's some stuff in there that the other papers didn't have. I read them all, and I must admit, yours was the best. How'd you get all that inside stuff?"

"I have a friend on the police force."

Valentine shook his hand and walked to the liquor cabinet where he poured himself a drink. "Get you one?" he asked as he pointed to a half-empty bottle.

"Scotch," the reporter replied without hesitating, "on the rocks."

"Very well," Valentine hummed. "Scotch on the rocks it is." He reached into the cabinet and produced another bottle. "I'll have to go to the fridge in the kitchen and get some ice."

"Don't bother," the reporter said. "It's fine like it is."

"Suit yourself," Valentine chirped as he handed the reporter his drink. The reporter received it and bowed his head in lieu of a spoken thank-you. Valentine pointed to a sofa. "Have a seat." The reporter seated himself, took a sip from his drink, and then placed it atop the coaster, which was resting on the small end table to the right of the sofa. "So," Valentine stated casually, "you have friends on the police force. That must be how you got here – a police helicopter." The reporter nodded to indicate that Valentine's perception was accurate. Valentine was still standing and looking down at the reporter. His drink was in his right hand as he used his left hand to emphasize his words. "Is that supposed to impress me!" he nearly shouted. "That you're friends with the police?" A quick gulp from his glass and then he put it next to the bottle on top of the cabinet. "I got no respect for the police. Every cop in this city is on the fucking take!" he exclaimed with his arms flailing in both directions. "On the fucking take or fucking stupid for not being so!" He turned toward the cabinet, picked up his drink, drained the glass in one gulp, and quickly prepared himself another.

The reporter took a sip from his own drink and calmly remarked, "Mr. Valentine, your assessment of our city's finest doesn't matter to me. Who's trying to kill you – or scare you – does."

"No one scares me, kid. You remember that," he said while pointing his finger. "No one scares me." He took a deep draw on his fresh drink, wiped some excess moisture from his mouth, and then put his glass down again. "I wasn't afraid of anyone when I was in the ring, and I'm not afraid of anyone now."

The reporter smiled, almost laughed as he finished his drink. He took a good look at Valentine for the first time, noticing his massive hands, each finger huge and menacing as he waved them in anger. His neck was bulky, and his shoulders and forearms, although slightly battered from the years of punishment, still had that rock hard rigidness. The reporter believed him when he said he wasn't afraid of anybody, but there was more to it as far as the reporter was concerned. Valentine's sudden outburst in regards to the police force had him slightly confused yet curious enough to want to find out why. "Mr. Valentine, you don't have to throw your swaggering might around me. I've seen you fight, and in the ring, courage was one thing you truly possessed. I know that if you could face your adversary, there'd be no problem. But level with me. This whole thing, it is frightening, and it does scare you."

"All right," Valentine said with calm exasperation. "It does scare me. Whenever you can't see your opponent, it has to be a little scary. But I'm not just concerned about my own well- being. The fucker, who tried to nail me, could have hit my wife."

"I understand," the reporter complied. "It's always difficult when someone innocent is put in harm's way."

"You bet," Valentine snorted. "She's done nothing wrong."

"I'm sure that you'd agree with me that your new found fortune has something to do with this," the reporter implied politely.

"The company," Valentine agreed. "It might have something to do with the company, but I can't see how."

"Before we go any further," the reporter interrupted, "could we talk a little about your company? I don't know that much about it since you haven't told anybody anything."

"What's to tell," Valentine said as he paced the floor. "I bought some stock. Bought it for next to nothing, and it hits, pays off big." He walked to the liquor cabinet and picked up the bottle of Scotch. "You want another?" he asked as he pointed to the reporter's empty glass. The reporter nodded and handed him his glass to be refilled. "Let me get you some ice this time," Valentine insisted as he trotted to the kitchen before the reporter could lodge a protest. When he returned with the ice-filled tumbler, he grabbed the bottle and hurriedly poured the Scotch over them. "This is good stuff," he claimed. "Aged to perfection. I don't drink it much, never really cared for Scotch; but I know good stuff when I see it." He waved his arm like a magic wand over his living quarters. "I had all of this waiting for me before I ever got here. It's the best; everything is the best you can get."

The reporter nodded in agreement as he received his libation from the pugilistic giant. "Was anyone hurt in the transaction?" he asked.

"In what way?" Valentine inquired defensively.

"You know, anybody get ripped off or stepped on or perhaps squeezed out?" He pushed his hands together to emphasize his last comment.

"No," Valentine replied, "nobody that I know about; and besides, killing me wouldn't help anyone."

"You got a will," the reporter asked, "or life insurance policies."

"I don't think I like what you're implying." Valentine's voice acquired a nasty tone as he plopped his drink down very aggressively. "Get out of here," he said in a threatening manner as he pointed to the door. "Better yet, why don't you go out the same way you came in?"

"I'm sorry," the reporter apologized. "I didn't mean to imply anything. I'll leave, but there is one thing I'd like to talk about before I go. I know that the police have told you a few things that didn't make the papers."

"I know as much as you know," Valentine said with disgust, "no more."

"I happen to know a few things that the other journalists were not privy to," the reporter rejoined. "Remember," he said arrogantly, "I have friends on the force."

"I don't know what you're talking about," Valentine retorted. His words were crisp and staccato as if fired from a pistol, but they lacked any sincerity at all; and the reporter knew this.

"Look, Mr. Valentine," the reporter said calmly, "anything you say to me is off the record." He crossed his heart. "On my honor."

"All right," Valentine agreed reluctantly. "Tell me what you know."

"The watch," the reporter replied with authority.

"So you do know a bit more than the others," Valentine conceded. "And like a good boy, you've kept your mouth shut." He smiled and then quickly stated, "Until now."

"Until now," the reporter agreed. "Have you seen it?"

"No, the police told me about it, but they said they need it as evidence, and I'll get to look at it later." Valentine was calmer now, almost bored, and the reporter knew that he would have to ease into the next area of conversation.

"Do the initials R.G. ring a bell?" the reporter asked as if he already knew the answer. Valentine did not respond at all since he was sure that the reporter would answer the question for him. He moved his hands motioning the reporter to continue. "How about Robert Gregory?" The reporter knew the connection, for he had read the articles and seen the telecasts; therefore, he remembered the name and how it fit into Valentine's past. "Those initials were on the back of that watch."

Valentine laughed. "Fixing fights is more his line, not murder. Besides, he's in jail. My testimony sent him up, and he's still got time to do."

"He would certainly have a motive," the reporter added as an afterthought.

"That he would," Valentine agreed, "but he's locked up. And even if he was loose, I don't think that chicken-shit little coward would ever come near me – armed or otherwise."

The reporter leaned back on the sofa and drained his glass. "Well, Mr. Valentine, there's not too much more we can talk about, so I guess I'll be on my way." He stood up and politely stated, "Give my best to your lovely wife."

"Yea, she's at the opera," Valentine quipped with snobbish tones. "Besides, my brother's stopping over, so you're right; you should leave."

The reporter glanced at his watch and snapped with surprise, "Your brother!"

"Yea, we got a lot to talk about."

"Is he in some kind of trouble?" the reporter asked indignantly.

"None of your business!" Valentine shouted. "Now get out of here before I really make you leave the way you came." He escorted the reporter to the front door where two bodyguards were waiting. First, he instructed one to go to the balcony and further insure that no one else had paid him a surprise visit. Then, he told the other to help the reporter on his way.

After leaving the building, the reporter waited patiently till both Valentine's wife and his brother arrived. "The hours some people keep," he said loud enough to get a few confused stares from some curious onlookers. Rather than return to his modest dwellings and sleep off what too much alcohol had produced, he decided to walk a little and let the night air clear his head. He hadn't gone far when he was approached by a lady of the night who blocked his path and refused to let him walk around her. "Hey, Blondie," she squealed while giving him an overall view of what she had to offer. "You look hungry; maybe I can feed you what you need."

The reporter smiled and took her hand in his. "The menu looks good," he said cheerfully, "but I doubt that I can afford the price." He hesitated, waved his other hand as if draping the territory, and then politely continued, "I don't live in this neighborhood; I was just visiting a sick friend."

"Baby," she stammered, "I'm way out of my usual region, but – believe it or not – I ain't looking for some rich guy – just somebody that will be nice to me." He dropped her hand gently and then gave her a long, puzzled look. "I'm hurting, you know," she stammered even more profusely than before. "I just want someone who can pay the cook. You break open your piggy bank, and you can help me out."

The reporter smiled again and then locked his arm with hers. "All right," he whispered, "I imagine we can work something out." They stumbled to the closest subway and then back to the squalor of his apartment, where together, they satisfied each other's needs. It was more than necessary yet never quite enough. She was different from the others, wanting more than just money, wanting much more; and she made him feel better than adequate. They took their time and made it last, made it last for a very long time, which almost made it right. By the time she left, both were completely gratified since the long-range needs were not as important as the immediate one; and for the first time in a long while, he felt content – if not with himself then with the world around him.

***

The slight pangs of a hangover and the fatigue of an exhausting escapade made the day a dreary mess; but fortunately, it was his day off, and a much-needed rest should have been the number one priority on his agenda. However, his curiosity had been aroused, and the first thing he did after a breakfast of stale doughnuts and instant coffee was place a long distance call to New York State Prison. After talking to the records department, he discovered that Robert Gregory had served only one year of his sentence and had been paroled for quite some time. The person with the motive would surely be the number one suspect now, but something was wrong. When the reporter asked for the whereabouts of Gregory, none were given. It was as though he had just disappeared. None of this made sense, and suddenly the reporter's mind began to spin out of control. Gregory had been out long enough that the police, Valentine, and just about everybody else should have known it. The reporter drank an additional cup of coffee, hoping to sublimate his system and perhaps sharpen his thinking. Annoyed by the abeyance, which a holiday always caused him, he called the police station hoping to find Jack.

"A reporter doesn't really have a day off," he told his friend on the force when he finally reached him and responded to the lecture about doing labor on what should be a day of relaxation. "I need to know a few things."

"Like what," Jack asked impatiently.

"Well, for one thing," the reporter snapped indignantly, "why was I – and perhaps Valentine – kept in the dark about Gregory's release from prison?" He aimed his pointer finger towards the speaker of the phone as if Jack could actually see that. "What, did he make some kind of deal with the feds or something?"

"What are you talking about?" Jack said, not being overly convincing with the tone of surprise in his voice.

"Stop it!" The reporter was fuming now. "Don't play games with me. I want to know what the hell is going on. Even I'm smart enough to know that a guy doesn't get his sentence cut that short unless he cuts a deal. Where is he now – witness protection?"

48

"It doesn't concern you," Jack snapped abruptly. He waited for a response, but when – much to his amazement – none was given, he continued speaking. "I know you want to get involved, but this is way out of your league. It's way out of my league too." He hesitated but not long enough for the reporter to say anything. "Please stay away from this," he expostulated. "It's bigger than both of us, and I really can't help you."

"You knew!" the reporter shouted.

"Yea, we knew," Jack said calmly.

"You knew all along," the reporter said allowing his fractious nature to take over.

"No," Jack quickly corrected. "A lot of people *did* know; that's true, but I've been in the dark as much as you."

"Bullshit!" the reporter spat into the phone. "You knew last night when you let me drop in on Valentine."

"But that was your idea," Jack reminded him. "Besides, would it have made any difference?" There was no answer. "I thought so," he said with slight relief. "Now, if you can get hold of yourself, maybe we can talk later."

"How much can you tell me? How much *will* you tell me?" he substituted instantly.

"Tony's at six," the reporter surrendered. Jack hung up, and the reporter fell back on his crumpled couch, hoping to get the sleep, which he now began to realize he should have gotten in the first place.

By the time Jack arrived at Tony's, the reporter was on his third round and already preparing himself for a fourth. His eyes were still a deep red from interrupted sleep, and his blonde hair was greasy and looked darker than it really was. The snow, which the weatherman had promised, had finally fallen and bits of it lay on the scalps of the many patrons who walked in and out of Tony's saloon doorway.

Jack shook the frost from his hat and tapped his feet together in an attempt to clear the frozen moisture stuck to the rubber heels on his shoes. He looked worn, and he felt exhausted from a tedious day; but he had promised to see the reporter, and he needed to talk to him, to find out how much he knew and what his conclusions might be. The reporter was intelligent; Jack knew this. He also knew that the reporter was not credulous when it came to most matters; and despite his improvident manner when it concerned his personal life, the reporter would never accept things on the surface alone. There was always more that he wanted to find out, and Jack respected him for this, even envied him to a point; but it was the recalcitrant side to his personality that seemed to come through more often; and this was frightening, for himself, for Jack, and for others who were concerned with the issues at hand.

"I let you have some fun, let you play detective," Jack said politely as the two settled down in the usual booth. "But now the fun is over, so just back off," he warned. "You can't lock horns with the powers concerned here." The reporter pushed his empty glass aside and folded his hands. Thumping ever so slightly, he started to rock the table. The words were there, but they just didn't seem to come out. Jack sipped his drink and smacked his lips to show satisfaction with the taste. "It was five years ago when all that stuff with Valentine and Gregory happened. You weren't even living up here at the time."

"So does anybody know where Gregory is?"

"*I* don't know where he is, that's for sure," Jack answered emphatically. "And that's the truth."

"What about Valentine?" the reporter inquired. "Why did he lie to me?"

"I'm not sure that he did," Jack said with uncertainty. "He was never the brightest guy out there even before he got popped in the head too many times."

"But someone would have told him – or should have at least," the reporter blasted. He twirled his sizzle stick and then tied it in a knot, a nervous habit he had picked up years ago. "It sure looks like someone is hiding or covering up something."

Jack sucked in his lower lip. "Yea, well, if that were the case, you never would have been given the information about his release so easily." The reporter just sat there silently with an almost disappointed expression on his face. "Maybe Gregory got some kind of deal. It happens all the time."

"Then why are you asking me to back off?"

Jack took a deep breath. "Because sometimes when you go looking for your dog, you come across another animal that isn't so friendly." He finished his drink. "There's too many things that don't concern you, and I don't want you to get hurt."

52

"But why?" the reporter asked beseechingly. "Why is this so important, and why has it made so many people nervous?"

"Who's nervous?" Jack decried.

"You for one," the reporter said.

"Fuck you!" Jack shouted. "I'm only trying to help you. I don't know what's going on, but someone put the word to me that you need to back off."

"They think I'm on to something," the reporter said with dissimilation. "They're hiding something and afraid that I'll figure it out." He rubbed his hands together. "They're afraid of me."

"Like they're afraid of a mosquito." Jack swatted the table. "You're just a nuisance that they can squash whenever they like. You're reaching for stars, man."

"Don't patronize me, Jack. If they want to squash me, then let them," he dared.

Jack stood up, finished any remaining liquid in his glass, and dropped a few bills on the table. "I've told you all I can, and I've warned you. It's up to you now." He hurried out the door into the cold damp substance that now engulfed the city. The reporter stayed for a moment, then did the same. As he walked away from the bar, he never looked back once at the sludge which trailed behind him.

***

For the next two weeks, he walked and he talked and he listened and he observed. From winos in the corner to young fighters in the ring, he spoke to them all. He got thoughts from some trainers at the various gyms and even bits and pieces from the guys who swept the floors. There were things he had not intended to uncover, but little by little, he was becoming convinced that there were more and more people involved in something wrong. There was not only a great deal of information to assimilate but the occasional roadblock along the way. Whenever he believed that he had found some true substance and enough information to formulate a good story, he was returned to covering sports again – describing tackles and touchdowns, hook shots and slam dunks, slap shots and saves. There was a time when this would have been his dream assignment, but now it had become the furthest thing on his mind. He truly believed that he was on to something – something more important than who won the Eastern division, but he received no help from anyone; therefore, he sat at his desk and gradually got covered by disposable coffee cups and sandwich wrappers as he awaited his next obstacle.

The start of the week was always a chore for the reporter, and this particular day was no different as he struggled his way to work. nursing a severe headache and a chronic upset stomach. He sat at his desk and attempted to lose himself in the pile of unfinished papers that lay on top of his filing cabinet, but the meditation didn't last for long as people started rushing everywhere, and noise and commotion filled the entire building.

"What's going on!" he shouted as he looked up from the disorganized collection of notes that sat before him.

"Haven't you heard?" a young copyboy yelled. "Valentine's been murdered."

"Murdered!" the reporter screamed as he jumped up. "When, how?"

"Poisoned," the copyboy said. "They rushed him and his brother to the ER last night. Looks like someone put something in the booze. They tried pumping his stomach, but it was too late."

"How about the brother?" the reporter asked. "Is he dead too?"

"Not yet," the enthusiastic boy answered, "but he's critical. It seems that he didn't drink as much to get the full effect."

"This is insane," the reporter whispered to himself. "None of this makes any sense at all."

His thoughts were interrupted when the boss commanded him to go through the tombs and come up with any information on Valentine – his career, his love life – anything at all – anything that they could pass on to the major publications looking to do a feature.

"I've been all through the tombs," the reporter protested. "All my research is intact. I won't find another thing."

"Do as you're told," his boss snapped. "I'm sure you can still find something significant."

"Right," the reporter said as he started for the tombs. How he hated this – more than anything, yet it was after a few hours of sifting through this nonsense that he came upon a discovery – one that would prove invaluable. Without saying a word, he ran to the nearest phone and put in a call to Jack; and within an instant, his friend was on the other end. "We need to talk, Jack," the reporter said in a monotone.

"Not now," Jack said impatiently. "You finally have something to write about."

"I know that," the reporter said calmly, "but you need to come by here and pick me up." His voice had become forceful. There was no answer, just the click of the phone being hung up; and in less than half an hour, the reporter was riding in a police car. "If you check the record," the reporter said, "you'll find out that Valentine is just a stage name." He started to laugh. "When I was a kid, there was a professional wrestler named Valentine – either Jimmy or Johnny – I can't be sure, but our boy probably got the name from him. Anyway, Giordono is the family name. I found it in an obit about Jimmy's father – Richard Giordono – R.G. Make any sense, Jack."

"Sounds interesting," Jack agreed. "Go on."

"I'm pretty sure that brother Joe took the Valentine name, so he could cash in on Jimmy's name," the reporter said with alacrity. "However, there hadn't been much to cash in on – until now, that is. I'm sure that with a little investigating, we'll find a will of some kind that leaves Joe with a big hunk of cash."

"What's his motive?" Jack asked.

"The usual," the reporter answered, "money, but for now, let's stick with the watch. It must have belonged to the father, and Joe dropped it when he tried to kill Jimmy."

"It's possible," Jack concurred.

"More than possible," the reporter amended. "While I was snooping around, I discovered that Joe had a problem with drugs, alcohol, and gambling. He owed just about everybody in the city."

"But murder," Jack said with skepticism. "Why didn't he just ask to borrow the money?"

"Perhaps he did," the reporter concurred, "but things don't always work out. Who knows? Maybe he just got desperate."

"So you're claiming that Joe murdered his brother."

"Exactly," the reporter said with confidence. "First, he tried to shoot him and when that didn't work, he came up with this poison idea."

"But Joe took poison as well," Jack reminded his friend.

"Which brings us to the poison. What better way to avoid suspicion than to take some for yourself – just enough to put yourself in danger but not enough to die. That way the whole thing looks like one big accident – and it takes away any suspicion on Joe."

"But Joe never was a suspect," Jack declared.

"And if his plan worked, he never would be. You got a better idea?" the reporter asked.

"Not really," Jack admitted. "Nice piece of detective work," he added as he clapped his hands softly on the steering wheel. "I don't think the boys downtown knew who to suspect. You've got something pretty solid here."

"I sure do," the reporter responded. "Too bad none of it's true."

"What are you talking about?" Jack asked with complete surprise.

"Come on, Jack. Everything is too perfect. It was too easy. The best way to get me off their tail was to send me on another tail – and not some wild goose chase either. No, whoever set me up did one fantastic job. They wanted me to find that information; that's why they planted it."

"Which information was that?" Jack asked as his expression changed.

"The information I just found this morning. I can't be sure when they wanted me to find it, but it wasn't there when I did my initial research on Valentine, or I would have found it before."

"Who is they?" Jack asked curtly.

"I think you already know the answer to that question," the reporter said vehemently. "In fact, I think there was a whole bunch of stuff that you knew. Stuff that you deliberately kept from me."

"Since you're so convinced that I'm a part of some conspiracy, why don't you fill me in on some of the details," Jack said resentfully.

"There were secrets, Jack, and not only with Valentine; but our ole pal Gregory had them too."

"Gregory?"

"You bet," the reporter stated with enmity in each breath. "He was just the go between for some big time…" The reporter paused and searched for the right word but reluctantly decided upon "operators." Jack gave an obstinate stare but remained silent. "Besides drugs and prostitution, gambling is another big source of revenue for those certain individuals who run the crime syndicates." He smiled and waved his hands nonchalantly. "But I don't have to tell you that because you're well aware of it." He put his hands flat on his lap. "Anyway, his job wasn't so much to fix fights as it was just to inform certain people about those which were already controlled. That way they could make the proper wager and get rich. That's when it gets interesting," the reporter stated anxiously. "Apparently some of New York's finest were a big part of this. It seems that they took this profitable information instead of a direct payoff for turning their heads on the other vices like drugs and so on."

"Yea right," Jack shot back sarcastically. "The whole thing sounds ridiculous."

"Not really," the reporter assured him. "Gregory would handle the bets for the cops if they wanted, or they could go to the bookie of their choice. But once the information was passed on …" He failed to complete his sentence, but his thought had been transmitted, and Jack nodded dishearteningly that he understood.

"So there were a few cops on the take," Jack said unrepentantly.

"A bit more than a few," the reporter declared.

"So where does Valentine come in?" Jack asked.

"For the most part, he was nothing more than a pawn. Mr. Gregory started to play games, took a little more than he deserved, passed on a little incorrect information and made some side bets of his own. So they set him up, paid Valentine a few bucks or maybe blackmailed him for some dumb thing he once did. I can't be sure, but whatever the reason, Jimmy testified, and Gregory went up the river."

"So just like that, you can assume that Valentine was not acting on his own behalf," Jack inferred.

"Pretty sure," the reporter replied emphatically. "He said a few things during our brief meeting which put some ideas into my head. Although he did say that Gregory fixed some fights," he sneered slightly between clauses, "he also had some harsh things to say about the men in blue."

"That doesn't prove anything," Jack said as he gripped the wheel and remained focused on his driving.

"Oh, it's not about proof, Jack. It's all conjecture. I can only guess as to why Jimmy testified."

"And I'm sure that you're gonna tell me it didn't stop there," Jack surmised.

"Afraid so," the reporter verified. "No, unfortunately Gregory had names – lots of them – maybe even a list someplace; and he presented it all to the D.A. as part of his deal." He shook his head as a display of his total disgust. "Too bad it was the wrong D.A. for he must have been on the take too," he said, not really surprised. There was an eerie silence as the reporter looked straight at Jack and then made a fist with each hand before resting them under his chin. "He's dead," the reporter said with perspicuity. "I guess they felt he couldn't be trusted."

"Disappeared," Jack corrected.

"I'll accept that," the reporter scoffed, "but he made copies of all his information and sent them to Valentine."

"How do you know that?"

"I don't really," the reported admitted. "I'm just making that up, but your reaction makes me believe that I might be on to something."

"Fuck you," Jack blurted out with contempt.

The reporter completely ignored him. "Take my word for this. Joe's not going to make it either, and his death will be ruled as an accidental homicide."

"This all sounds rather convoluted," Jack declared. "You should be a mystery writer."

"Not a bad idea," the reporter agreed. "The more convoluted, the better it is to hide what they want to hide."

"It's still a little farfetched, don't you think?" Jack appealed.

The reporter dismissed him and continued with his elaboration. "It reads like an Agatha Christie novel. Too many things just kept falling into the right position, and then it dawned on me that it had to be a set up." He nodded his head. "They wanted Valentine dead and they wanted it to look like Joe did it, so they ordered a hit and left the watch to implement Joe. Now, I'm not sure if the 'hit' failed or if it was also part of the set up, but that doesn't matter. I just know that there was a set up. Valentine's told about the watch but he never gets to see it, and that's because it's a fake. Somebody – either very high up or maybe working for the paper – makes sure that I know about it and leaves me a convenient trail of breadcrumbs." He paused and then said very deliberately, "For all I know, it could have been you. The more you told me to stay away, the more I would dig – and you knew that." The reporter hesitated, allowing his words adequate time to sink in and then began to shake his head approvingly. "It was beautiful," he continued. "I have to compliment whoever it was that concocted the scheme. When Joe supposedly tries to kill Jimmy again with poison – and succeeds, it will all fall on Joe. But here's the best part, the part with real imagination. Let's not frame Joe entirely. Let's make it appear as if he almost pulled it off. After all,

Joe might have motive, but by taking some of the poison himself, he would have an alibi. However, he gets careless, and takes more than he should have, and his beautiful plan backfires." He began to rub his hands together. "Five'll get you ten that we hear about Joe's demise in a little while, and along with that, there will be incriminating evidence that points to him as the killer." He gave Jack an expression that implied, "Am I right?"

"You might have something," Jack said with chagrin. "But why kill Valentine?"

"I'm sure that he had information, and they didn't trust him either," the reporter said with feigned anxiety. "That and the money he used to buy that stock. It must have been dirty money – dirty money that he wanted to hide. It might have been money he got for his testimony against Gregory, but that's total speculation. However, I wouldn't be surprised if a few lawyers got rich on this one."

"Again, it's possible," Jack conceded, "but not likely."

"Aw come on, Jack, it's more than possible and it's damned likely. People in high positions can do all sorts of things with the right manipulation – and that's what we're dealing with. It's hard to win the game when the opposing team writes the rules." The reporter pressed his hands together and rested them on his lower lip. "Take my word for this," he continued. "Joe's not going to make it either, and his death will be ruled as an accidental homicide."

"So tell me something," Jack requested politely. "How'd you figure this out?"

"I talked to a lot of people, Jack, and little by little things started to come together." He smiled. "But to be honest with you, a lot of it was just speculation on my part combined with some dumb luck." He scrunched his mouth and attempted a smile. "I found some old betting slips and a few things that the bookies thought were unimportant." He sighed. "There were also a few – shall we say anonymous sources – who got burned in a few transactions and were more than willing to fill me in on some things."

"You can't trust people like that," Jack declared.

"Perhaps not." He looked directly at Jack. "But nowadays, I don't know who I can trust."

"And how did you know that someone was setting you in the wrong direction?" Jack inquired, trying to remain calm.

"How come the detectives didn't find out about Valentine's real name?" the reporter countered. He laughed. "I might be a good detective, but I'm not the only one."

"So what do you do now?" Jack inquired with aplomb.

"It's time to make a difference, Jack, because in some ways we're all guilty – you, me. When we get word that stuff's going on, we just turn the other way. I saw it all the time as a sports writer. We constantly ignored things to protect someone's image, but this is much worse. Who would we be protecting this time?" He rolled his eyes and vigorously shook his head. "It's all wrong when the guys who are supposed to protect people are the ones who should be locked up."

"Not all of them," Jack said, almost as though he were asking for forgiveness. "I'm sorry. I'm truly sorry. There was nothing I could do."

"But you did know about some things, didn't you?" the reporter pried. There was no response, but Jack's eyes blinked in the affirmative. "You can do something now."

"No, I can't!" Jack shouted. "I can't do a damn thing!"

"Well, I can," the reporter said as he reached for the door handle. "I can blow the lid right off the top of the police force and all those involved."

"You don't have enough to get anybody."

"Maybe not," the reporter concurred, "but I've got enough to initiate one hell of an investigation. It might take a while, but I can get it done."

"No you can't," Jack said. "Your editor will never print it."

"That's right," the reporter said with aversion. "He stopped me from uncovering something every chance he got, but there are other papers. I can go to one of them."

Jack shook his head. "You can't be sure they'll print it either; and if they do, are you convinced that people will believe it?"

"They'll believe it if they want to," the reporter answered with assurance. "The public likes this kind of stuff, and I doubt that anything would happen to me." He shrugged his shoulders. "It would only convince the public that much more."

"They don't always kill people," Jack said. "Sometimes they just discredit them. You go public and you're probably finished." He took a deep breath and seemingly begged the reporter to listen. "You said it yourself. You can't beat them when they make up the rules."

The reporter opened the door as the car came to a complete stop and stepped outside. The cold didn't seem to bother him as he stood on the sidewalk starring at the door he had purposely left open. "It makes no difference!" he shouted. "I know I'm through one way or another; but it's only a career, and I've got my conscience to wrestle with." He pointed. "And so do you." He put his foot on the door, pushed it closed as hard as he could, and then walked away.

Part 3
The Teacher

While his gas tank was being filled, the teacher looked around and noticed that not a whole lot had changed since his departure some three years ago. When the tank was completely full, he walked into the grocery section of the station and purchased an overpriced drink to quench his thirst and replenish his body with any energy that may have been lost.

"That'll be five dollars, Mister," the young attendant growled as if he were being forced to do something against his will.

"For the drink!" the teacher gasped.

"No, for the gas and the drink," the attendant shot out in disgust.

The teacher looked at the establishment's young employee and acknowledged his gaffe. "I guess I didn't need as much gas as I thought."

"Guess not," the attendant said, actually sounding friendly. He never looked up as he placed the five-dollar bill in the appropriate slot and never said another word. The teacher gave a slight wave to show his appreciation and then returned to his car.

Things wouldn't get underway for several hours, and there were several places where he could go to waste a sufficient amount of time. However, he knew where he needed to be, and within ten minutes, he was back on the campus where he had spent four years: four years studying and four years preparing for life. There had been a few additions and some minor renovations; but for the most part, everything looked the same and *felt* the same too. He could still pass himself off as a student if he wanted to, but the momentary thrill of convincing some eager young coed that he still attended classes from the other side wasn't worth the bother. He thought about visiting some of his old professors; but since he hadn't made the time to visit them during his two year tenure at the high school, it didn't seem appropriate to do so now. He just kept walking and taking in the sights of a new crop of youngsters who had the same ambitions that he once had. The time passed by more quickly than he could have imagined; and before too long, he was on his way again.

He had been to things like this before, and too often they turned out to be glorified reunions and not much else. He hoped that it would be different this time because there was no one he really wanted to see, and more than anything he wanted to pay his respects.

71

Popularity forced the proceedings to be moved from a smaller funeral home to a much larger church. With so many people on hand, he hoped that an inconspicuous entrance could be followed by an abrupt yet polite exit. It was Ed's daughter who contacted him because she knew how close he and Ed had been, and he sincerely hoped that she had kept the news of his impending arrival to herself.

There hadn't been a lot of them, but Ed's daughter was one of his supporters; and the reason for that support made no difference to him at all. Whether it was out of loyalty to her father or because she really believed that an injustice had occurred, she maintained her belief in him nonetheless.

By the time he found a parking place and then made the hike to the church entrance, the service had already begun. The family had decided that having a single memorial in place of a wake on one day with a funeral on another would best serve everyone. Ed's wife had passed away some years earlier, so all arrangements were made by the surviving son and daughter. Since the son and his family lived in a different state, the brunt of the responsibility fell on the daughter and her family. The teacher couldn't honestly remember having actually met the son; and if he had, it was very unlikely that the son

72

would remember him. In fact, the teacher was hoping that very few people – if any – would remember him. His departure from the town had not been a pleasant one; and when he left, he made a promise to himself that he would never return. Ed's death had changed all that. He couldn't stay away from paying his respects to the man who had given him his very first teaching job, and to the man who did not desert him in a time of need.

There were a few staring faces, but he couldn't be sure if they were expressions of recognition or just the miens of those who wished to honor Ed. The teacher made no acknowledgments as he took his turn and strode to the front of the church where he shook the hand of the son and embraced the daughter. "I'm glad that you made it," she whispered in his ear. He nodded his head, returned to his seat, and patiently listened to one tribute after another. When he was convinced that he had spent a sufficient amount of time, he left the church quietly and returned to his car. Before he could turn the ignition key, there was a tap on his door and a pair of hands settled on the open window frame. "I didn't really expect to see you here."

"Ed was a good man," the teacher said with assertion, "and I needed to be here."

73

"Yes," the other man said with equal assertion. "You probably did." Then he glanced over his shoulder as if looking for someone in particular. "Let's go and have a drink. I think we need to talk."

Zander's Bar was a dingy little place; but the drinks were cheap, and the din produced by the clientele wasn't so deafening that two people couldn't hear each other talking. "So tell me, Henry," the teacher said as he hoisted his beverage. "What do you want to know?"

"I see that you're drinking coffee these days," Henry said with mock approval. "I didn't know they sold coffee in this joint."

"I think this came from the boss's office," the teacher suggested.

"How does it taste?" Henry asked.

"I've had worse. Besides, it's my new vice," the teacher lamented. "I know I drink more than I should, but we all have to have some bad habits."

"True," Henry said. "I have a few of my own. By the way, you didn't happen to run into an old friend?"

"Like whom?" the teacher asked, unable to legitimize his query.

"Frank," Henry said with authority

"I didn't notice him," the teacher said with no emotion in his voice at all. "Besides," he added, "I don't think Frank knew Ed all that well."

"Last I heard, Frank moved out West someplace to live with his sister. I guess he couldn't afford to make it." Henry's account came as no surprise to the teacher at all. "And you know what happened to Jillian," he added.

"Yea, I heard." The teacher found it hard to say these words and even harder to keep his composure. Although he hadn't seen or heard from her since his departure, he never stopped thinking about her. "Maybe Frank had something to do with it."

Henry's expression shifted to total confusion. "What would Frank have to do with it?"

A noisy sigh was all the teacher could produce. "I was just thinking out loud; forget that I said it." He then gave an open-palmed gesture, and in an icy tone declared, "I guess we've all moved on."

"That's a fact," Henry said, "but some of us moved without any explanation at all."

"I can't give you a reason for why people left like they did," the teacher said sarcastically.

"I'm talking about you, and you know it." The teacher nodded but said nothing since his expression revealed it all. "The new school year begins," Henry continued, "and you're nowhere to be found. You're supposed to get married over the summer, but it doesn't happen; so most of us assume that had something to do with it." He took a long sip from his drink, put the glass down on the table, and leaned forward to get as close to the teacher as possible. "But we ask anyway, at least those of us who cared. Jillian wouldn't talk to anybody, and the principal said your decision to leave was personal."

"It *was* personal," the teacher reinforced.

"Right!" Henry lengthened the word before taking another drink. "But we do a little digging, and we discover that there may have been more to it."

"Like what?" the teacher asked while looking over the rim of his coffee mug.

"Disciplinary action," Henry said with a slight hesitation in his voice. "Just rumors, but from pretty reliable sources."

"Then just leave it at that," the teacher demanded as politely as possible.

Henry put his hands together, formed a steeple, and began wiggling his fingers. "Look," he said with authority. "You don't have to tell me a damn thing; but I'm pretty sure that if there was any kind of disciplinary action, it was trumped up total bullshit."

The teacher snickered and drank the last of his coffee. "All right," he said, "I owe you that much; but your knowing won't change anything, and it might even make you a little nervous."

"I'm all ears," Henry said, "so let's have it."

Scholarships had been hard to come by; therefore, when a small college offered him one for his track skills, he accepted it without hesitation. Besides, he thought, a trip to the South would do him a lot of good. While some of his old friends were shoveling snow to clear the driveways, he'd be sitting on the beach getting a suntan. It was hot in Florida, and it was humid; but eighteen years of harsh winters made the tradeoff more than bearable.

Those first three years at school couldn't have been better since his track skills kept him active and healthy while his achievements in the classroom were reaching an all-time high. A part time job at the local lumber company took over for any expenses that weren't covered by his scholarship and even put a few dollars in his pocket for a rainy day. Then there was Jillian, the beautiful dark-haired coed with whom he had fallen madly in love. She was born and raised in Florida and attended the college because it was close and convenient. His Northern accent – while it may have annoyed some of the local residents – intrigued her, and his abilities in and out of the classroom as well as those on and off the track, made him even more appealing. By the time their third year of school had rolled around, they were the perfect couple: the All-American athlete and his beautiful girlfriend.

Things changed during the fall of his senior year, and these changes forced him to make new decisions and to set new goals with his life and career. After a long bout with lung cancer, his mother had finally succumbed to the disease and left him with no family at all. A torn meniscus during an early morning practice put him out of commission for the entire cross-country season and all but doomed his chances for success during track season later in the year. His scholarship, however, remained intact; and his injury did not disable him enough to give up his part time employment. Meanwhile, things with Jillian could not have been better. There was talk of marriage and even a spring weekend spent looking for a place to live. There were also going to be job openings at the local high school where he was currently doing his "practice teaching"; and he felt confident that his credentials and background would make him the front-runner for one of the positions.

"It's all roof," the teacher said as he looked at the A-frame, which had gotten Jillian's attention.

"That's the way they make them, silly," she said as she led him to the front door. "They're very comfortable with an upstairs loft and two downstairs bedrooms." She smiled as she looked directly into his deep blue eyes. "And they are very affordable."

"You don't expect me to buy this place!" he said unable to control his apprehension.

"Not right away," Jillian said. "You rent to own, and when the time is right; you take it over."

"You'd really be comfortable in a place like this?" he asked with sincerity.

"I'd move in with you right now," she said while playfully stroking his arm.

"If your father would let you," he interrupted.

"If Daddy would let me," she conceded with compunction in her voice. "But that doesn't mean I won't be a constant visitor." She hesitated but only slightly. "An overnight visitor."

The teacher smiled and then laughed. "It'll be easier than sneaking you into the dorm at night."

"For sure," she cooed, "but not as much fun."

Together, they examined the property; and together, they decided that it would be a good fit – for the both of them. With no place else to go, the teacher knew that his future was set; but all decisions hinged on getting a job at the high school. Interviews were often granted to college students who were doing their internships; and with salaries on the low side of the scale, many institutions were looking to fill their available slots with cheap labor.

With less than a month left in his college career and with two months left in the high school semester, he was given the interview he desired.

Ed Stansky was a first year principal, originally from Ohio, but a Florida resident for close to twenty-five years. The forty-six year old – former basketball coach – liked the teacher from the time he began his internship and told him so. "You've done very nicely here for us," Stansky said as he rapped the eraser end of his pencil on the top of his desk. "As good as some of our veterans." He stopped abruptly as if to amend his statement and quickly said, "This may be my first year as a principal, but I've been a teacher long enough to know talent when I see it." He hesitated again, only this time it was to emphasize his point. "And you, my man, have talent."

"Thank you, sir," the teacher said.

"Call me Ed," Stansky said insisting that the interview be informal and that the teacher be more relaxed. "This whole thing is just a formality as far as I'm concerned. However, I am required to follow procedure. The job has been properly advertised, and references for you and all the other applicants have been checked out." Stansky leaned forward and spoke just above a whisper. "I wanted you to work here from the first time I met you, so I'm delighted that you want to stay down here rather than go back North.

"I have no family up there," the teacher said solemnly. "But down here I can start my own."

Stansky smiled. "Yes, I know all about you and Jillian. She was a student at this high school; which I know you're aware of, and a pretty popular person in the community." His expression immediately changed as he asked the question, "How do you get along with her father?"

"It's an uneasy peace," the teacher said. "I try not to discuss politics or even sports with him."

"Good move," Stansky said with approval. "He still acts like it's 1947 instead of 1967. Sometimes I think he keeps some deserted slave quarters out on that ranch of his just as a reminder of what he would call the good ole days."

The teacher gave a brief smirk but then nodded his head to indicate a slight disagreement. "I don't think he's that bad, Ed; but he does have some strong opinions which could be interpreted as racist."

"He's still jumping for joy over the Yankees finishing last, and he never shuts up about those heathens from Indiana who stole the national championship," Stansky said to change the topic to something less important. "I can hear him like it was yesterday," he uttered with a certain degree of aloofness. "Just singing the blues: 'Those bums didn't play anybody at all but got a free pass from all those Northern sports writers.' Oh yea, I can still hear him." Then he laughed and quickly added with an overdose of sarcasm, "Hell, who can respect a college that makes its football players attend class?" For a full twenty seconds he just stared into space as if absorbing his own comments before refocusing on the interview. "I'm sorry," he said contritely. "I have a tendency to get carried away." He folded his hands and leaned back in his chair. "You'll teach history and gym, coach cross country and track; and unfortunately, you'll do it for very little money." He extended his hand with a polite request, "Deal?"

The teacher received the principal's hand and responded eagerly, "I'm looking forward to working here."

Stansky stood and led the teacher to the door. "Contracts will be drawn up for you to sign later, but in the meantime, enjoy your graduation. Do you have a place to stay?"

"I'm renting a place," the teacher answered, "and I'll keep my part time job."

Stansky laughed as he opened his office door. "Reminds me of myself from a few years back. I had to moonlight from time to time. Well, anyway, have a good summer, and I'll see you in the fall."

The teacher hurried to his car and raced back to the college where he met his roommate and several other students who were waiting to hear the news. Since they all belonged to the religion which insisted on celebratory convenience as its daily worship, they headed to the college bar and hoisted a few in triumph. "So, will you be getting laid tonight?" his roommate asked with a complete lack of respect for anyone within earshot.

"Is that your sneaky way of asking me whether I'm going to kick you out or not?" the teacher asked between sips on his draught.

"Don't worry, Frank," one of the other collegian bar patrons said, "one of us will put you up for the night." With that, they all laughed, clanged their mugs together in a mock salute, and ordered another round.

Graduation was as nice as a graduation could be; but with no family to attend and give him the obligatory hugs and kudos, he felt somewhat alone as he crossed the stage. There were several parties afterward, which he attended; and a late evening with Jillian when the two of them made love for over an hour. These things convinced him that his future was bright and that his past was just that – passed.

He was able to increase his hours at the lumberyard, and this enabled him to meet his financial obligations of rent, damage deposits, and utility bills. The A-frame turned out to be more comfortable than he had imagined, and his nights with Jillian – although still clandestine to feign innocence for the sake of her father – were most rewarding. He knew that he wanted to spend the rest of his life with her; and with or without her father's approval, they would be married some day.

The biggest disappointment of this academic hiatus occurred with the news of Ed Stansky's heart attack. It was not fatal, but it was serious enough that doctors insisted he go on permanent disability. The teacher was assured that his job was still safe, but he still had to meet the new principal who replaced Ed. Thomas Carter had been an assistant principal for six years and was not happy when he was overlooked for the position that fell to Stansky. He didn't dislike Ed Stansky, but he believed that it had been unfair when Ed was made the principal. Carter didn't trust outsiders, and as a local boy with deep roots and connections, he always believed that he had been the logical choice to run the high school. Now he had his chance, and he was going to make the most of it. Whereas the interview with Ed had been a most pleasant experience for the teacher, the conversation with his successor was nothing more than a power play and a reminder of who was now in charge.

"I'll be honest with you," the somewhat belligerent Carter said, not masking his feelings in any way. "I may not have hired you if I had been in charge, but I will honor my predecessor's decision and keep you around." The teacher wasn't sure if he should thank him or say, "Thanks for nothing." Therefore, he didn't say anything at all, but his expression must have revealed some contempt. He was sure that all previous hiring decisions could not be reversed and that Carter was just throwing his weight around.

Like all new teachers, he knew that he would make his share of mistakes; but his confidence was very high because of the success during his internship. In many ways, he didn't feel like a rookie. He wasn't happy with Ed's replacement, but he knew that acceptance and tolerance of the situation were very important.

His year moved on as expected. Cross country season produced a few state qualifiers, but what should have been accolades became nasty taunts from the football team that cross- country was simply for those not rigid enough to tough it out on the grid iron. The coaching staff never threw any barbs at him directly, but they made it obvious that "his" sport wasn't a "real" sport. Despite their lack of appreciation, he attended all the Friday night football games that were played at home and even made it to a road game or two when the trip wasn't so bad. However, there was no reciprocation; therefore, Saturday's early cross-country meets were attended only by team members and their parents. Monday morning announcements glorified a football win and gave kudos to a hard fought loss regardless of the score. However, any mention of the cross-country team was brief since those prepared announcements, which he gave to the person in charge, had to be edited for time.

Gym class was a snap during the fall since half of his two classes were filled with football players who were routinely excused from any activity that might negatively influence their performance for practice that afternoon. This simplified his grading system since all pig skin participants received an automatic "A" while those who did actually participate worked hard enough to earn one.

He had to modify his presentation during his history class and be very careful when discussing current events. Anything too political was not allowed. Actually, anything too political, which did not coincide with the administration, was not allowed. Although this disturbed him greatly, he did his best to stay within the boundaries, which had been set for him. Occasionally he would sneak in a topic or two that would get him branded as some type of agitator by an angry parent who did not want her children hanging around with the wrong kind. However, the law was on his side in most cases; and as long as he kept his discussions balanced, he managed to get away with a few themes here and there.

By the time Christmas came around, he was ready to sit back and enjoy some leisure time. His coaching supplement did not replace the extra money he received when working at the lumberyard, but the additional hours, which coaching required, forced him to abandon this part time employment.

Despite the constant hassle in trying to make ends meet, he was pretty happy with his existence. Most of all, he was very happy with how things between him and Jillian had developed. Her overnight visits were a regular occurrence, and her sexual appetite had increased to a level that nearly matched his own. Her job at a local law office kept her gainfully employed, and together they were able to splurge on a few other delights besides their time in the bedroom. They did their best to be as discreet as possible; but before too long, their affiliation became the worst kept secret in town. No one seemed to care; and even Jillian's father turned a blind eye when it came to his daughter's relationship. He and his daughter's favorite suitor were certainly not friends, but they had developed a mutual respect for each other, if nothing else. If his daughter was happy, then Jillian's father was happy; and it was more than apparent that his daughter was happy.

It was during their private New Year's celebration that Jillian and the teacher decided to go "public" with their relationship and announce their plans for getting married. Their early evening love making session had been followed by some Chinese take-out dinner and an inexpensive bottle of Champagne. By the time 1968 arrived, they were both feeling the effects of the sparkling wine and therefore engaged in more sensory activity to welcome the new year.

"Are you still with us?" Jillian asked as she moved her hand across the teacher's chest.

"Barely," he said in a loud whisper. "You wear me out, lady"

She spit some air in his direction and then slapped his stomach as she rose from the bed. "There's some left-over food in the fridge. Do you want some?" she asked as she started down the stairs, which led to the kitchen.

"I guess it's true what they say about Chinese food and how you're hungry a half an hour later," he shouted so she could hear him.

She interpreted his response as a "yes" and returned with enough for the both of them. He leaned against a propped up pillow and watched Jillian as she walked slowly across the room and then sat on the edge of the bed. "You must have some Chinese in you," she said seductively, "because I'm always ready for more, less than half an hour later."

"Let's eat first," he said; "so I can build up my strength. "Besides," he chided playfully, "that statement is racist when you think about it."

"And yours wasn't" she said sarcastically. With that, she took a spoonful of refried rice and pushed it before his mouth. "Eat first," she tantalized, "play later." By the time morning arrived, each was satisfied with the other's performance.

"Do you really want to marry me?" Jillian asked cautiously.

"Of course I do," the teacher answered, well aware that her question was not at all serious. "You wanna elope tonight?"

Jillian knew that his last statement wasn't serious either, but she responded anyway. "My father would kill us if we did that."

"That reminds me," the teacher exclaimed. "Where did you tell him you were last night?"

"Does it really matter?" she answered quickly. "He knows that I was with you."

"Tell you what," he said assuredly. "Why don't we let him off the hook?"

"What do you mean?" she inquired, honestly confused.

"I know that we can't elope, but we could set a date."

"Yes, we could," she said triumphantly. "And for appearance sake, we'll make the engagement at least a year long."

"Is appearance really that important to you?" he asked, unable to hide some disappointment.

"Not to me," she retorted, "to my father."

It was decided that a year from June would be the perfect date. He would be completing his second year at the high school, and she would be well ensconced in her job. It would also give her family the necessary time to prepare for the overblown, overstated, and overdone celebration that her family deemed so important when dealing with these matters.

There were those who congratulated him in the formal sense and those who indicated that he was merely making things legal, and there were those who said nothing at all because they couldn't care less. By the time track season was underway, there was enough to keep the teacher's mind occupied and away from any doubts that he and Jillian had made the right decision.

Track received a little more respect than cross-country since several members of the football team partook in the activities. However, when spring football neared, the track team took a back seat and suffered a few unnecessary losses. There was no need to protest, for it all fell on deaf years. Attendance at a county track meet could not measure up to an exhibition game between the school's red team and black team. It was all about tradition, and the teacher better wise up.

Summer couldn't come fast enough, and fortunately there would be some part time work at the lumber yard to help with the nonexistent summer pay for high school teachers. It was also a great opportunity to do something that required very little brainwork at most. Some heavy lifting and good old-fashioned manual labor were just the remedy to exorcise a person from the world of academia. It would also serve as a reasonable incentive for one's return to teaching when the fall session began again. This was just what the teacher needed.

His nights with Jillian continued, but those hard days at the mill were enough to force some early evening retirement and slow down those bedroom romps. Jillian accepted these new recreational terms and decided to rely more on quality than quantity; and by summer's end, all was well.

His second year began pretty much the same as his first year had begun. There were the useless meetings that took up so much time during the teacher's planning week and the endless lesson plans that clearly indicated all those goals and objectives, which proved an educator's real value to the system. There had been some "voluntary" practice sessions for the cross-country team over the summer and then those mandatory sessions when the season began. Despite the typical lack of support that he had become so accustomed to, he enjoyed the season and declared it as a success.

The first two marking periods had flown by and before he knew it, the Christmas season had arrived. He sat in his usual spot at the dinner table during the celebration, which Jill's family provided, and took his usual position when it came to the family debates. He said nothing political at all and reluctantly kept silent when those sports franchises, which he secretly admired, got trashed by the colloquial experts.

To honor her mother's request and to continually appease her father, Jill was forced to attend a huge function on New Year's Eve. Naturally, she was expected to have her fiancé with her; and naturally he attended. The couple would have preferred to bring in 1969 by a different means, but each accepted this obligatory plight and treated it as no special occasion. They had spent many nights alone together, and they would spend many more in the future.

Frank Stewart had been the teacher's roommate in college; and although they hadn't seen much of each other since graduation, they were still considered close friends. Therefore, Frank's unexpected arrival in late February was a welcomed one, and his request for a place to stay was not refused.

"All I can find is part time work," Frank lamented as he sipped on the beer, which had been offered to him earlier. "Seems no one is interested in a music major."

"Have you ever thought about teaching music?" his friend asked him.

"Sure," Frank answered. "but you have to be certified, and—." He paused and took another hit on his drink. "I'm not."

"I wish I could help you," the teacher said with sincerity.

"Just letting me crash here for a few weeks will be enough," Frank said gratefully. "I'm sure I'll be able to find some decent employment and a place of my own."

"There is some work in the area," the teacher confirmed, "but you might have to put in some extra hours to make ends meet."

"I'll do whatever it takes," Frank promised, "and I won't be a burden to you at all. I can sleep on the couch in the living room and never bother you and Jill."

The teacher laughed. "Jill and I are not married. Not yet."

It was Frank's turn to laugh. "I know, but she spends a lot of time over here."

"True," the teacher conceded, "but she is not officially living here." Together they concluded that Frank's short visit would not affect anything, and together they clanked their bottles to celebrate the moment.

Two weeks turned into two months; and before long. Frank's inhabitance had become a malignant cancer. He had not found a job, and his efforts to do so had become nonexistent. If not for Jill's compassionate nature, Frank would have been out on his own, and because of her insistence, Frank stayed, and stayed, and stayed.

When track season began, the teacher was forced to put those personal issues aside and concentrate once again on overworking and getting little appreciation for his time. Before season's end, the team had accumulated enough victories to be the conference champion but faltered some in the regional meet and left the field with a bit of disappointment. There was some chatter that the team would do better next year, but when spring football began, there was talk about the football team and nothing else.

While the teacher had to deal with the growing menace, which his permanent boarder had become, it turned out to be a distant second to the problem that was facing him at work.

"He's already signed with the university," the head football coach said between expectorants of tobacco juice into the Styrofoam cup, which acted as a spittoon and sat on his desk. "You can't flunk him."

"He's already flunked, Wayne. I've been telling you since the beginning of the year. You didn't care as long as he remained eligible." The teacher took a deep breath. "And I don't know how he managed that, but I'm only concerned about my class."

"Listen," the coach said. "If he has to go to summer school and make up your class, it'll put him behind in his training schedule."

"That's not my problem, Wayne."

"Look, Ace," the coach said with no attempt to hide his condensation. "Think of the embarrassment it will bring to this kid and to his family."

"Is the university aware that he can't read, Wayne? I mean he can't read at all."

"X's and O's, track star, X's and O's." The coach leaned back in his chair and took one final shot at the cup, which he was now holding in his hand. "Football may be a bit more complicated than putting one foot in front of the other like your kids do, but it ain't rocket science."

"Grades are due on Friday," the teacher said abruptly. "His 'F' stands, and that's just the way it is!"

"Suit yourself," the coach said with aplomb. "I wanted to do this the easy way. That's why I came to you first, but I don't have to talk to you about this, and you're going to regret your decision."

"Is that a threat?" the teacher asked with a certain level of belligerence.

"Not at all," the coach replied confidently. "It's just the way things are done around here."

The teacher turned and walked from the room. His overall anger was apparent as he passed two students in the hallway and ignored them when they paid him their respects. The obvious sneers from some of the football players and a leering smile or two from members of the coaching staff were true indicators that the fix was in. He submitted the 'F' as promised; but when final report cards were issued, he discovered that not only had the grade been improved from an 'F' to a 'D' but his name had been replaced by a more accommodating teacher. This made it appear as if the student in question had never been in his class at all.

The teacher's outrage was equaled by his total disbelief that such a thing could actually happen, and storming into the principal's office did not help matters. "Were you aware of this!" he shouted as he threw a copy of the report card onto the principal's desk.

"Don't you come in here and yell at me," the principal said as if he were scolding a young child.

"Knock it off, Harvey," the teacher said, ignoring any attempt by the principal to quell his anger. "You can't do this, and I'm not going to stand for it!"

"You have nothing to say in the matter," the principal said with complete authority. "Besides, it's over and done with and too late to change it. Now, get out of here and leave me alone. I've got work

to do."

"You haven't heard the last of this!" the teacher exclaimed. "This

is wrong, Harvey. Totally wrong, and you know it."

"Taking away some poor sharecropper's chance for success is

wrong. Have you even thought about that?" The principal looked

straight at the teacher the way a boxer stares at his opponent in the

center of the ring before the fight begins. "Something like this

makes our school look very good in the eyes of the public, and no

one – not you or some other agitator – is going to put any kind of

black mark on this achievement."

"Come on, Harvey," the teacher interrupted. "We do these kids

a real disservice when we just push them through the system."

"Not this boy," the principal shot back. "This kid really has a

shot. A shot of going all the way to the pros."

The teacher shook his head vigorously. "And those kids who

have been promoted just so we can get rid of them?"

"We don't do that!" the principal countered.

"Are you kidding me, Harvey?" His expression was aghast with a combination of bewilderment and disgust. "We've had students who spent three quarters of the year serving in-school suspension who still managed to pass everything."

"That's not impossible," the principal suggested.

"It's not impossible," the teacher agreed, "but it's highly unlikely." He assumed a calm demeanor and carefully calculated what he said next. "It's about numbers, Harvey. It's about numbers, and it's about funding. I get that, but to pass someone who is functionally illiterate and send him off to college simply because he's a decent football player, is completely unethical and should be illegal."

"Are you finished?" Although the principal's words were slow and articulate, the teacher refused to respond. "He's no longer your responsibility," the principal continued. "Now get your moral compass out of my face and leave before I have you drug out of here."

The teacher smiled slightly and silently laughed at the principal's poor verb usage. "Ed Stansky wouldn't have allowed this."

"Well, why don't you just go and ask him."

"I'll do better than that," the teacher said triumphantly. "I'll go to the newspapers. They'll love a story like this."

The principal just laughed. "The public would be on our side; especially when it deals with someone who could help one of our major universities win a national championship." He pressed his hands together and then released them gently. "People take their football very seriously down here, and you need to learn that and learn it well." His expression reversed itself and became completely serious. "Not only will you *not* contact the newspapers, but you're gonna regret that you ever threatened me by saying that you would."

"So what does that mean? You gonna fire me?"

"No," the principal said in a slow raspy whisper. "Firing is too easy. You'll be hearing from us, and you're going to regret the day you ever walked in here."

Before going home, the teacher stopped and picked up some food at the local grocery store. No matter where he turned, eyes seemed to be following him. It was nothing more than his imagination, which had created this paranoia, he thought; but when he got home and put in a call to the lumber yard, the paranoia increased. There would be no summer job for him this year. Of course, this could have been nothing more than a coincidence, but it was eerie just the same. Things didn't fare any better when Jill came over, and she appeared to be on the principal's side.

"All you had to do was give him a passing grade!" she yelled when he told her of his impending dilemma. "It's about loyalty and school spirit —" she broke off but then came back with a rush, "and school pride. Don't those things mean anything to you?"

"Of course, they do," the teacher answered trying not to sound unreasonable. "But there is a little matter of right and wrong. You can't pass someone when he can't read."

Jill just threw her arms up into the air and increased her already puzzled expression. "How did he become a senior in high school if he couldn't read?"

"Good question," the teacher responded. "I almost didn't notice it myself since he came to class so infrequently. I think the fact that he got this far has a lot to do with why they don't want this to hit the papers."

"Are you really going to the papers?" Jill asked.

"We'll see," he answered, not feeling comfortable enough to mention the principal's threat in regards to what he had said. "First things first. I've got to find a summer job since the lumber yard is not hiring, and I'm afraid I'm either going to tell Frank to leave or charge him rent."

"He doesn't have a job yet," she said sympathetically.

"I don't either," he said dryly, "so keeping him aboard might be difficult."

The month of June proved to be the most difficult of times. A few hours a week at the local packing plant was just enough to clear some of his bills but not enough for him to make any progress. With Frank's refusal to take on a similar position, it was time for Frank to leave.

"I'm sorry, Frank," the teacher said with mock sincerity. "I can't accommodate you anymore. You're not only eating me out of house and home, but you've been running up some huge long distance charges. Since everything is in my name, I get stuck with those things."

"I'm gonna pay you back," Frank said despondently. "As soon as something comes my way."

"You could always work at the plant like I do," the teacher said, well aware of what Frank would say.

"I can't do that kind of stuff because of my condition, and you know that."

"I've already lent you more money than I can afford," the teacher said, knowing full well that repayment on his interest-free loans would never see the light of day. "It's just not worth it anymore, Frank."

"So you're just going to throw me out on the streets?" Frank's words were more of a whine than a plea, but the teacher didn't care one way or the other. He knew that his decision was right and that he had to follow through with it.

"I'll give you till the end of July."

Without warning, Frank grabbed the front of the teacher's jersey and gave a panic-stricken scream as he ripped the garment down the front. "You can't do this to me!"

The teacher took Frank's hand and removed it from his freshly torn shirt, and for one brief moment he could feel his anger rising and his temper getting the better of him. He wanted to hit this man, wanted to hurt him; but he couldn't, for in front of him stood a pathetic creature who needed pity more than animosity.

"I wish that I could help you, but I've got some problems of my own," the teacher said as if Frank's outburst had never happened. "The end of July." The teacher had no idea how prophetic his words were. Money was tight and things with Jill had become terribly strained, but there was a greater tragedy awaiting him: one that would affect his life as well as his career.

The teacher had convinced himself that going to the papers was the right thing to do. Surely, he believed, a story of this type would whet the interest of some editor and pique the public's interest. It was true that the area's population was overindulgent when it came to football, but even they had to believe in social justice. Besides, in many ways, the athlete in question was a victim — a victim of a system that had failed him a long time ago, the victim of a system that would fail several others if it wasn't repaired. Unfortunately, he never got the opportunity to submit it. Before the month of June had ended, he was accused of indiscretions that could cost him his teaching license and even force him to spend some time in jail. The principal had been right. The teacher regretted the day he had walked into the office.

"We have affidavits from several students claiming that you bought them alcohol on more than one occasion. We also have statements from several teachers who have — shall we say — always been suspicious of you."

"Let me guess," the teacher said defiantly, "football players and members of the coaching staff."

"We also have a friend of yours who will testify that he saw you supplying kids with beer while having a party at your residence," the principal added, ignoring the teacher's earlier comment. "I believe you know a Frank Stewart."

The teacher almost gagged on his own words. "Yea," he said with malice. "I know him." It was amazing how quickly and with how much precision this network had acted. It was almost like the plan itself was always in operation and just waiting for the moment when it was necessary for complete implementation. Did Frank go to them, or had they approached Frank? It didn't really matter, for whatever the case; the teacher knew that he was beaten.

The deal was very simple. The teacher's contract for the following year would not be renewed, and he would be permitted to resign quietly. No charges would be brought against him as long as he remained silent about the fabrication concerning the athlete's performance in the classroom. As part of the agreement for his silence, he would be issued a general letter of reference that claimed he was a qualified employee if nothing else. Refusal to comply with these demands would result in criminal charges, which included contributing to the delinquency of a minor. With the threat of all this hanging over his head, he had no choice but to agree with everything that lay before him.

There were whispers. There would always be whispers, but all the gossip that spread and permeated the small community said the same thing: something bad had happened and one of the high school teachers had been forced to leave.

The teacher actually tried to make a go of things and work on his damaged relationship, but what little chance it may have had, quickly died as the rumor mills put the final nails into the coffin of an arrangement, which had been unstable for quite some time. What had once been a slow process had accelerated to a dangerous speed, and with this velocity came an assortment of hate filled comments and misguided accusations. He couldn't be sure if the intent behind all the vitriol was designed to make him suffer even more or if its purpose was to alleviate him of any prolonged anguish. All he knew was that it hurt; it all hurt just the same.

Trying to convince himself that it was all for the best didn't help at all, and the morbid fascination of bringing bodily harm to somebody only clouded his judgment when it came to handling other important matters. His job was gone, and with its demise so fell another dream. There had been disappointments before, and he had always managed to recover; but this was different, much more intense and to a certain degree even a little frightening.

When he returned from a weekend of solace and a period for some soul searching, he found that his home had been ransacked and severely damaged. He could only surmise as to who the perpetrator was, but there was no way to prove it and no immediate friends to assist him in doing so. It was a fitting conclusion to a terrible series of events and furthermore convinced him that it was time to move on.

Henry sat there for a moment and let his system digest what he had just heard. His words were not deliberately harsh, but he had no regrets with how he presented them. "I'm sure you've heard about the stats your favorite player has put on the board."

"I have," the teacher said flatly. Devoid of all emotion, he added, "It's too bad that he can't read those stats himself."

Henry's face transfigured into a smile. "So you put some light on why you left so fast, but there are still a lot of unanswered questions."

"Like what?" the teacher asked.

"You mentioned that there had been problems between you and Jill, but you never said if she believed all that bull shit."

"If you're talking about the alcohol situation, I never brought it up to her." The teacher just shrugged nonchalantly. "There were a bunch of rumors going around, but there were so many, I don't know what she believed and what she didn't."

"And what about Frank?" Henry inquired. "I had no idea that he did what he did. How could a good friend like that turn on you so easily?"

"You'd have to ask him," the teacher responded without hesitation.

"With all the trouble he was having with getting a job," Henry said, "maybe he did it for money."

"Perhaps," the teacher acknowledged. "And maybe he took his thirty pieces of silver and then hanged himself."

"You can only hope," Henry said with a supplementary laugh. "You can only hope." His eyes had a measuring look as he stared at the teacher. "But there's more to the story. There's something you're not telling me." Rather than respond, the teacher just pursed his lips, pressed his first two fingers together, and placed them against his mouth. It was as if he were acknowledging defeat, presenting the inevitable; and Henry had his answer. "They had an affair," he said with contempt. Once again, the teacher allowed his expression to speak for him. "So he betrayed you in more ways than one." Henry swallowed hard and cautiously asked, "Do you think that had anything to do—"

"I'd rather not speculate on that," the teacher interrupted.

Henry just nodded, got up from the table, and shook the teacher's hand. "I'm sure it was no accident that Jill's family was nowhere near the funeral."

"I'm sure it wasn't," the teacher concurred.

"So where do you go from here?" Henry asked.

"I don't know," the teacher said with lack of conviction. "Still a few things I haven't tried yet."

"Good luck," Henry said. "I hope you find what you're looking for." They said nothing as they left the building and walked to the parking lot. The teacher climbed into his car as Henry got into his. The pain had returned; and for a moment, the teacher wanted to put his head down on the steering wheel and sob like a baby. Henry pulled out of the parking lot first, but the teacher was not far behind him. They both drove away quickly, and neither one looked back as they headed in completely different directions.

Part 4
The Poet

If he had been an artist – an artist at any level – he'd have painted pictures that expressed how he felt. If he had been a musician, he'd have composed music that clearly displayed all his inner emotions. However, his talents lay elsewhere; so he wrote stories – stories about everything from science fiction to serious drama. There was romance, remorse, and a trip to the afterlife. His characters played sports, saved lives, and escaped earthquakes that brought the end of the world. It helped pass the time and served as an honorable companion to those things he read, but there was something about poetry – its lack of rules, the freedom which it gave, and how easy he believed it was to create. Therefore, he wrote poem after poem: blank verse, free verse, and even some Haiku.

No one would read his stuff. He knew that, but he didn't care; for it wasn't about what others thought. It was about him. There were so many things that he wanted to forget, but there were too many things that he just couldn't let go. It may have been painful, but it was necessary – necessary for him to keep it fresh and to never let it heal. That would be wrong. Something had to be done; and he knew that until he did something, he'd never have real peace of mind. In many ways, it was a cleansing process that helped him cope with all that had gone wrong, and it was the best medicine right now.

His favorite poet was Rudyard Kipling, and he often read his works for inspiration; and now he felt inspired and with the help of Mr. Kipling, he could put it all down, put it down in the form of a Kipling verse and let no others judge it for its worth. Although he did his best to follow the pattern and emulate the style, he missed in places; therefore it was flawed, but it didn't matter. It had meaning to him and only to him; and as he put the words onto the paper, it became very clear – what he was and what he must do.

The Ballad of Him

One may think the best is here
When a close friend's livin' near
And all the good things are yet to come together;
But when it's 'bout surviving,
He'll be sneaky and conniving

And he will stab the back of 'im who's helped ya.

In the humid tepid air

Back when I resided there,

I worked from day to day to make ends meet.

Of all who failed the test,

One failed beyond the rest

Was a wretched soul whose name I will not say.

Just say: Him! Him! Him!

Underhanded shabby useless limb.

No simple job was kept,

Or single tears been wept,

For nothing did you take time to pursue.

He took what others gave.

Not a cent would he save

Till soon he had no property at all.

So I let him stay with me

For a friend I thought he'd be

With a promise to pay me what he owed.

No contract was ever made,

Yet quite often he delayed

While he just loafed and watched himself get fat.

He never lent a hand,

Just took a friendly stand

As he squandered all that sat upon his plate.

For it was Him! Him! Him!

With the bills which piled beyond compare.

Not a handout he'd refuse

Or a companion to abuse,

Lowest of the low, whom we care not to name.

Then it went from bad to worse,

And soon I began to curse

When the things around me started to unfold.

Allegations soon were made

And an evil trap was laid,

So suddenly before the bench he would stand.

He declared that things were true,

And he swore upon it too

That now I had done myself a big disgrace.

For the truth was all I'd plead,

But he failed a friend in need;

And then he preyed upon what meant the most to me

It was Him! Him! Him!

Took advantage of the situation then.

When confused to him she'd turn,

He perverted her concern

And made me hate till I could hate no more.

On the day I threw him out,

I could hear him cry and shout:

"To the streets you'll make me live without a cent."

Yet he never once denied

The words which he supplied

That had brought me tumbling down so very far.

And though he had a turn,

Her respect he couldn't earn;

And never would she look me in the eyes

So I went my merry way

Somewhere else to earn my pay

And do my best to put the past behind.

It was Him! Him! Him!

The name that's put some shame upon all others.

Each moment that goes by

I am hoping he will die.

Someday I'll get the chance to bury him.

He left in such a haste

But took the time to waste

Those belongings to which he could never claim.

An act without remorse

It set him on his course

To find a place where he could live rent free.

I know that later on

There'll be a place where he has gone

To be getting all his goods from other ghouls.

They'll be burning his damn soul

In that deep and ugly hole

'cause they've saved a spot in hell – just for him.

So it was Him! Him! Him!

With the name that I'd just as soon forget.

Though he tried to defeat me

And lied so he could beat me,

I'm a much better man, better off than him.

Part Five
The Student

The alfalfa stretched for miles, or so it seemed on the two thousand acres that cut across the state and ran directly to the base of the mountains. The best kind of fodder was alfalfa, and the cows who ate it roamed in a different part of the pasture close to the trees and away from the blistering sun.

There never seemed to be enough rain to suit the owners, but fortunately, she was not one of them. This was just a place for meditation, for remembering. She carefully opened the letter and read the contents very quickly, making sure not to miss a sentence. The penmanship was good; therefore, she was able to enjoy all that was written. His letters were never long but always filled with information.

They were both still grieving for a mutual friend, and these letters helped her with that grief. For a moment, it was as if nothing had happened. She looked at the perfect sky and marveled to herself about how perfect it actually was. As a slight breeze picked up and the ocean of grass made wave after wave circling towards the natural borders that the hills and the small river made, she gave everything a panoramic glance. It was truly beautiful. Her eyes returned to the letter, searching more carefully now, hoping to find something that she missed the first time or maybe to enjoy something else all over again. These letters were the only connection – the only bond that she and her friend had. He never called and never seemed to be in one place long enough; but he wrote, and she wrote back, mailing the letters to his mother who then forwarded them on to him.

She was never really sure how old his news might have been, but it was always fresh to her. Each correspondence was like a tale, a small journey back in time to that place which they had in common. To her, he would always be a friend; and to him, she would always be the student – the student who learned more in one year than most people learned in ten. It was that year about which she was thinking now as she absorbed each morsel of the written meal before her. That year, that year, she kept thinking. How she remembered that year!

1

It was a cold day when I left for college, but the real chill that I felt down my spine was not the result of the weather. I had never been a good student in high school, and I didn't expect my performance at

122

college to be any different. It was my father, his money and his influence that got me into college; and because of his push, his drive, I could feel the pressure. I lacked maturity and confidence, and my parents believed that college would change all that. It would make me more responsible, enable me to get a grip on myself and force me to grow up a little. The challenge was there, but I wasn't sure if I could meet it, and I was scared – very scared.

After landing at the airport, I just stood around feeling lost and lonely; but fortunately three other girls were in the same predicament as I, and with sheer luck and a lot of curiosity, we all got together and split the cab fare to Citra University. Money was no problem in my family; but Daddy had me on a budget, and for that first year in school, there would be no car and only a limited monthly allowance. Splitting the price of a taxi to the school was the first step in trying to make my money go a little further.

Each of us had a different reason for coming to the California coast, and not one was better than the other was. The tall blonde from Chicago wanted a little sunshine; so California seemed like the best place for her, and I couldn't have agreed more. The trip was pleasant; and since we were able to see much of the scenery (orange

123

groves and the like), I understood why people were drawn to this state. It had its smog, and the cities had crime; but there was an alluring sense about the mountains and the valleys and the presence of homes and clubs and organizations that belonged to a state, which its inhabitants called golden.

There was a short brunette who believed that it never rained in Southern California and told us that we'd all love her home town of Seattle if we enjoyed rain 363 out of 365 days a year. Obviously, she was looking forward to a little drier climate.

The West coast fascinated the tall redhead from New York City, who used to visit California every summer and was very excited about spending the winter in the land of surfers and movie stars.

I told the girls how fortunate I was just to be going to college and that I was looking forward to it. There were things that I was leaving behind, but they were personal and I saw no need to discuss my private matters.

As it turned out, the small brunette and I would be staying at McGegor Hall, the standard freshmen dorm for all the young coeds who wanted clean carpets and somewhat liberal visiting rights. The red head bragged that living at the Roget would put her closest to the campus tavern while the blonde snubbed us all by residing at the Brentwood apartment complex. Brentwood was only one of the several apartment complexes owned by the college; and although they were very expensive, they were well worth it. Since the college showed absolutely no authority over them at all, she knew what she was talking about when she said, "That's where the action is!" As soon as I could save some money or con my father one way or the other, I was going to move out of McGregor and into my own apartment as well.

Our arrival at the campus was typical. Returning students were being greeted by friends, and they all seemed quite sure of themselves as they went to all the right places. Those of us, who were new, certainly showed it by acting totally lost.

Despite my inability in locating my dorm or the college administrative office, I felt good about the place. It had a grand, almost majestic look with its well-groomed lawns and precisely trimmed trees; and all the buildings were new looking, freshly painted, or chemically cleaned. In addition to all the greenery and elaborate housing, there was a very good transportation system – shuttle cars and buses that ran frequently – all paid as part of our

125

tuition. I was impressed but a little frightened since it was like a world within a world, a city in itself.

By noon of my first day, I had settled in my room, a private room. It was the one thing that Daddy thought was best for me. "No problem with noisy roommates bothering you when you try to study," he said. And no problem with studious assholes bothering me when I'm trying to party, I thought. It was a big enough room and it had been kept in pretty good condition.

Thanks to Citra's alert transit system, I was able to find the college laundry where I got fresh linens and a receipt to have my laundry done. Each floor in the dorm had washers and dryers for all those emergencies that always seemed to arise on Friday evenings or for those few individuals who were ambitious enough to do all of their own washing. Except for that occasional last minute spot removal, I would let Citra's clothing engineers see that my outfits and underclothes were always suitable for wearing.

The small brunette, with whom I had shared a cab, was named Kerry Callahan; and not only were we in the same dorm, we were on the same floor as well. Therefore, when I had completed my tasks for the day, I went to her room to check in on her progress. "How are we getting along?" I asked as I walked through the door.

She was in the middle of making her bed and looked at me with an exasperated expression on her face. "Well, if it isn't Ms. Geralyn Garr from New York State," she said. "Why I haven't seen you in almost an hour. We both laughed as I assisted her in making the bed. "You're not settled in already, are you?" she asked.

"Sure am," I answered while making a mess at attempting a hospital corner.

"You gonna get the phone hooked up in your room?" she inquired while staring at the instrument which sat on the table closest to the window.

I nodded affirmatively. "Need to call the folks and let them know that their little girl is all right," I said sarcastically.

"I'll wait for my roommate to arrive," Kerry remarked casually. "Maybe we can split it."

"Do you know who she is?" I asked.

"No," Kerry replied. "I just hope she isn't some rah rah or a real slob; you know what I mean?"

127

"Well," I said, "if she turns out to be a real pain in the ass, maybe you can get a private room later in the year."

"I'll have to wait and see," she said as she walked to the huge dresser, which stood close to her closet. "Um," she said while opening the top drawer. "I can't believe I didn't ask you before. Do you smoke, Gerry?"

"Why? You need one?" I said quickly. "There's a machine outside my door."

"I don't mean cigarettes," she carped. "I mean pot."

"I'm from New York," I said mordantly. "Everybody back there smokes pot."

She laughed. "Do you have any?" she asked somewhat delicately.

"I was able to smuggle a little, but not too much," I said apologetically. "We're going to need to make some connections and find a supplier."

"That's for sure," Kerry confirmed. "There's probably plenty of stuff all over the place."

"Oh sure," I agreed. "Tell you what. Let's go to the bar and loosen up a little, and maybe we can catch on to where we can get set up." I smiled politely and then said, "We can always come back and smoke a bit later."

"Sounds good," she sang out. "Besides, it'll give us a chance to check out some of the guys."

"All right then," I announced loudly. "Finish up here, and let's go."

"But do you know how to get there?" she asked.

"Who needs to know," I said, waving my hands in the air. "Just tell the driver where you want to go."

In less than half an hour, we were seated at a comfortable booth listening to some acid rock and working on our second beer. One of the worst kept secrets about Citra was its laissez-faire attitude when it came to underage drinking. Since all of the bartenders were students themselves, the last thing they wanted to do was ask for proof. In fact, most of them encouraged overconsumption with the hope of taking an inebriated coed back to a quiet place after hours for some casual sex. Beer and wine were the only beverages the bar served, so my taste for rum and cola would have to be postponed for a while. We also learned rather quickly that several of the bartenders were the college's best suppliers when someone was interested in getting a much stronger buzz than alcohol could produce.

When our need for food became more urgent than our desire for companionship, we shuttled to the cafeteria and arrived just in time to get some finishing on a thing called lunch.

"We should have stayed at the bar," Kerry complained, shoving her plate away from sight. "Pretzels and beer nuts would have been better than this shit!"

"Cafeteria food always sucks," I said with authority, "but it's free; and if I want to purchase other – important – things," I winked, "I need to save some money."

"Let's go back to the bar," Kerry pleaded. "We shouldn't have left there in the first place." I just smiled but said nothing. "We might as well take advantage of the situation," Kerry lamented because tomorrow we have to get our I.D. pictures and go to some stupid orientation. Besides, we might be able to score some stuff later."

"I don't know about that," I said skeptically, "but we can still go back and get hammered."

"I wish my stereo would arrive," Kerry whined. "We could listen to some tunes while getting stoned."

"Remember," I reminded her, "I don't have that much, but we'll have plenty of time to listen to some tunes. My parents are also shipping a stereo and a TV set."

Kerry laughed. "Your parents certainly don't want anything to interfere with your education," she said with a roll of the eyes.

"Well," I said carefully, "they probably think that by sending me my own entertainment center I'll stay in on Friday and Saturday nights. That way I'll never get in trouble." I shook my head and curled my lip. "I've been sneaking out of my house since I was thirteen years old and on the pill since fourteen."

"And your parents don't know?" Kerry asked, bewildered.

"They have their own cocktail parties, so they are not the most observant," I said with a malicious tone.

"I'm on the pill myself," Kerry said, "but I'm still pretty selective."

"Nothing will slow me down if I don't want it to," I said, "but let's not worry about that now."

We returned to the tavern, drank ourselves silly, and bargained for a few extra joints that we would both smoke later. By three o'clock, I was asleep in my room listening to music on the stereo, which hadn't arrived. When I awoke, I went to Kerry's room and discovered that she didn't look much better than I did. I could tell by the additional baggage that her roommate had arrived but was nowhere around. Unlike me, she had not been sleeping; and she wanted to spend the rest of the evening toking and telling me about her roommate.

"Her boyfriend's a sophomore, and she seems to know pretty much what's going on," she said as she filled her lungs with the intoxicating vapor. "Those orientation sessions they hold are a lot of bullshit."

"Are we gonna go?" I asked as I rolled over on my bed.

"To the first one," Kerry blurted out as she released a belch of smoke. "To the first one."

"But why?" I asked.

"To check out some of the people; that's why," she said with laden demeanor.

"And this is the suggestion of your roommate?" I asked.

"It is," Kerry concurred. "And here's the best part about my roommate. Her boyfriend!"

"Her boyfriend?" I asked somewhat confused.

"Her boyfriend," she repeated. "He knows all the best connections and he has quite a few interesting friends that would love to meet a couple of girls with the right attitude."

"You mean like us," I declared.

"Exactly," she agreed. "And tomorrow, they might be there checking *us* out when we check *them* out."

"Sounds pretty cool," I cooed. "Let's do some exploring tonight."

"How?" she demanded.

"Let's ask the bus driver," we said in unison, but we were both too high to try it.

2

The next day all the freshmen lined up and had their pictures taken. Each mug shot was then encased in plastic, and along with some typed-written vital statistics, became our student identification cards. Each person was claiming that his or hers looked worse than the next person's did; when in reality, they all looked sub human. I had circles under my eyes, and my dirty blonde hair looked just that – dirty. By ten o'clock, it was time for the first orientation; and most

133

of us felt no worse but looked no better. Just as Kerry had predicted, the sessions were nothing more than decent opportunities to meet people; and it was during the first session that I was introduced to Kerry's roommate, Carol. We sat with two other girls at a small table, which could have easily accommodated a few more.

"Do you believe this garbage?" the girl sitting next to me asked with contempt. "Husband hunting girls and sex seeking boys! What gives that asshole the right to say something like that?" Her remarks were in direct reference to the professor whose rude manner and comments were a feeble attempt to serve as our wake up call. "He sounds like my old man," she continued, "and I'm not going to stay around and listen to any more of this bull shit."

As she head for the door, Kerry asked, "What about student advisors? They assign them during this session." However, the disgruntled student paid no attention to Kerry's alert and continued walking toward the door and eventually through it.

"I'm getting a cup of coffee before they start," I commented and walked over to the table that held a large coffee urn and several dozen Styrofoam cups. I had barely taken a swallow of the mud-like substance they were trying to pass off as coffee when the next speaker came in and started to get things organized. We were set up into alphabetical groups and given lists, which indicated which concentrates reported to which faculty advisors. These sessions were torturous, no doubt, but they did enable us to get a head start instead of finding out about advisors during registration at the end of the week. No student could register for classes before a faculty advisor signed off on a student's schedule, and no faculty advisors would see a student until all the orientation sessions were completed. When my last session was completed, I managed to get an appointment for early Thursday morning. This enabled me to slip out to catch a shuttle back to my dormitory. As I sat on a bench waiting for my mode of transportation to arrive, I noticed that across the street, there were two students who were sitting under a large tree in an attempt to escape some of the heat. One was short with red curly hair and a bright smile on his face; while the other boy, slightly taller, had long blonde hair that appeared to be darkening with age. His sullen expression never changed while his rapid hand movement showed only the slightest indication of emotion. It appeared that he was explaining something to the red head, and with each exaggerated gesticulation, the red head increased his look of pleasantness. The

135

slight wind, along with a few passing cars, made it hard for me to eavesdrop; but I concentrated on hearing them and I was able to pick up a word or two.

"It's no different … if you pay attention. Each teacher … his own system." Despite the several gaps, which ran throughout the dialogue, I was able to understand the spirit of his message. I smiled and forgot that I was staring at them when the blonde looked at me and cracked a slight grin. My momentary embarrassment was spared when my shuttle arrived, so I jumped on quickly but looked out the window. I tried not to be so obvious as I watched the blonde resume giving his advice as I was carted away from the area.

When I got back to my room, I discovered that the rest of my luggage had arrived; therefore, I spent the rest of the afternoon unpacking while I listened to some music. When I was satisfied that I was totally settled, I went to Kerry's room where I noticed two stereos and a large color TV. "Wow!" I exclaimed as my eyes floated around the room. "I see that the rest of your luggage arrived."

"Only the clunky looking stereo by my bed belongs to me," Kerry said with a giggle. "The really expensive stuff that's not set up yet belongs to Carol."

"And where is Carol?" I asked, noticing her absence."

"Who knows," Kerry said. "She'll be back later. She has her own car, you know."

"If she's so rich," I inquired, "why doesn't she have a private room?"

"I asked her that," Kerry said. "As it turns out, she plans to spend most of her time living with her boyfriend; and having a roommate will lead her folks to believe otherwise."

"What a deceitful little bitch!" I cried out with admiration.

"And here's the best part," Kerry added with glee. Since she's gone so often, it's like having a private room." She put her hands up in a stopping motion. "I do have to do one thing for her from time to time."

"Like what?" I asked with concern.

"If her parents ever call – on the phone that we'll be getting next week – I have to play a little diversion for her."

"Such as?" I interrupted.

"Oh, claim that she's in the shower and that she will call back or that she's out with friends. I just get a message to her at the boyfriend's, and she calls her parents. No one is the wiser."

"And for that, you get all these little goodies," I asked, "or does she take all this stuff over to her boyfriend's?"

"She says that her boyfriend has all she needs, so this stuff stays here." She gave me a toothy grin and then shrugged her shoulders. "Maybe I can rent out the other half to some indigent and make a few bucks." Her words were as silly as her expression and in no way intended to be taken seriously.

"Fantastic," I said with a twinge of jealousy.

"But it gets better," Kerry added. She walked to the small dresser by her bed and opened the top drawer. Inside sat a tin container that looked like it held talcum powder or something similar. However, it was filled with a dozen or more perfectly rolled joints – all of a considerable size as well. "I told you that her boyfriend had the best connections," she said as she handed me two joints.

"Now, I really am jealous," I said seriously.

Kerry laughed. "We're going out later," she said. "You wanna go?"

I took a deep breath and practically apologized. "I don't think I'm up to it tonight." And I wasn't. I fell asleep around nine and slept right through to eight the next morning.

I was able to make my appointment quite easily and discovered – much to my chagrin – that regardless of my major, I had to take a heavy load of compulsory courses. It took close to an hour for my advisor and me to complete the construction of a schedule, which offered no conflicts with time or educational requirements. Then I had to go and register as quickly as possible with the hopes that none of my classes would be closed out, forcing my return to the advisor's office where we would start the process all over again.

Because of my promptness, I suffered no shut outs for any of my classes; and with very little difficulty, I was able to get in one of the three lines at the registration window. While I was there, I noticed the same two boys from the previous day, but this time I was very careful not to stare. Red and curly was sitting in a corner while "Blondie" stood in the line furthest from mine. When it was his turn at the window, I noticed that he was pointing to the red head. Then he received two packets instead of one and carried one to his friend. This seemed rather odd to me at the moment, but I let it pass and rushed up to the window when my time arrived. I was handed a large envelope, which contained computer cards for each of my classes and a list that informed me of the necessary corresponding texts. When I turned around, the two boys had already left; but I observed them later at the college bookstore where I purchased the required text for each required course. Both were seated at a table in the far corner of the adjoining lounge with a pile of books in front of them. Once again it appeared as if the blonde were giving advice as the two were thumbing through the pages of one book very carefully, stopping periodically as the blonde pointed things out.

I was tempted to walk over and eavesdrop once more but thought better of it; so I took my own handful of books, struggled to the bus stop, and rode back to my dorm. I plopped my books in a heap, and watched some quiz shows. I smoked one of the joints, which Kerry had given me, and discovered that it was better stuff than what I had. The room spun around nicely, and fortunately I had enough snacks to satisfy my appetite later. Kerry may have stopped by to ask me something, but I didn't really remember. All I knew was that I felt good – very, very good – and suddenly realized that the college experience was going to be fantastic. I spent the next day catching up on some sleep while those less eager than I, had to apply for late registration and settle for whatever was left behind. It was a holiday well spent.

3

Kerry was going out with her roommate on what amounted to nothing more than a blind date; but she promised that if she found someone, whom she thought I'd find interesting, she would turn him on to me. "I'm not crazy about blind dates," I told her. "I'd much rather meet someone at a party or pick a guy up at a bar."

"What if he's handsome and rich?" she asked.

"I appreciate the offer, but don't knock yourself out trying," I answered as I pushed her out the door. I was pretty confident that no such man of my dreams would appear anytime soon, so I was content going to Friday night's college dance by myself. I had very little interest in dancing, but I figured that it would be a good opportunity to meet people – and to meet them on my terms.

The dance – or college mixer as some called it – was held in the auditorium and turned out to be more crowded than I had anticipated, thanks in part to the two bands working on alternate shifts and a

141

temporary but very large bar which served beer or wine to those who could produce the proper identification – or in most cases, the appropriate bribe. Some only needed a wink and a smile while others were required to drop some extra coinage to cover the already over-priced drink. Either way, there was an enormous amount of underage drinking; and any college personnel in attendance seemed to look the other way. The smell of pot stayed outside with the usual collection of stoners, who always attended these functions. I had indulged a little before I left, so one or two drinks were all I needed to remove most of my inhibitions.

I was drifting around when I noticed those two boys again, and this time I decided to find out a little about them. I walked very casually to where they were sitting and looked at them both with equal measure, trying to appear more enthusiastic than aggressive.

"Hi," I said, "my name is Geralyn Garr."

Both looked at me and acknowledged my presence. The redhead remained seated and very politely introduced himself as Jim MacIntyre but insisted that I call him "Mac." The blonde stood up and offered me his hand. He was also polite but slightly abrupt as he shook my hand and said, "Steve Connolly."

"Well," I said, "are you guys from around here or what?"

Steve answered quickly, "We're both from New York, and you?"

"Upstate," I answered, never considering that my answer could indicate California and not New York.

They both nodded. "It seems like everyone is," said Steve, obviously aware that I too was from the East. He then motioned toward a vacant seat. "I'm sorry; I've been very rude. Would you like to sit down?"

I accepted graciously and planted myself in a chair that was not too uncomfortable. "Are you freshmen?" I asked.

"Of course," Mac responded with a laugh. "Upper classmen never come to these things."

I felt a touch embarrassed. "I don't know," I said in a feeble attempt to recover, "there might be a few." I looked around as if I were surveying the area. "But I should have known that you were freshmen because I saw you at one of the orientation sessions," I lied.

"Mac and I paid very little attention to those things," Steve said, not masking his displeasure for the program at all.

"I know what you mean," I agreed. "They were pretty boring." I was about to ask them what their majors were when I noticed Kerry among the crowd, and it appeared as though she was looking for someone. I ran over to meet her, and she showed signs of relief when she spotted me.

"Gerry, I can't believe I found you!"

"I thought you and the roommate were hooking up with her boyfriend and some other guy?"

"I am," she said, "but we need another body."

"No way," I said harshly. "This sounds like a blind date."

"Don't look at it that way," Kerry pleaded. "Look at it like a party – a party where a lot of fun lies ahead."

"What kind of party?" I asked with my curiosity aroused.

Kerry started tugging on my arm. "Look we've got a ton of pot, some coke, and who knows what else."

"Sounds interesting, but why do you need me?" I asked.

"Carol and her boyfriend engineered the whole thing. Originally, it was just one guy coming down from San Francisco. But he has a friend with him, and that friend is the one who supplies all the stuff."

"So you need me to entertain the friend," I said defensively.

"Something like that," Kerry replied.

"And I imagine that I've got to put out for this guy."

"That's up to you," Kerry answered quickly. "Don't tell me you've never been in situations like this before. Besides, we're not being sentenced to prison or anything. We get to spend the night at a nice apartment, and we get to smoke a little, snort a little …" Her words faded away.

"I'm still not sure," I said.

"You've got nothing to lose," Kerry said, raising her voice to be heard over the din of the crowd. "If the guy turns out to be a creep, you still get high for free. And," she tilted her head, "if the guy is worth it, it's double your pleasure, double your fun."

"But San Francisco," I said with a low whine. "We can't be sure if these guys are normal."

Kerry moved her body in exasperation. "They're friends of Carol and her boyfriend, so I doubt they're serial killers."

"And how long have you known Carol?" I asked in desperation.

"And how long have I known you?" Kerry shot back.

"Touché," I granted Kerry. "Just let me do one thing, and I'll be right back."

"We're parked outside on the south side, be there as quickly as possible."

I walked back to where Steve and Mac were sitting and a little sheepishly said, "Say, fellas, a friend of mine just came in, and she wants me to go someplace with her; so I'll see you around, huh."

"No problem," Mac said as he looked up. Steve, however, just gave a nonchalant shrug and nodded his head.

As I ran to meet Kerry in the parking lot, I looked back for an instant and saw Steve and Mac marching toward the bar. I noticed that Mac had a very noticeable handicap, which affected his walking; and if not for Steve leading the way, he would never have gotten through the crowd. It then dawned on me that this was the first time I had seen Mac in anything but a sitting position. My concentration was broken when I noticed Kerry by the exit door waving frantically. "All right," I shouted, somewhat annoyed. "I'm coming.

Kerry led me to Carol's waiting car, and within seconds, we were on our way. Between hits on the joint that Kerry started passing around, Carol did her best to convince me that I was in for more fun than I could handle. She spoke non-stop about her boyfriend Bill and his two friends; and if they were all as good looking as she described, we were indeed going to have quite an evening. "Here we are," she said when we completed the half hour journey and pulled into the parking lot of the most expensive apartment complex in the entire area.

I could not believe the size of Bill's apartment as I walked through the front door or at the amount of the electronic equipment that graced the inside. "Some place, isn't it?" Kerry whispered as we seated ourselves in the living room.

"I'll say, but where's Bill and the two guys we're supposed to meet?" I had hardly finished my sentence when the front door flew open and in pranced three very attractive males. The first one to enter was tall and sandy haired with blue eyes that suffered from a red tint around the white. When he grabbed Carol and kissed her passionately, I whispered to Kerry, "That must be Bill."

"No shit," she fired back. "Oh by the way, the ugly one's yours."

"What!" I said, caught completely off guard and trying to imagine whom she could possibly have meant.

"Gotcha!" she squealed with delight. "It's already been arranged that Greg is with me."

When Bill finished greeting Carol, he turned and pointed to the pair at the door. "This is Tom and Greg," he said. Tom was shorter than Bill, had hair that was a little lighter, and eyes which were as brown as any I had ever seen. At this point, I didn't care who had been designated for whom, but I was certainly attracted to Tom and delighted when he came and sat by me. Greg was the shortest of the group but the most muscular. He had dark hair with eyes that matched and seemed delighted when he saw Kerry. The feeling was apparently mutual as Kerry looked at me and gave me a smile of approval.

I was already high from the joint we had smoked on the way, and any inhibitions I may have had previously, all but vanished. When Bill lit up another joint and passed it around, I could feel the intensity growing inside of me with an overwhelming urge to attack Tom. The music, which had always been playing, grew louder and louder; and the lights in the speakers flashed with each beat of the melody, almost creating a hypnotic effect. By the time the cocaine came out, I was ready for anything. It was here when Bill explained that an earlier trip to get the coke was the cause for their unexpected tardiness. I couldn't care less, for everything was peaking; and as I did my first line, I could feel my soul leaving my body. I had only used coke a few times previously but always felt that it added necessary stimuli to most occasions, so without hesitation, I did one more line. Tom took my hand and gently led me to one of the bedrooms, where suddenly I drifted to the top of the highest mountain and sucked in a mouthful of cool, fresh air as my body transformed into a beautiful flower. My soul had reunited with my body, and the two became focused on what I was doing. Very little was said, for we both wanted the same thing – just a casual moment of total togetherness with no strings or commitment. I opened my petals and accepted Tom to the fullest; totally aware that things for the moment were always the best and that nothing would last forever.

We spent the next three days at Bill's smoking, snorting, and appreciating the high priced equipment as we all made the same journeys to paradise. Faces became blurred and merged as one with Tom becoming Greg and Greg becoming Bill and Bill becoming Tom. When we left on Sunday, we were so wasted that we barely made it to our rooms. I fell asleep at six and stayed asleep until breakfast.

4

I finished breakfast around eight and then started for my first class, naturally unaware of where I was going. While getting directions from an upperclassman, I noticed that most of the students were walking around bleary-eyed, hung over, or both. My first class was composition, and all freshmen were required to take it, along with a foreign language, a math or science, a fine arts course, and good ole physical education. After meeting these requirements, a student could complete the curriculum with a chosen course – an elective or a concentrate. I took accounting since I knew I would need it later.

Regardless of one's major, the college considered composition to be very important; however, I hated it and found it extremely difficult as well, especially this course. I had always thought that composition was supposed to be writing – not grammar and mechanics, which it appeared we were getting.

In an attempt to see how much or how little we knew, the instructor had given us a diagnostic test; and he expected us to do it. I remembered some of the material from elementary school, but since I never had it in high school, I was really out of it.

Steve Connolly was in the class, and for the first time, I didn't see Mac close by his side. As I was fumbling over my paper, I noticed Steve just sitting there with a bored expression while his test paper was turned face down. He's going to make one hell of an impression on the teacher, I thought. Why wasn't he working like the rest of us? I thought.

I didn't waste any more time watching him since I had enough trouble as it was. At least I finished the paper, which was more than I could say for most of the class. This would not count as a grade, thankfully, so we were told to exchange papers with the person next to us and wait for the answers. I took Connolly's paper and was surprised to notice that he had actually completed it. When the instructor gave us the answers, my fifteen out of thirty wasn't that impressive; but Connolly's perfect score was. I handed his paper back to him; and before I could ask how he had done so well, the teacher started yelling at us to get our attention.

"You are all wondering why you are taking grammar in a freshmen composition course. I'll tell you why," he grumbled. "Before you can write a composition, you have to learn all the basic fundamentals. Why do you think I took a nice leisurely stroll around the room – for my exercise? Of course not, I was observing you, and you, class; do not know the basic fundamentals."

We sure didn't, and for the rest of the period, this crotchety man before us waved his huge wrinkled hands, flashed his large bushy eyebrows, and pushed his fifty years of life and his well-trained mentality at us from all directions. I only hoped that some of his wisdom would trickle down on me. I left the class slightly shell shocked but not the least bit afraid of the man who convinced me that he really wanted to help us. As we filed out to the upper breezeway, I took the opportunity to speak with Steve. When I asked him how he had done so well on the handout, he just looked at me with a solemn stare and said, "It all goes back to when I was in the sixth grade. I had one heck of a teacher when I was in the sixth grade."

"And you retained all of it?" I asked with skepticism.

"Most of it," he answered quickly. "I've used a lot of it over the years, so it tends to stay with me."

"Over the years!" I exclaimed with obvious bewilderment. "Doing what?"

"In high school," he answered abruptly. "We used it when I was in high school." Then he looked directly at me and raised his eyebrows. "Didn't you?"

"Not that I remember," I admitted, "but I was busy doing other stuff."

"I see," he remarked curtly, "but you must have done well enough to get into college."

"Oh yea," I said, too embarrassed to admit that my father's money had more to do with my acceptance than my SAT scores. "I applied myself whenever it was necessary."

"That's the case with most students," he responded with authority. "Back in that sixth grade class, we were lined up on a daily basis and quizzed unmercifully. To an eleven-year-old it was like the firing squad." He took a deep breath and then let out a sigh. "We were seated in straight rows that alternated from boy to girl; and if you missed a question, you had to remain in the back of the room when the next row got up there. Needless to say, you stuck out like a sore thumb."

"Sounds awful," I said.

"Oh it was," he replied. "All of your friends would make faces, embarrassing the hell out of you while the teacher was barking out questions one after the other." He paused for a second, pressed his lips together, and widened his eyes. "It was quite effective though because I really learned something." He shrugged. "But that was then. Teachers no longer use fear as a motivator or humiliation as a learning tool."

"What school was this?" I asked with sincere curiosity.

"It was a small private school," he said somewhat evasively. "You probably never heard of it."

"I thought you said you were from New York." This caught him off guard although I was the one who was totally perplexed.

"I live in New York, but I was educated somewhere else." His delivery was brusque and his tone was rather exacting, so I decided not to pursue our conversation any further. We gave each other polite farewells and went our separate ways.

My next class was Spanish – from 10:00 to 11:00 – and I knew that I would have trouble because I was just naturally terrible when it came to languages. I had taken Spanish in high school but ouched my way through with a low D that came as a result of cheating on

154

most of my tests. From 11:00 to 12:00, I was free for lunch, and then went to biology at 12:30 and to my lone accounting class at 2:00.

Monday, Wednesday, and Friday were my toughest days since I had a full load of classes; and Tuesday was mildly difficult with a ninety-minute fine arts class, a biology lab session, and the class I dreaded most – physical education. Thursday was by far, the easiest day on my schedule with Introduction to Theatre (my fine arts class) being the only thing on the docket. I had purposely scheduled my accounting class as late in the day as possible, so I wouldn't oversleep and miss the only class I considered important.

As far as I was concerned, classes were merely a good way to pass the time of day. Night was the all-important part of my twenty-four hour section on the calendar, and I made sure that I didn't miss a bit of the action. Tom and Greg stayed down from San Francisco for two weeks before they had to return to *their* college, and Kerry and Carol became my constant companions during that time. I spent more time at Bill's apartment than I did at my own room, and each night was a party while each morning was a chore to get up. Somehow, I managed to show up for all my classes during those first two weeks, but I had comprehended nothing.   Part of the arrangement between my parents and me was that I manage to pass everything, and I was already falling behind on several of my assignments. I didn't want to give up this sweet college life that I had already grown accustomed to, so I had to put in a little effort for my parents to keep footing the costs. I wasn't too worried, however, since it was early; and there was plenty of time for school.

Tom and I had continued our causal relationship until his departure, and we each made a half-hearted promise to keep in touch – something that neither of us intended to honor.

5

I was a more active student during my third week, but catching up proved more difficult than I had anticipated. This attempt to accept academia made the week go by very slowly; and when the weekend finally arrived, I was looking forward to it. As usual, Carol was spending the weekend with Bill; and with Tom and Greg gone, Kerry and I thought we'd just loaf around the campus. On Friday night, we went to the campus bar, where we met the tall blonde from Chicago. It was the first time we had seen her since we split the cab fare.

"Well, fancy meeting you guys here," she said as she pointed to an empty stool. "I don't believe I remember your names," she apologized.

"That's all right," Kerry said sympathetically, "we don't remember yours either." We all laughed as we reintroduced ourselves and discovered that her name was Margaret.

"So, what have you guys been up to for the last few weeks?" Margaret asked.

"Not too much," I said. "There were some guys down from Frisco visiting Kerry's roommate's boyfriend, and …"

Margaret laughed and mimicked the way I had spoken by saying, "Kerry's roommate's boyfriend?"

"That's right," I answered as I smiled and then snickered a bit. "Kerry and I spent the better part of two weeks with them."

Margaret raised her eyebrows in an orderly fashion. "Sounds pretty decent," she remarked. "So are you just warming up for more of the same?"

"Hardly," I asserted, "they left for Frisco last week."

"Well, then," Margaret said with a bounce to her voice, "you and Kerry need to stop by the apartment tomorrow night."

"What's the occasion?" Kerry asked.

"No occasion," Margaret answered. "Just thought you'd like to stop over and get wrecked. There'll be others coming."

"Sounds good," I sang gleefully.

"Will any boys be there?" Kerry asked.

Margaret forced her lips together so her left eye closed and nonchalantly said, "Who knows?"

"Don't worry about it," I interjected. "I think I can survive without a man for the weekend." I looked over at Kerry. "It'll be a nice change to just hang out and get blitzed."

Kerry leaned over my shoulder and started laughing. "Besides," she whispered, "it'll be nice to give your back a rest."

"All right," I shot back, trying to keep my voice low. "I'm sure you and Greg were just holding hands."

"What was that?" Margaret asked, trying to get in on the conversation.

"Nothing," I answered. "Just some sick humor from my friend here." Again, I pointed to Kerry. We all laughed, bought a round of refreshments, and spent the entire evening drinking, playing the usual selection of bar games, and rejecting several invitations to parties in which we were not the least bit interested. I didn't remember what time I went to bed, but I slept till noon.

When I finally rolled out of the rack and looked out my window, I decided that it was too beautiful a day to waste indoors nursing a hangover. I knew that the college had a swimming pool, but I hadn't really seen it except from a distance; so I grabbed my suit, a towel, and some lotion, hopped on the first bus arriving, and landed there in no time.

The pool area had a modest crowd of sun worshipers, complete with the oily bodies and the already darkened skin. An occasional diver would display his acrobatic stuff to any spectators in the crowd, who were willing to look up; and a few marathon swimmers were fighting the throng of floaters and bathers in an attempt to swim the length of the pool since members of the swim team were using the special area with the roped lanes. There were radios everywhere, each playing a different station, which made the entire complex sound like a carnival.

As I entered, I spotted Mac sitting on a lounge chair listening to the program of his choice; and it was no surprise at all when I saw Steve sitting in the chair next to him. Mac appeared pale as though he had not been in the sun very much, and his body looked fragile. Steve was wearing a T-shirt, so I couldn't observe his tan – or the lack of it – but even through the garment, I could tell that he had a rigid body with finely honed muscle. I had never really looked at him before, and I was realizing for the first time that he was actually quite handsome. Whenever I saw him during the one common class we had, he was usually wearing some baggy garment that did little to accentuate his physique. He also had the habit of sitting near the front of the class, and I always opted for those desks in the last row; so more often than not, I saw nothing but the back of his head. He was also very quick to leave at dismissal, and I rarely got to speak with him. Here at the pool, he appeared a lot less studious and a lot more relaxed. His fluffy blonde hair was blowing in all directions making him look every bit the beach bum, and I got the feeling that he spent a good deal of his free time in these surroundings.

"Well, Steve," I said as I walked over to greet them both, "you look different without a book under your arm. I never seem to see you anywhere but in composition class." They both looked up and smiled. "And, Mac, I haven't seen you since that Friday night dance."

"I've been working pretty hard these last few weeks," he said while turning the radio down. "I have a project due next month for my film class."

"Hmm," I groaned. "I thought about film for one of my fine arts requirements, but I took theater."

"I'll take theater next semester," he said complacently. "They're all pretty much the same."

"That's true," I agreed, "but I'm not sure if I'll take film or not." I looked over at Steve. "And how about you?" I asked.

"I'm taking TV media for one of my fine arts requirements," he answered quickly.

"Not that, silly," I said with a chuckle. "What have you been up to lately?"

His eyes widened and showed their blue. "Just hanging around," he said, "and going to class."

"Sounds dull," I moaned.

"Oh it is," he remarked. "Can't you tell how dull we are?" They both laughed and pointed to an empty chair. I put my carrier under the seat and sat down.

"It sure is a nice day," I said as I inhaled the air. "I need to come here more often."

"It's the best as long as we don't have a smog alert," Mac said as he struggled to get up. I put my hand out to offer some assistance, but Steve waved me off. "I'm gonna go and soak for a while," Mac said as he finally got to his feet.

"Fine," Steve replied. "Have fun." Mac hobbled to the shallow end of the pool and carefully lowered himself in.

"Are you roommates?" I asked, quite sure that they were.

"Yes, yes we are," Steve said. "We have an apartment at the Regency."

"Sounds nice," I said. "Do you have a car?"

He nodded. "We just picked one up the other day – not a brand new one but good enough to get us around."

"Couldn't handle waiting for the buses each day," I said but immediately regretted it.

"Something like that," Steve replied, apparently not offended at all. "It's easier for Mac."

"Does Mac drive?" I asked, once again afraid that I had been rude. "I'm sorry," I quickly interjected before Steve could respond. "I shouldn't be so nosy."

"It's fine," Steve said, making me feel less awkward. "He drives when he has to but not too often. The car is designed to accommodate him, but he prefers to let me handle the wheel."

"Speaking of getting around," I said cautiously, "would I be out of line if I asked you what is wrong with Mac's legs."

"Certainly not," Steve said, putting me completely at ease. "He has cerebral palsy."

"Oh, I'm so sorry," I said.

"Don't feel sorry for Mac," he demanded. "He never feels sorry for himself, and he doesn't expect others to feel sorry for him either."

"I didn't mean anything by it," I apologized.

"I know you didn't," he assured me, "but Mac is pretty independent, and he wants to be treated just like anybody else."

"That's why you stopped me from helping him," I declared.

"Exactly," Steve said. "He likes to do things on his own, but from time to time, he doesn't mind a little assistance." He clapped his hands gently and then interlocked his fingers. "If people start to feel sorry for him, he *will be* offended. He knows what he wants out of life, and he's not shy about going after it." I didn't know what to say, so I just smiled and folded my arms. Fortunately, Steve – once again – put me at ease as he narrowed his eyes and wrinkled his lip. "How about a trip to the bar for a drink? I'm buying."

"Sure," I said as I stood up, "but what about Mac?"

"He can come if he wants," Steve assured me, "but I doubt that he will. Just let me tell him where we're going, and he can join us later if he wants."

As I gathered my things, he walked over to the pool and gave Mac the message; and within a few minutes we were comfortably seated and drinking our beverage of choice. After a few beers for me and a ginger ale for him, I learned that Steve ran track for his high school but played football and baseball independently on the weekends when each sport was in season. He liked to play golf, read, and watch every kind of sport on television; and like me, he was looking forward to the school's upcoming football season and fully intended to be at every home game. He was open in his conversation, but there seemed to be some missing pieces. There was a subtle mystery about him – a mystery that led me to believe that he was much more than he appeared to be.

"How long have you and Mac been friends?" I asked.

"I've known him since high school," Steve answered, "and I'm a family friend as well."

"And that's why you're here," I said, feeling exceptionally perceptive.

"I'm here to get an education," he interrupted with a slight rise in pitch.

"There's more to it," I continued. "You're here to watch out for him. I can see it when the two of you are together. You're his mentor, his advisor, his …"

"His friend." Steve completed my sentence with a critical ring to his voice and gently put his glass down.

"Now, I know for sure that I've offended you," I said assuredly yet timidly.

"It's all right," Steve said. "I do look out for him, but I do it because he's my friend. But believe me when I tell you that I'm here to get an education."

"Fair enough," I said as I drained my glass, "and you're confident that Mac could make it without you."

"He's not the problem," Steve said, starting to show some emotion. "*We're* the problem – you, me, and all the other people who can walk without any difficulty. We make it tough on people like Mac because we patronize them and cater to them and destroy their whole sense of worth. Mac'll make it just fine, just as long as people allow him to be self-reliant."

"Very profound," I announced.

"I didn't mean to ramble," he said somewhat embarrassed. "Let's get another drink if you want and then go back to the pool."

"I'm good," I said. "Let's go back now.

When we returned, Mac was back in the lounge chair blasting the radio. "You look like you're getting a little sunburned," Steve said.

"Yea, I am feeling a little tight," Mac said while he stretched. "Maybe we better head for home."

"Good enough," Steve said. "Gerry, can we drop you anywhere?"

"No thanks," I said. "I'm going to change and go for a swim. It's still early, and that's why I came here."

"We'll be seeing you," Steve said.

"Later," Mac said with a smile.

I watched them all the way to the parking lot until I could see them no longer. As always, Steve led the way. After a quick swim, I soaked up some sun for about an hour and then returned to my room and got ready for my night at Margaret's. The shower was cold, but the water was refreshing as it hit my partially sunburned body. I stood under the spray for an eternity, letting my mind wander with each jet of water that hit my face and back. I was giving myself a cheap thrill as I thought about Mac and Steve and the entire afternoon; but my mind was getting confused, so I blocked it out and concentrated on the cheap thrills alone. When my wet experience was over; I put on my robe, lay on my bed, and stared at the ceiling – hoping that my evening would be worthwhile.

I met Kerry at six, and we arrived at Margaret's by 6:30. Three joints into the evening, we decided to watch an old movie on television – a sad one that made me cry. Sometimes it could become embarrassing; but I cried quite easily during tearjerkers, and there was nothing I could do about it. Too many times I saw a situation in a movie that reminded me of something in real life, and just like that, the tears started flowing. I let things bother me when I shouldn't have, but I never seemed to get things under control.

Margaret and a few of her friends watched the movie but didn't seem to take much in since they continually stared at the set, into space, or at each other. Kerry fell asleep before the feature was half over, and she looked so calm and content as she lay on the couch, never moving a muscle and breathing so gently until we woke her up around midnight with the intention of crashing the party three apartments down. We were all set to make the scene when a large fight broke out, and we didn't bother to find out what caused it. However, we were able to witness the arrival of the campus police and their apprehending of two boys involved – one with a broken arm and the other with a bloody face. I could only watch for a few moments before I felt my stomach starting to churn; and even when Kerry and I rode the bus home later, I couldn't get that bloody vision out of my head. The sight of violence always sickened me and often caused me to vomit. When I got back to my room; I plopped on the bed, turned on the radio, and let the soft music lull me to sleep.

For some reason, on this particular Sunday, I decided to act like a student and actually worked the entire day, finishing several reading assignments and reports that were due; but it was torture, and I felt it.

My studious attitude carried over through the week as I slugged through my classes. My most successful course was accounting – not only the easiest but also the most important as far as I was concerned, and composition was my most unsuccessful with hard work and a hard teacher who expected a great deal from his students. Spanish was a joke, thanks to a moronic instructor, who couldn't control the students or catch them at the act of cheating; and biology was no more than note taking with a test on every other Friday. Since part of the grade – a big part – was based on lab participation, I did my best not to miss any sessions. Kerry was taking the same biology course that I was but at a different time; therefore, we often swapped notes and took turns skipping an occasional class. The teacher was a total bore, but he was smart enough to give each of his classes a different version of his bi-weekly assessment; or we would have been swapping those out as well. I hated my physical education course, and I hated the teacher even more. Since I was fortunate to eat just about everything and never gain a pound, I saw no need for the weekly aerobics and asinine volleyball games in which our instructor insisted we participate. We were promised that future classes would include swimming, bowling, and even golf; but swimming was the only one that caught my interest. Finally, there was my theater class, by far the most interesting and most enjoyable of them all. I expected to hate the course when I first signed up for it; but thanks to Dennis Stottlemeyer – a thirty-something, very liberal thinker, who demanded no more than class discussions, impromptu skits, and some role playing – the class became pure joy. With Dennis (who insisted that we call him by his first name), we were all able to get up close and personal. We learned that he was a big contributor to Community Theater and had even done some summer stock with a famous person or two. Whenever we did skits in class, it was obvious that he was no stranger to acting. It was his unique interpretation of Malamud's Yakov Bok that blew me away and prompted me to stay after class as often as possible and learn even more fascinating things about his past.

Each teacher had his own policy concerning the number of cuts that a student was permitted to have, but Sottlemeyer had none. All of us could come and go as we pleased; and with no hand out assignments or tests, this made it even easier. I was never quite sure how he could figure a person's grade with his unorthodox methods, but I never questioned the policy. As it turned out, theater became the one class that I never wanted to miss, and Dennis Sottlemeyer probably knew this was the case with most of his students.

I was doing my best to give all my classes an equal amount of attention, but each class seemed to demand more than the one, which preceded it; and by day's end, I was completely exhausted. Thankfully, I was able to wind down rather nicely with my seemingly endless supply of marijuana; and thankfully, there was always something to do on the weekends – if time permitted.

7

There was something about a football game, a certain magic in the air that I could always feel. The time of the year had a lot to do with it; and even when the seasons didn't change so drastically, I knew when autumn was upon me – and with autumn, came football. The noise of the crowd, the band, and the cheerleaders all added to an excitement like none other; and I could feel the adrenalin flowing and my heart pumping with anticipation for the pre-game and post-game activities – as well as for the game itself.

My high school football team had compiled a record of 29-8 during the four years that I attended, and I must have gone to every home game. There were always pep rallies and parties whether the team won or not, but a winning team made the celebrations more enthusiastic and kept the stadium crowded with delirious fans, who cheered a play or booed an official. Not all of us really understood the rules of the game; we didn't have to. All we needed to do was follow the lead of the masses that *did*, and keep pace with their banter and chants of victory, glory, and high esteem.

Citra had a reputation as a good football team in its division, producing a winning record for the last three seasons; and we may not have had as much hype or media coverage as the larger universities, but in our own way, we were big time.

The weekend of our first home game had finally checked in with the arrival of Friday night and a collection of parties that made my head swim. A large open field, which adjoined the college, was lined with kegs of beer and spotted with an occasional bon fire.

Meanwhile, every apartment complex was having a party of its own. There was even a party on the roof of the library. People everywhere, noise that shattered the eardrums, singing, dancing, bands playing – it was one wild orgy, and I loved every minute.

Carol took Kerry and me to Bill's where we got stoned out of our minds and then left to hit every other place in existence before we got separated at who knows where. The last thing I remembered before passing out was crawling into the back of some van with a guy named Marvin. When I finally woke up, I discovered that the van was parked about a block from my dorm; but I couldn't be sure if it had been parked there all the time or if someone had driven it while I was asleep.

Marvin was still asleep – or unconscious – when I climbed out the back of the vehicle and somehow managed to walk to my room. I wasn't sure if somebody had spiked my cola with more than rum, but I was having one hell of a time. The floor was spinning at a rapid motion that kept increasing with each step I took; and my clock radio, which read 4:22, suddenly vanished into thin air. My bed melted into a puddle of water and washed me into the bathroom, and the windows rattled while the floor swallowed me whole. Lights kept flashing before my eyes as I kept falling deeper and deeper; first, they were dim, then bright, finally blinding – but always flashing. There was no end to it, nothing in sight that would cushion or prevent my plunge; and then I became thirsty. My mouth was dry, but this couldn't compare with the pounding of my heart or the racing of my pulse; and I was now convinced that someone had given me the substance to put me in this spiral. Suddenly, my fall became a flight, a flowing with wings – and it was beautiful, almost angelic. I was sucked into the abyss but only for a moment, for it would end; it had to end; I knew it would end.

8

The game started at two, but the stadium had been filled since one with fans abiding to the unwritten rule that all members of the student body had to be drunk or stoned before entrance. Many devotees of the sport, drank during the game itself to keep their minds refreshed from the pre-game libation. There were those who used goatskins filled with wine – and in a ceremonial ritual, sans the raccoon coat and straw hat – flaunted the freedom of a new age with the style of an old one. Others just relied on flasks containing stimulant to ward off California's 80-degree chill factor, while most of us took occasional hits on a joint or two, so we could always keep the score. With the exception of a late fourth quarter drive, the game was totally lopsided in our favor and resulted in a 35-7 win.

The parties on Friday night were tame compared to the goings on that *followed* the game. People drove their cars down the street and blasted their horns continuously – some in corresponding rhythm with the chants from the cheerleading squad who led the parade and others with no regard to any organized incantations at all but merely to create enough noise and contribute to the mayhem. As this tornado-like jamboree tore across the campus, the streets were riddled with empty booze bottles; and the singing and dancing lasted for hours.

I was a little more careful than I had been the night before, and this time I was with Keith instead of Kerry. I had met Keith during the game, and we decided to celebrate as a pair. Therefore, we covered all the places that we could and then ended up at his apartment where an all-night party robbed us of all our senses and destroyed any rectitude that might still have glimmered somewhere between us.

When I left the next morning, I must have stepped over a dozen bodies spewed about the living room and the hallway. I caught the first shuttle back to my dorm where I spent the rest of the day with my head draped over the toilet, emptying my insides until there was nothing left. The pounding in my skull and the blurry vision made me realize that Friday's trip had become Saturday's crash, and now on Sunday I was regretting my curiosity. I managed to pick up a copy of the newspaper, which had been delivered to my door, and noticed that the front page had a corner denoting the team's triumph. Citra had won the game all right, but the students and a huge chunk of the campus had lost. Destruction had become entertainment in the form of a victory dance, and no one seemed to care, for the season was just beginning.

9

There were several things about the whole football extravaganza that I never remembered and other things that I did my best to forget. Marvin, the creature with whom I had spent my Friday night, was never seen again; and I even wondered if he had really existed in the first place. If he was more than a figment of my imagination, he couldn't have been a student – at least not at Citra. He was either a local townie or a visiting patron that came along for the ride in order to score with some naïve drunk, who passed herself off as a college freshman.

Therefore, Marvin was a blur; but Keith was a perfectly focused picture, vivid in my memory and as complete as my recollections allowed. As it turned out, he was as interested in me as I was in him; so we began to see a lot of each other. I was more impressed with his sharp sophomore wit and keen interest in campus politics than with his six-foot frame, blue eyes, and sandy brown hair. The Cockran family was worth a small fortune, and Keith wasn't afraid to spread some of it around by taking me places and doing things that were utterly fabulous. Since he was a very good student, his family had put no restrictions on how much money he could spend; and since he was a good student, he was able to help me a great deal in the area of academics. We studied together and we played together; and for both, we gave it our all with an intensity that always hit the maximum level. With each experiment, I reached new horizons and saw things on a higher plain. Keith had given me a desire for unreserved achievement and stressed that everything had to be taken in as a whole, as a total thing. With this new attitude, my grades not only improved, they began to flourish. I informed Keith about my own financial situation and how my parents had me on a tight leash, but he didn't care at all. "When you have me," he said flatly, "you don't need them."

We continued to attend the football games and the usual parties, which followed as the team marched to a 9-1 record. "Winning teams create a winning atmosphere," Keith recalled, and I felt very much a part of that; and with the arrival of Thanksgiving, I no longer wanted to go home. A rock concert in San Diego and a trek with a dozen other students was a better way to hold on to the magic in the air that I never wanted to release.

Several of us had pooled our money together and rented a decent sized truck that would serve as our mode of transportation. A few of the boys would take turns driving while most of us would sleep on the mattresses and pillows thrown in the back. We were guaranteed a safe ride with enough stops along the way to get supplies and use the restroom facilities. Since we planned to leave the Tuesday before

Thanksgiving, I was sure to save any necessary cuts and to complete as much of my work as possible. The days could not go by fast enough, and when Tuesday evening arrived, I was more than ready to go.

Bill and one of his friends picked up the truck and met the group of mutually enthusiastic participants at the front of the cafeteria. Carol was there, of course, along with Kerry, Margaret, and naturally Keith. The rest of the team was rounded out with several others that I did not know but was sure I would become acquainted with by the time we reached our destination.

Singles piled on one side and couples on the other; but before too long, singles joined with other singles and *became* couples, and the few odd numbers, who were left out, didn't seem to mind at all. I shared a small mattress with Keith, where we lay and listened as vehicles went by in the opposite direction and blinked as an occasional light flickered through the small crack that the opening in the door provided; and for the longest time that small glimmer served as our total luminary until someone turned on a battery powered lantern, which gave the entire area a radiance. It was hot but we tolerated it as we tried to occupy our time. A few joints were passed

179

around, but the poor ventilation made the usual soothing effect *less* soothing and *more* annoying; so most everyone ceased indulging. Keith turned on the radio that rested by the head of our mattress with all our supplies, and the choice of soft jazz quickly put me to sleep.

I was having a peaceful dream when a banging noise on the back of the truck woke me up. It was Bill opening the door and informing us that we had pulled into a small rest area just off the highway. He advised us to make use of the bathroom facilities and just about anything else that this small oasis provided. We all rolled out of the truck and went to our respective places of calling. Within ten minutes, we loaded up and started on our way again. We had picked up cans of soda and some packaged goods to supplement our food supplies, along with some toilet paper that was lifted from the stalls. There would be a number of uses for it as well as for any empty containers, which would quickly accumulate. It wasn't as hot now, so most of the couples started snuggling up together and indulging on the joints that once again were being passed around. Bill had been relieved from driving, so he and Carol now occupied a space of their own. The lantern had been turned off and eventually the radio. Keith was able to fall asleep, but I was having some difficulty.

However, after concentrating on the sounds of the highway and allowing the vibrations to hypnotize me, I finally drifted off. This time it was a sound sleep with no dreams at all, and I slept that way until Keith awoke me and said that our destination had been reached.

Things had been organized well. We had all signed our names on a register before the trip began, which not only served as a check to make sure that everyone had paid, but acted as a way of making sure that no one would get left behind for the return trip. We all went our separate ways, promising to return to the truck by 6:00 PM on Saturday. It was now ten o'clock Wednesday morning, and the concert would begin at four and continue till four on Saturday.

Bill and Carol vanished immediately; and Kerry and Margaret, – with their newly acquired companions disappeared as well. Therefore, Keith and I set out to find a spot of our own. We took a blanket, the radio, some binoculars, a jug of wine, twenty sandwiches, several joints, and a small but comfortable tent, which provided some shelter and served as a form of cheap entertainment as I watched Keith setting it up with a degree of difficulty. We located atop a grassy knoll about two hundred yards from the stage, shared a joint, listened to the radio and got a little sun. If it got too hot, the tent provided the required shade to make our environment a bit more bearable. By the time the concert began, I forgot about any of those little discomforts and promptly joined in on the experience. For the next seventy odd hours, Keith and I watched some thirty different bands perform; smoked ten joints; finished a jug of wine; ate sandwiches for breakfast, lunch, and dinner; were introduced to over forty people; sat through five hours of rain and tramped through two feet of mud; fought off mosquitoes; made love twice; hiked to the woods seven times; suffered a slight case of sunburn; pushed and shoved in a crowd for two hours; and waited in the back of the truck for four. We ended up leaving much later than originally planned; but we didn't mind a bit, for the concert was definitely a worthwhile adventure.

"How did it feel slumming with the poor folk?" I asked Keith as we rolled up our gear and stuffed it in an appropriate bin.

"You tell me," he said. I laughed and then swatted him playfully. "Even us rich people have to rough it once in a while," he said complacently. "That's half the fun. We can't travel in limousines all the time, you know."

"It *was* fun!" I declared ardently. "And you're right. Riding in the back of that truck was a blast. I hope the ride back is as good."

"Believe me when I say it isn't," Steve lamented. "But you'll sleep well."

On the way home, we decided to do just that rather than sharing our exploits and rehashing about how much fun we all had. Our drivers were spelled more frequently on the return trip, and even Keith took a turn; but nothing could rock those of us who stayed in the back as we all faded off into slumber with our merry little boat bouncing on the waves of the highway and drifting into the direction of our school.

10

Throughout the country, the end of Thanksgiving always meant the start of Christmas season, and college was no exception to this practice. However, it was difficult for me to get into a true holiday spirit without the snow in the air and with the presence of a bright blue sky instead of a gray and dingy one. Besides, the semester was drawing to a close, and that meant final exams. I had come too far to let it slip through my fingers now, so more investment in academics trumped the appealing gaiety of Santa and his elves. I had managed to maintain decent grades in most of my courses – some with the help of Keith and others with a little luck and perhaps a sharp eye. Accounting was a potential B, theatre a cinch A, biology and composition hard earned C's, and Spanish an underhanded C or C –. If I received passing scores on my exams, I would maintain these grades; and I had *every* intention of doing that. P.E. was a B – provided that I didn't miss another class, and I had *no* intention of doing that.

The exam schedule had been posted, so I was able to make my reservation for a flight home; but I had to admit that going home did not hold the interest it once had. Keith and I were doing fine, and a little change would be good for both of us; but four weeks away from him would seem like an eternity. Since I had been spending so much time at his apartment, I was forgetting what my dorm room looked like; and with exams right around the corner, I planned on spending even more time at Keith's just to get prepared – emotionally and intellectually for those final assessments.

Between the studying and long tutoring sessions, Keith and I still managed to find the time to attend a party or two and even went to the huge Christmas dance – a semi-formal event, complete with seasonal decorations, plenty of holiday spirits, and even an artificial snowstorm.

When the dance was over, Keith and I took a long ride down a dark country road and parked the car; so we could walk, look at the stars, and just talk. "What do you like best about this time of year?" I asked.

"It's hard for me to say," he answered. "I guess it's just the time of year itself." He looked up at the sky and took a deep breath. Then he smiled to indicate his total appreciation of the beautiful sight that stretched before us. "Everyone seems to be happy and looking forward to something."

"Like going home," I interrupted.

"That or maybe a trip to some place exciting that really has the Christmas atmosphere." He paused, took my hand, and then whispered gently, "I wish you could come to Switzerland with me."

"That would be nice," I said. "I've never been to Europe."

"We go to some very special place every year," he said, almost apologizing. "But this year I'll be thinking of you most of the time."

I smiled, hugged him, and kissed him softly. "I'll miss you too," I said, "but it won't be forever, and just think how nice it will be when we get back." I had almost convinced myself that these words were sincere, so I was sure that Keith believed in their authenticity.

"That's true," he sighed. "It does give us something to look forward to."

I kissed him again. "I've met a lot of great people here, but you're the one who's special. And when all those relatives come to my house and tell me how proud they are and all that other crap, I'll tell them they can thank you."

"Don't get goofy on me," he laughed.

"I won't," I promised. "It's just that next week we've got exams, and then I'm heading home for four weeks." He led me back to the car, and we drove off, continuing to take in the beauty of the warm winter night. We made love that evening without a thought or worry concerning the present or the future. We studied the next day and throughout most of the week. With my head crammed with as much as it could possibly hold and my pockets stuffed with well mapped out cheat sheets; I was prepared for my exams – all of which were complicated, fun, boring, interesting, and finally over.

Keith took me to the airport to see me off; and since planes always made me nervous, upon take off, I could feel a pounding in my chest along with sweaty palms and a fluttering stomach. Every bump, turn, and air pocket had me worried, and they revived my recurring dream of crashing in the desert and my roaming endlessly in search of food or water. As the plane travelled north, my delirium switched from an arid landscape to a large blizzard that covered me up and made it impossible to push the make shift sled constructed from pieces of the plane's fuselage. This morbid fatalism continued until the plane landed, and the only sounds I heard were the polite words from the stewardess as she sang, "Hope you had a nice flight." After a quick greeting from my parents and an eternity waiting for my luggage, we started for home as I lied about my experience at school; listened to my father's usual lecture with no interest at all; and totally ignored my mother's monotone lamentations about garden clubs, social groups, and civic meetings.

The weather was chilly but not as cold as I expected; and the absence of snow was a major disappointment for sure; but vacation was just starting; and behind me, I put the thought of classes, grades, teachers, and students. By midnight I was asleep in my own bed, exhausted from the long trip, and weary from all the useless conversation. I was content and looking forward to four weeks of no responsibility whatsoever.

11

Christmas day was about what I expected with a few variations: Mother's banquet was smaller, fewer relatives showed up, and most of the little kids who had run around the house on previous occasions were now considerably grown up.

There was so much that I wanted to do during this month long hiatus from college, but there weren't enough hours in the day. Too many bars, an abundance of parties, reunions, and just plain loafing around seemed to occupy most of my time with a few movies, a concert in the forum, a dance or two, and one hell of a New Year's Eve rounding things out nicely.

I had spent most of the time with my old boyfriend, but circumstances had prevented us from having any real quality alone time; therefore, when December 31 came about, we shared a motel room and brought the new year in appropriately. I told my parents that I was going to a party with several of my friends; and since they

188

were going to do some heavy celebrating of their own, they showed very little concern about my whereabouts.

My boyfriend and I had made an arrangement before I left for school, but now I was afraid, afraid that things would get out of hand and I would lose the sure reliability of someone steady if things didn't work out back at Citra. We smoked some grass and made love a few times, and then lay in bed, relaxing and watching celebrations on television as one year ended and another one began. "What happened to us, Jimmy?" I asked. "You didn't write me very much at all."

"Gerry, you know that before you left, we discussed things and decided on no strings, no attachments." He paused as he lit a cigarette. "Did you stay out of trouble?"

"What's that supposed to mean?" I replied belligerently.

"Don't get angry," he said calmly. "It's just that you don't have your dad to bail you out if things get touchy."

"I don't even have a car," I said flatly, "so that's not gonna happen again. Besides, no one was injured; so no harm no foul."

"Did you go out with other guys at school?"

"No," I lied, afraid that the truth was not appropriate right now.

189

His eyes narrowed, and his forehead wrinkled as he glanced over the bridge of his nose to stare at me. "You mean you didn't go out with any boys at all?"

"I met a few people," I said defensively, "but it was all very casual."

He smiled and took a drag on his cigarette. "Well, that's too bad. I went out with plenty of girls, and I'm planning to go out with plenty more."

"Did you fuck them all!" I shouted as I rose from the bed and put on a robe.

"I'm not even going to respond to that," he said while sitting on the edge of the bed. "I'm just saying that whatever you do – or whatever you did out there in California, it's fine with me." He gestured for me to come and sit by him. "All I'm saying is this: we have fun together, and we both make each other feel good. And if you need me, I'll always be around." He smiled. "Come on," he pleaded, "I won't bite."

I turned slowly and faced him, now feeling very sorry and somewhat resentful that I hadn't told the truth, but I had been lying to him for years, so it came very naturally to me. There had always been others, others long before I left for college. If I told Jimmy about them and about everything that had happened at Citra, it might hurt him; and that was what I wanted to do more than anything right now – hurt him the way he had hurt me. However, I was weak, and my needs outweighed my desire for revenge; therefore, he stood up and led me to the bed where I sat with my arms folded. He kissed me very softly on the cheek, causing a slight grin to appear on my face. "That's better," he said calmly. "Now unfold your arms and give me a hug."

I wasn't sure if it was my desire, the effects of the pot, or a combination of the two; but I complied, and our embrace became passionate with the both of us falling back upon the mattress. He was ruthless, but he knew it was what I wanted; and although my pain had not diminished completely, it was subdued enough to make me forget that our lives were on opposite ends of the continent and that any chance of having a lasting relationship was an impossibility. "I love you, Jimmy. I always have, and I've always been loyal to you." I whispered the words as I bit his ear and hoped that he would feel guilty – guilty enough to equal my anguish. It was the best way to hurt him – to hurt him without depriving myself of what I always needed. By the following afternoon, my thoughts were elsewhere.

My grades arrived during the last week of my vacation and turned out to be the best – although belated – Christmas present I could have gotten: C's in composition and biology, a surprising A in accounting and an expected A in theatre, a B in physical education that I *worked* hard for, and a B in Spanish that I *cheated* hard for. My parents were proud and I was delighted.

With my head still spinning, I was back in California; leaving the cold behind me along with the family pressures, noisy relatives, and any final thoughts concerning Jimmy. It felt so good as the plane came up on that strip of runway, allowing me to see Keith at the gate and immediately removing all my distress.

12

I spent my first full day back at the confines of Citra settling in and preparing for new classes. Thanks to pre-Christmas prep and early registration, there wasn't a lot for me to do. Composition II, Accounting II, and Spanish II were required courses; and I did my

192

best to acquire teachers I preferred and at hours that would accommodate my active social life. Chemistry would show up on a mandatory list sooner or later, so there didn't seem to be much sense in putting it off too long. I could take bowling as my physical education requirement and decided to do so, and I jumped at the chance of having Sottlemeyer for Intro. to Film with all the expectations that came as a result of his excellent Intro. to Theatre course.

Four weeks away from Citra were not enough to change it at all: people hustling, new arrivals, meeting friends; and all of it so familiar to me now that the panic and fear, which had so overtaken me back at the beginning of semester one, now seemed silly by all accounts. I was far from a weary, aged veteran, but at least I was comfortable; and thankfully, there would be no orientation classes.

I had made three trips to Kerry's room before I finally caught her napping. "Hey, kid, get up!" I shouted as I kicked her on the bottom of her heels.

She opened her eyes and sprang to her feet. "Gerry!" she exclaimed as she hugged me. "How was your vacation?"

"Fine," I answered. "Just fine, and yours?"

"Great." She reached for a pack of cigarettes, opened it, and handed me one. "How'd you get from the airport?" she asked as she lit her smoke and then mine.

"Keith met me," I said with a sparkle in my voice. "He's trying to change one of his courses to a different time, or he'd be here now. Carol pick you up?"

"Yea, Bill and her arrived late last night. They're out screwing around as always. Who knows where?"

"Or just plain screwing," I added.

"Probably," Kerry coughed as too much smoke filled her lungs. "But what the hell. I get the benefit of using all her neat stuff while she's out playing footsie with William. Did you see that guy over vacation?"

"Jimmy?" I said abruptly. "He's an asshole. Besides, it was over between us long ago."

"And your folks?"

"The same ole' shit," I said with a grin from ear to ear. "They were so proud of me when my grades came in. I had the two of them fooled from day one. They actually think I spent most of my time with my nose in a book. Speaking of grades, how'd you do?"

"No aces, but nothing lower than a C. Oh, by the way," she said with a sharp inquisitive tone, "did you check your mailbox yet?"

"What the hell for?" I said while giving her an exasperated look.

Kerry's forehead tightened, and her face looked straight ahead as her eyes shot upwards. "I got a reply from the sorority."

"Really?" I asked, barely above a whisper.

"Really," she answered, saying each syllable clearly and distinctly and forcing me to read her lips.

My voice rose about three decibels as I shouted, "Are you kidding?"

"I'm serious as hell," she replied. "Did you send them your résumé before you went home?"

"You know I did," I answered as I felt my pulse quicken and my heart start racing.

"Well, then let's go check."

Within moments, we were in the lobby; and I was fumbling with my key as I nervously opened the door to my P.O. box. I pulled out the envelope with the sorority logo in the corner, opened it quickly, and read the contents to myself. Kerry became impatient and asked excitedly, "Well, what does it say?"

I took a deep sigh and formed a sad look on my face but quickly changed to a happy expression as I read aloud: "The sisters accept your résumé and invite you to try out for their sorority."

Kerry jumped up and down. "This is fantastic!" she shouted. "Let's go and celebrate." And celebrate we did, for we knew that it wouldn't be long before our nights would be spent appreciating the finer tortures of the second year sisters who still felt the sting of last year's hazing. I was so hung over the next morning that I barely rolled out of bed to start a day of important activity. I limped through the day and crawled through the evening, never bothering to have dinner or even brush my teeth before I fell asleep. I swore off booze but not pot, and my dreams of a slower paced day became a reality as I coasted to the weekend and watched it float by amidst soft music, a comfortable enhancement, and Keith.

13

In order to gain entrance to a sorority, one would have to go through the most rigorous initiation that a group of human beings could possibly dream up. For thirteen days we were forced to participate in some of the most insane and hideous events imaginable. It was fittingly called "thirteen unlucky days of hell" and I would go through those unlucky days in order to reach the highest pinnacle in college – acceptance.

Day One: Monday

It was a cool, overcast evening as Kerry and I went to the introductory meeting at the sorority hall – a beautiful structure that seated almost two hundred people with chairs set up for almost that number.

Kerry and I arrived around seven and sat in the front. By 7:15, the seats were more than half-full with eager but somewhat apprehensive individuals, whose faces showed the strain of the day and the anxiety of their not-so-certain futures. The only person I knew was Kerry, but there were several familiar faces, which I had seen in class and was sure that I would see a lot more as my hell session neared its inception.

At 7:30, the meeting opened with a blaring presentation by a stereotyped arch villain who looked a lot like a Nazi storm trooper. She was wearing glasses and a tight fitting, somewhat masculine looking outfit that I was sure was all part of the act. "May I have your attention, please," she said, using mock deliberation that was not surprising to me. When the commotion settled, she continued. "You are all about to embark on a trial for acceptance to the best sorority on campus. We are very proud of our sorority, and only those who display the type of qualities we are looking for and who seem worthy, will be accepted." There were a few rumblings and some slight chatter coming from the crowd, but it ended abruptly when our illustrious presenter shouted, "The first rule you all must abide by is this. No one is allowed to talk at a meeting when current members are present unless you are given permission." The place had now become so quiet that it felt a little eerie. I looked at Kerry but didn't dare make a sound. She was smiling, and I could tell she wanted to laugh.

The "Gestapo" agent in the shades continued with her absorbing recitation. "You will address all current sorority sisters as Ma'am, Miss, or Ms. Now read the list that we are about to pass out and then meet us here tomorrow night at eight o'clock. No excuses will be accepted, and no one will be late." She nodded politely and then said, "Good night, and you may now speak if you wish." She was gone before I even looked up. I grabbed the paper with the list of rules and read them carefully.

1. All pledges must honor a curfew of 11:00 unless performing an initiation process.

2. No pledges will be allowed to date during the entire rush.

3. All pledges (whether living in apartments or dorms) will eat dinner at the cafeteria and

must meet there every night at seven, unless told otherwise.

4. All pledges will be assigned Big Sisters later in the week, and you will be expected to

perform certain duties such as washing her car, cleaning her room, or doing her laundry.

Kerry and I didn't bother to browse around and examine the lack of refreshments; we hustled out the door to a spot where we could chat privately. The breeze had picked up considerably and almost blew the paper out of my hand. "What do you think?" I asked almost shouting to be heard over the whipping wind.

"I got a kick out of the group leader," she said with a quiet laugh. "And some of the rules are a bit much, but I think we'll make it. A lot of it was just overly dramatic bullshit to psych us out."

"Probably," I agreed, "but we still better be prepared for the worst." It started to rain, so we ran in pursuit of a transit. By the time I reached my room, I was chilled to the bone. A hot shower not only warmed my slightly frigid bones but relaxed me enough so I fell asleep quite easily.

Day Two: Tuesday

After a grueling day of classes, night fell upon us; and with a slight fear, Kerry and I approached the meeting hall where our paranoia turned out to be one of a logical nature. The same girl who had led the first meeting gave a repeat performance and informed us that we would be put into small groups where a designated leader would instruct us about the blessed events that awaited us this night.

No one talked, and the leaders did not introduce themselves, only motioned as we followed. There were approximately ten of us to a group, and each group piled into a different van. No one moved a muscle as the vehicle chugged on its way to a destination, which only the driver knew.

In what seemed like an hour but was actually not even half, my group arrived at the school's soccer field. At the far corner, there was an entrance to a large grove that was considerably overgrown due to neglect. Blindfolded, we were led cautiously to its deepest part where, after having our masks removed, were given orders to go back to the soccer field. Kerry looked at me and smiled deliriously. We trudged a few hundred yards through the muck and the weeds until we were out of the leader's earshot. "Shit!" Kerry shouted as she looked at me with glazed eyes. "How the hell are we going to get out of here? I was never a Girl Scout!"

"It can't be too bad," I said with a false sense of security. "Our group leader walked in with us, and she has to get out too."

"Yes, but she has a flashlight," Kerry said derisively, "and she probably marked a trail on the way in."

"You want to hide and try to follow her?" I asked with desperation in my voice.

"Not a bad idea," she answered quickly. "But if she catches us, we'll probably get bounced out."

"If we don't find a way out," I said in a panic, "we'll starve to death!"

"Now, don't say that!" she shouted loud enough to cause an echo off the trees. "There's a way out; we just have to think."

"Where are the others?" I asked not hiding the fear. "I've just noticed – we're alone."

"We must have lost them in the darkness," she said while rotating her head and looking around. "Looks like it's just you and me kid."

"Well, what do you suggest?" I asked calmly, somehow believing that Kerry could get us out of this mess.

"Let's start moving," she said with authority. "Maybe we'll come to a path or a trail that can lead us out of here."

So we wandered aimlessly for twenty minutes bumping into trees and into each other, never sure of what we were doing or what we would do next. My feet were wet, and the darkness was so frightening it was almost as if the blindfolds were still around our heads. Fatigue started to set in, so I placed myself on a dry rock and greedily reached for one of Kerry's cigarettes. As I lit it, I noticed the moon making a brief appearance from under the clouds. I kept staring at it, absorbed in its brilliance when suddenly an idea popped into my head. "The moon!" I shouted excitedly. "Kerry, it's the moon."

"So the moon's finally out," she said unimpressed. "Now, we can see the trees when we run into them."

" Aw hell," I said. "We could make torchers if we had to." I held up my book of matches as evidence. "It's not just the light," I added, quite proud of myself, "but the direction."

Kerry looked at me with a confused expression on her face. "The direction?" she inquired.

I spoke more calmly now. "When we were about to enter the grove – before they put the blindfolds on – which direction was the moon facing?"

Kerry put her thumb to her bottom lip and pondered for a moment and then suddenly lifted her head and smiled. "To the right. With us facing the entrance to the grove, the moon was to our right."

I nodded my head. "Exactly. So all we have to do is face in the direction, which has the moon to our *left*, and keep walking that way."

"But doesn't the moon move?" Kerry asked timidly.

"Sure, you dope," I said with a grin, "but not that much in just an hour or so."

"Then let's hurry," she said while rising from the rock where she had joined me, "before the clouds cover the moon again."

It took about an hour, but eventually we made it back to the soccer field where I fell to the ground and rejoiced. Three others were already back, but none of us spoke. I took my shoes off and then squeezed the water from my socks. They were almost dry by the time everyone returned from the woods. "Good job," the leader said in a non-complimentary manner. "If we had to go and get you, you would have been done." It was obvious that some other groups still had this little hike before them so we were informed not to speak about it to anyone. We were also told to be at the hall by seven the next morning. We would have to get home on our own, but that was the least of anyone's problems as our leader climbed into the van and left ten ragged looking girls standing on the soggy turf.

Day Three: Wednesday

My head had hardly hit the pillow when I heard that alarm sounding in my ear, so I lumbered out of bed and made my way to the shower where I washed my aching body with torpid motions. In five minutes I felt relieved enough to meet Kerry and head for the meeting hall; but it didn't last very long, for before we had even arrived, I started to feel my energy drain.

At five minutes to seven, we were seated in our assigned areas. I noticed several empty seats and began to wonder about the other activities, which occurred the previous evening. I couldn't imagine them being much worse than what we had already gone through. My trance was broken by the stomping of several leaders walking to the podium and dropping bags of clothing to the floor. Funny hats, baggy pants, and sloppy looking shoes became our attire for the day as we were ordered to dress up. No matter how hard any of us searched, we could find nothing that fit. Everything was at least a size too large, making us all look as ridiculous as possible.

"I always wanted to be in the circus," Kerry whispered while adjusting a wide brimmed hat.

"Looks like the entire rush group gets to take part in this one," I said as I noticed more people walking in.

"You never looked lovelier," Kerry remarked, paying close attention to the large green blouse that ran from my neck to my knees. I just groaned and walked away. We had to go to all of our classes dressed in this foolish manner as well as report to the cafeteria for our mandatory dinner.

Unfortunately, Wednesday was my heavy day for classes, so I was never more embarrassed as I walked the hallways and went from room to room. There were a few snickers but most people ignored us, all well aware that we were pledging a sorority. However, there was no easy way for me to attend Sottlemeyer's class. Nothing was said, and very few stared; but the knowledge that he was looking at me dressed in garments suitable only for a freak show was just too much. When the class ended, I ran from the room and returned to my dorm where I would have stayed the rest of the day if not for the required appearance at the cafeteria.

The day's activities were enough to satisfy our fearless leader, so we were given the night off. By eleven o'clock I was fast asleep, knowing that I didn't have to report to the hall until seven the next night. It was a very pleasant relaxation.

Day Four: Thursday

We were split up into our little groups again, and my group was ordered to wait while the other groups filed out. Once we were alone, we were handed overcoats that felt damp and looked like Salvation Army rejects.

"Why are these things wet?" I whispered to Kerry as I climbed into the awkward garment.

"I've got a funny feeling that we're going to find out real soon," Kerry said quickly.

She was right and I half expected it when we were driven to the lake, marched out on a wooden pier, and ordered to jump. My bones were already chilled from the damp coat, and the instant blast of icy water that hit my feet as I jumped, made my body go numb. Those non- swimmers in the group were able to put their fears to rest since the water level barely reached our shoulders. However, I could feel the mud squish between my toes, and the overcoat kept floating up around my neck making it difficult for me to move. I struggled but somehow made it to the pier and climbed out.

"Very good," our group leader said while I stood on the narrow edge. "But who told you to get out." Before I could respond, a firm shove had me back in the lake gasping for air and fighting the surface. I stood quietly and waited for any directives. "Return the coats to the hall and wait for further instructions!" rang out in the darkness and echoed across the lake. By the time we landed on a dry surface, we were all alone.

"Is this it?" Kerry asked disgustedly.

"Isn't this enough?" I responded nastily. "They may not let us on a shuttle looking like this, which means we may have to walk back to the hall." There were no further comments as we all wrung out the coats and started on our way. Fortunately, a shuttle did pick us up, and we arrived at the hall within minutes. There were now ten girls sitting in the seats where we usually sat.

"Now what," Kerry groaned.

An attractive blonde walked over to me and smiled. "I'm your big sister," she said. "I'll see you on Sunday. Good luck."

I returned the smile and said, "Thank you," even though I had no idea what she meant. I threw my jacket in a heap with the others and gladly accepted the fact that we were allowed to leave. A hot shower and two cups of coffee helped bring back the circulation, and a short joint put me to sleep.

Day Five: Friday

The sorority seemed to spare no expense in making our initiation as tough as possible; and when Friday night arrived, they proved just how much they were willing to invest towards pledge discomfort. Three victims to a car, a blindfold on each person, and it started again. Only this time I wasn't with Kerry, and it made me feel that much lonelier; for loneliness was the name of the game on this excursion. Three different stops occurred; and at each point, one pledge was let out. I was the last one released after what seemed like a three-hour ride and told to be back at the hall by two o'clock on Sunday. I removed my mask and stepped from the car. As I watched the vehicle zoom away, I noticed the heavily congested area and began to wonder just where I was and wondered why I had been given a night and a day to make it back to the sorority hall.

Before we had left the hall, all of our belongings had been collected and put into a large envelope. I was wise enough to know that wherever we were going, a little money would come in handy; therefore, I hid a twenty-dollar bill in my shoe and was lucky enough that none of the sisters had any desire to do a strip search.

I took the bill from its secret cache and then asked a passer-by for directions to the nearest bus depot. I had no intention of asking where I was, but it didn't take me very long to figure out that I was somewhere in downtown Los Angeles. I spent the night at the station since no buses were leaving in the direction of Citra until the morning; and although it was somewhat drafty, it appeared to be safe from those nasty elements, which so often plagued a city. Therefore, I waited patiently and dozed off occasionally till I could purchase the first available ticket to Citra – or at least as close to Citra as my twenty dollars would afford.

After taking the bus as far as my money allowed, I used the better part of my sixth hell day utilizing some free transportation. It took over a dozen rides and close to five hours on "hitchhiker's highway" but I made it back to my room safe and sound. Kerry arrived about three hours later, looking just as haggard as I felt. She too had been dropped off in L.A. but didn't have the foresight to sneak a little money with her. She spent Friday night on the beach with a bunch of high schoolers and all day Saturday taking advantage of the same free transportation system that got me home. When she arrived at the dorm, I was awake and wanted details of her plight; so we traded stories and then went to sleep. My bed was certainly more comfortable than the depot bench, and my room was a lot quieter. With no shuffling noises or flashing lights to distract me and with the soft sound of a door closing or a voice in the hallway, I was lulled into a perfect slumber.

Day Seven: Sunday

Two o'clock arrived with an undesired velocity even though Kerry and I had enjoyed lunch and a chance to catch up on some schoolwork. I was able to get only a modicum of assignments done before it was time to discover what bestial form of existence was waiting for me on this so far pleasant Sunday.

I glanced around the hall very carefully upon my entrance and noticed that the number of pledges had dropped off slightly. I wondered what had happened to them and speculated about what was yet to come for those of us who had stuck it out so far. My thoughts returned to the present with the sight of my big sister advancing towards me. "I'm glad you made it," she said with approval.

"So am I, Miss" I responded with a careful lift to my voice. "So am I."

"Come with me," she said quickly, changing her expression to one of authority. I followed her to the outside parking lot where I was hustled into an orange Triumph and rocketed to the Baldwin Apartment Complex in a matter of minutes. Handed a set of keys, I was informed that apartment 18 needed cleaning and that I was the person to perform the task. When I was done, I could do as I pleased as long as I made it to the hall by seven. In an instant, she was gone and I was left to my assigned chore.

I picked up clothes, books, and empty beer containers; swept the kitchen floor, vacuumed the carpet, and cleaned the bathroom; made her bed, dusted the furniture, and scoured the oven; put away food, took out garbage, and even washed the windows. I'd seen messy places in my time, but this was a topper; yet somehow I got the impression that it was all premeditated – a mere product of prearranged, deliberate uncleanliness.

By six I was done, and by seven I had graduated from the ranks of a common, household maid to the ranks of a common, everyday waitress. For two hours, my group – which had now been reduced to six girls – served food and drink to those sorority sisters who had decided to have a modest Sunday night banquet. When the feast had ended; we spent another two hours cleaning tables, mopping the floor, and washing dish after dish after dish.

I was so exhausted by the time I made it to my room that I could barely change before I fell asleep. I let the next day's morning classes slide, along with any thoughts of a late breakfast or an early lunch. I was not to be disturbed.

Day Eight: Monday

This was the easiest day of the initiation but not because the sisters had some compassion or because they were running out of things for us to do. Compassion was not one of their virtues; and running out of things to do, would never happen to those creative minds who caused us pledges so much misery. Actually, they were just being lazy.

We were responsible for making banners and noisemakers to entice the crowd at the basketball game into raucous ovations for the home team. I wasn't very excited about basketball, but yelling a few cheers and shaking a few cans filled with beads was certainly easier than hiking through the woods or hitching a ride from L.A.

With each break in the action, we all stood up and gave a "rah rah"; and every point by Citra brought on a volley of rattles, clumps, and bangs – each louder than the time before. Halftime was the only embarrassing moment when our display of the homemade banners was subjected to the booing, laughter, and flying objects of the crowd. The final score was the home team: 88, the visitors: 79, and the sorority pledges: 0.

Day Nine: Tuesday

God intervened on the ninth day of hell – because it rained. I didn't know what the original intention was, but I was positive that an alternate activity of some kind would be quickly arranged. However, as we stood and waited for the rain to stop, it became apparent that the sorority pledge masters were not entirely flexible.

The big sisters took over and used the opportunity to have their rooms cleaned or laundry done, but my big sister just told me to go home and stay in my room; and like a good little sister, I did as I was told.

Day Ten: Wednesday

Miracles happen only once; and on the tenth day of hell, it did not rain. A brisk wind and a full moon added just enough eeriness to our night's assignment, which took place in a cemetery. Armed with only flashlights and note-taking instruments, we were driven to one of the smaller cemeteries that was situated on the outskirts of the campus. The girls who dropped us off told us that they would be back in an hour, and during those sixty minutes we were supposed to copy down the name and date which appeared on each and every headstone. There were approximately a hundred tombstones; and if we didn't complete this task, we would be thrown into the lake again – something that none of us relished on such a cool evening.

The lake, however, became the last thing on my mind as I tiptoed from one plot to another, never quite convinced that a ghost – real or otherwise – wouldn't jump out from behind a grave marker and scare

215

the hell out of me. Every time the wind whistled, I began to shiver with fear. Despite the nervous anxiety, I managed to finish my assigned chore in about forty-five minutes. The tombstones were close together, so there wasn't much walking; but my hands had been shaking so badly that I had trouble reading my own handwriting.

We all sat by the cemetery entrance where we compared notes and made sure our lists were in order. Some girls even copied other lists to fill in the gaps on theirs while some of us were so paranoid we believed that hidden cameras were everywhere. None of it mattered because it was all for naught. No one came to pick us up after an hour. In fact, we weren't sure if anybody was coming back at all. As we waited, each second seemed like a minute, and each minute seemed like an hour; but we still waited, each of us afraid to start home for fear of the consequences that would surely be given us. Therefore, we waited some more, and it got windier, and we felt colder and more scared; but we continued to wait. Each time we saw an emerging headlight, we stood up – hopeful that this would be our ticket home; and each time as the lights went by us, we sat back down and waited some more. A second hour had passed and then a third when finally our transportation arrived. No one stood up for we were all convinced that it was another false alarm, another ray of hope which would dash away and sink our spirits some more. The group leaders didn't even look at what we had written, just told us to throw the papers away. As I climbed into the back of the van, I realized what the true test had been.

Day Eleven: Thursday

We picked oranges on this day. We didn't squeeze them, we didn't eat them, we just picked them. From noon till four we picked them off the trees, from the ground, and even out of the transport trucks. No one was expected to be there for the entire four hours since many of us had afternoon classes, but everyone was expected to put in a one-hour shift and then be there on the soccer field by four o'clock. Using the fruits of our labor, we spelled out the sorority letters on the field; and from the highest balcony on the science building, we could see our work of art. The Greek letters standing out in bold design was truly a thing of beauty.

"Makes sense; doesn't it?" Kerry asked sarcastically in a whisper that only I could hear.

"What's that?" I whispered back.

"All over the world people go without food," she said, "and we use oranges to make sorority letters."

"Christ!" I snapped, "you sound just like my father. Besides, people can still eat those after they've been on the ground." Kerry didn't answer. She just picked up her large satchel and walked away. I stood there and looked at it, cherished it, and was pleased that I was part of it; for it was a part of me; it was ours.

What started out as nothing more than a glorified lesson on how to become a migrant worker turned into an absolute nightmare. I should have known better than to think that we would get off so easily.

At eight o'clock, we climbed into our usual mode of transportation and went about five miles from the outer reaches of the campus to a lonely looking horse farm. There we were blindfolded and forced to walk through one of the holding pens.

I walked very slowly and carefully, but it didn't matter because eventually I came down on something which was most certainly not the ground. Frantically, I started to run, well aware but not concerned that there was no place to go. I bumped into other girls, causing some to fall and falling twice myself; but I kept running, and it seemed like each new step brought an unwanted reward. I fell once again, and this time I stayed on the ground, buried my face in my hands, and cried like a baby.

Less than three hours ago I had been proud of my accomplishment, but now I was ashamed and humiliated as I wallowed in some filthy remains. They built us up just to break us down, and I was definitely broken. For the first time since this hell session had begun, I wanted to quit. I wanted to quit and tell the sorority leaders what they could do with their organization. It just wasn't worth it anymore.

They hosed us down and gave us some liquid soap to cleanse ourselves before they let us back on the vans. I was quiet on the return trip, and no one tried to talk to me – not even Kerry. She just stared at me and I was sure that she wondered what was going on inside my head but was afraid to ask. Even if I wanted to, I couldn't have told her; for I wasn't sure myself. I was filled with mixed emotions right now, and I needed a bath, very badly.

When I got to my room, I showered and scrubbed my feet thoroughly. Then I sprayed the shower with disinfectant. I couldn't sleep, so for hours I just lay there and stared at the ceiling never thinking once about horses or sororities.

Day Twelve: Friday

Kerry had to coax me out of bed on the twelfth day of hell session because I just didn't want to go. She made me realize that quitting now – with only two days left – would make the first eleven days a total waste. I got up, but I wasn't very eager to discover what new variety of pain and humiliation had been dreamed up for us.

We didn't have to pick oranges or trudge through horse manure, we just had to collect aluminum cans. This didn't seem like much of a chore, but I had now become accustomed to any late surprises that might be looming in the future; so I took nothing for granted.

Embarrassment ran rampant as we proceeded to beg, bargain, borrow, or steal as many aluminum cans as possible. We were expected to do this before class, after class, and even during class.

By the time four o'clock rolled around, I had had enough of looking for cylindered containers made of a bluish-white metal that is highly resistant to oxidation, but for some reason I decided to visit the college bar in pursuit of more. Since the bar was an obvious choice, I was counting on the other girls staying away for just that reason. However, when I entered, the bartender informed me that some girls had gone through about an hour earlier and emptied all the trash barrels of the precious metal. I noticed a few littered tables and decided to help the establishment by clearing them.

Things were moving along smoothly until I came to a table where a tall, lanky boy sat. He had either sat at a dirty table or consumed quite a bit of beer because the table supported about ten empty cans. I smiled at him as I picked them up and threw them into my bag. "Want this one too?" he asked as he sipped the beer he was holding.

"Sure," I said, "when you're finished with it."

"What's it worth to you?" he asked with a lecherous yelp as he wiped brew from his upper lip.

"Forget it," I said as I started to walk away. I had my back turned when I felt his hand grip my wrist. I tried to pull free, but he increased his hold even tighter. "Fuck you, creep!" I yelled as I slapped his hand and managed to break free.

"Listen, bitch," his voice turning nasty now. "I don't let people talk to me like that." Before I could move, he had both hands wrapped around my arm. My bag fell to the floor, and cans were rolling everywhere. Now I was frightened.

"Let go," I pleaded but in a very calm voice.

"No way, cunt." His eyes were red and glaring, his breath heavy as he spoke.

From the corner of my eye, I could see the bartender approaching, but before he was in range to offer any assistance, I heard the words, "Let her go, Drew," from behind my shoulder. I forced my head around and spotted Steve Connolly.

"Steve!" I said, showing great appreciation at the sight of him. "Where'd you come from?"

"Hi, Geralyn," he said so matter of factly that he almost sounded bored. "How have you been?" He removed the hands from my arms without any struggle and forced the perpetrator to sit back down.

"Fine," I said, catching my breath. "I'm glad to see you, but really – where'd you come from?"

"I was sitting in the corner. I come in here often while I'm waiting for Mac to get out of class."

"Well, once again," I added, "it's good to see you."

"Not to worry," Steve said. "Obviously Drew's drunk."

"No, I'm not," Drew said, his speech now noticeably slurred.

"Drew," Steve said somewhat sternly, "you've been drinking since two. Now come on. We'll go get Mac and then I'll drive you home."

"Is he a friend of yours?" I asked.

"Not really," Steve said as he helped Drew up. "Just a routine I've gotten into."

"Thanks, Steve!" the bartender shouted. Steve just waved and headed for the exit.

"Yea, thanks, Steve," I said, still sounding a little shaken. He nodded his head and kept walking. I could still feel the hands on my arm and see the red piercing eyes looking directly into mine. My heart was racing, and I was afraid that I might hyperventilate. "Say, bartender, could I have a beer?" I requested as I approached the counter.

"It's on the house," he said with a smile. "I think you could use one."

I gulped it down and felt my nerves steady just a touch, but I was still shaking. For the second day in a row, I had had my fill of the sorority and its designated epochs of hell; and the day wasn't even over yet.

On this particular night, we had to report to the hall at six o'clock. I was sure that it was some type of dinner detail; and although a dinner was involved, it wasn't the kind of detail I imagined.

After we boarded the vans, we were given ski masks and told to put them on. "Are we going to rob someone?" Kerry asked.

"Of course not," one of the leaders said. "You're going to streak through the cafeteria."

"No way!" one girl shouted as she stood up and ripped off her mask. "You have no right to treat us this way. We're not whores." With that, she jumped out the van door and walked away.

"We've given you these masks so no one will recognize you," one leader said, totally ignoring the girl who had departed.

"I'm not doing it either," I said to Kerry. "It's just not worth it."

Kerry handed me a cigarette. "Why do we go through with this?" she asked rhetorically. "Because we want to be in a sorority, and there is only this and one more day left before we get accepted."

"But is it really worth it?" I asked seriously.

"I won't quit now," Kerry answered. "I have to prove to these assholes that I can take it. That I'm as good or better than they are." Her words seemed to trail off as she let her head fall back against the wheel well and bury her face in smoke.

Prove what, I thought to myself. Being as good as the sorority leaders couldn't mean that much. I didn't even know the name of the girl who had left, never took the time to learn since I was sure I'd get to know her later; but now she was gone and sure to be the subject of some ridicule amongst the entire Greek community. I was so proud of the shred of dignity I had kept, but it couldn't match up with the dignity she demanded. "You look like a fucking crook in that mask," I said.

"I know," Kerry agreed. "Let's get this over with."

Several laughed but many didn't even look up as some very well built female bodies danced by the tables that sat on a cold tiled floor. My feet were freezing as I raced to the back exit and jumped into the conveniently awaiting van, which ensured our getaway and our anonymity.

Before Kerry removed her mask, I looked at her and jokingly asked, "So do you want to rob someone while we're at it?"

"Get fucked," she said sardonically.

"Please," I said, "I've got to make it for one more day."

"One more day!" Kerry shouted and banged the side of the van in unison. Instantly, the van filled with the chant of, "One more day! One more day!" It got louder and louder each time, and then I visualized the face of the girl who had walked out. I continued to see her face and hear her words; but by morning's arrival, she was no more than a blur, and I was content with myself all over again.

Day Thirteen: Hell Day

My alarm went off before six; and since I had taken a shower the night before, I felt no need to do so as I rolled off my bed. "It's hell day," I said to myself.

"It's hell day!" Kerry shouted as she banged on my door. "It's hell day!"

"It's hell day," I responded as I opened the door.

"That's right," Kerry repeated, "but after hell day, it's all over and we're in."

We're in," I thought to myself. I wasn't sure if it was really possible. One more step was all that we needed to take, but it was a

226

big step – a giant leap over a chasm that would swallow us up if we fell. The pit of my stomach was like a cocoon, and I weighed the possibilities, not quite sure if fear or anxiety was the thing bothering me the most.

I remembered all the little goodies I had, which could make the final parts of this session go by faster and more easily. I decided it was time to pull out all the stops and be prepared. It was time to dull the senses entirely, so the punishments would be softer. I had convinced myself that hell day would be the worst day of the entire thirteen – the ultimate disaster and fitting end to the pain and suffering, which we had been subjected to – and so very often. The sorority could give me all it had, throw its best punch, and kick its swiftest kick. I wasn't worried because I wouldn't feel a thing.

At 7:30 a trip through the mill resulted in aching knees, sore hands, and a strong desire to stand up.

At 8:00 we were forced to eat a mash concocted by the sisters.

At 8:30 we all got sick.

At 9:00 we were taken behind the cafeteria where we were pelted by rotten fruits and vegetables.

At 9:15 we all got sick.

From 9:30 to 10:30 we got tarred and feathered – with maple syrup substituting for tar.

From 10:30 to 11:00 we did our best to remove all the residue that had stuck to our bodies.

From 11:00 to 12:00 we marched with rock-filled sacks on our backs.

At 12:00 we ate lunch in the cafeteria.

At 12:30 we all got sick.

At 1:00 we ran barefooted through a pile of crushed ice.

At 1:15 we crawled through it.

From 1:30 to 2:30 we sat on the sorority bench in spaced intervals without making a sound.

At 2:30 we had our nails, hands, arms, faces, and feet painted with water base paint.

At 3:00 we were hosed off and drenched with soapy water.

At 3:15 we all jumped into the lake.

At 3:30 we ran through a pile of oranges.

At 3:45 we ran through mud.

At 4:00 we were hosed down and taken to the boat house on the lake.

There we witnessed our tormentors scattering broken glass onto the floor in the back room. Then barefooted, blindfolded, and unaware that the glass had been replaced with potato chips; we were forced to enter. Since no one would enter willingly, we were pushed until we could feel the crunch under our feet and the slivers between our toes. At this point, we were told to unmask so we could discover the ruse. Then after howls of laughter and congratulatory embraces, we were instructed to go back home and prepare for the all night celebration. Hell was over and we had been accepted.

I stood in the shower for a long time. There was no hurry tonight, no deadlines to meet, no schedule to follow. The party began at eight; but if we weren't on time, it didn't matter, not this night. The party was for us, and we were ready. There was eating and drinking and access to all kinds of stimulant; music, and movies, and games of chance; a great deal of yelling and a hell of a lot of passing out.

At 3 am we all got sick.

14

When morning came, following the day of acceptance; I was weary, aching, and looking at the world through bloodshot eyes. My stomach was queasy, and my head was pounding; but it didn't slow me down. By eleven o'clock, I was on a shuttle heading in the direction of Keith's. I had only been able to stare at him from a distance during the rush or talk to him on the phone; and it nearly killed me inside not being able to get closer, feel his warmth, his touch.

When he answered the door, I almost laughed at him. He was half-dressed with his hair sticking out in different directions and his eyes almost closed. As he yawned and smiled, he said, "Yes," stretching it out to fill a full ten seconds.

I ignored his humor and walked into the apartment very slowly, looking in all directions as I moved around the perimeter. "Is anyone here?" I asked.

"Just me," he answered quickly. "Why do you ask?

"Because I can't believe that one person could create this mess all by himself." I put my arms around him and hugged him tightly. "I don't think I'll ever let you go," I said softly. His response was favorable, and we tumbled to the floor. Thirteen days had separated us, and now it was time to catch up. Love, hallucinations, television, and food filled the day; only making me crave that the days be longer. This fantastic feeling of being in the sorority and having not lost Keith in the process had me higher than a kite. Even Keith's momentary resentment of being second to "that girls' club" couldn't dampen my spirit. I had it all, and I never wanted to lose it.

By the time I arrived back at my dorm, it was well past ten. Kerry was lying on her bed when I crashed through the door and surprised her. "Hey, sister, how was your first day of freedom?" I asked.

"You didn't waste any time, I see." She jumped from her bed. "Spend the whole day at Keith's?" she asked, already knowing the answer.

"You bet," I replied. "How about you?"

"Carol's – er Bill's," she said and then laughed.

I laughed with her. "Gotta smoke?" I asked. She threw me the pack.

"We've been so busy with pledging that we've been out of touch with the rest of the world," she said, now standing by the window. "You won't believe what's been happening."

"Like what?" I asked, not really caring and more concerned with lighting my cigarette.

"It seems that there has been some embezzling up at the top around here."

"Yea," I acknowledged. "I caught some bits and pieces, but I was always too tired to check into it. So tell me. What's going on?"

"One of the guys over at Bill's works for the paper, and he said there's going to be a big investigation into the pilfering of funds."

"By who at the top?" I asked, suddenly curious.

"The very top," she retorted. "The president of the college himself."

"How did they find out?" I inquired, now sitting on the edge of the bed and motioning for Kerry to do the same.

"Well," she replied as she sat and faced me, "it seems that someone in the accounting department leaked out the information."

"Oh, I love a scandal," I chirped with delirious delight as I rubbed my hands together. "Is the paper going to print a story?"

"You mean the school paper?" she asked.

"Any paper," I said quickly.

"Apparently, the outside papers want to hold off for a bit, but our paper is going to print the story and an editorial – backed up with statistics and everything. They got some pro who used to work for a paper to write it, and it's supposed to be pretty good."

"I can't wait," I said. "When does it come out?"

"Tomorrow," Kerry said, "if all goes well."

"What's the problem?" I asked.

"The people on the paper have been working around the clock – and on the sly too. It seems that Sethman wants to close the paper down."

"How can he do that?" I asked with disgust.

"He's the fucking president of the college," Kerry shot back. "He can do a whole lot of stuff."

"It sounds like he's afraid of something," I speculated.

"That would be my guess," Kerry agreed as she got up and once again moved to the window. "It'll be interesting; that's for sure."

"No doubt," I said, preparing to leave the room, "but how does all this concern us."

"We're part of the school's biggest sorority now," she said slowly and emphatically. "We have an obligation to help in any way that we can."

"I suppose so," I concurred.

"There's no two ways about it, Gerry. We need to get involved, so be alert and ready to help." Her words came across as a command.

"Sure," I said defensively. With that, I gave a polite farewell and left the room.

15

It was amazing what the school paper revealed. It had photo stated copies of the budget reports, copies of the bills, and even receipts and cancelled checks. There was testimony by an undisclosed source that proved more damaging than anything else did however. This unnamed whistle blower had provided records, which showed that one million dollars could not be accounted for. It was also revealed that the president of the college had two private homes, several automobiles, and a membership to a very exclusive country club. He had also taken several trips abroad. It all seemed virtually impossible on the president's declared salary. When the figures had been broken down precisely, a huge discrepancy was obvious. The paper pulled no punches in pointing the finger at Dr. Sethman and attacked him quite viciously with its editorial.

The President's Private Slush Fund

By T.J. Kingsley

Doesn't it seem a little strange that a man can spend more than 50% above his annual earnings? Dr. Robert Sethman (by his own accord) does not come from a wealthy family. How often have people had to sit and listen to the preaching about the "humble" beginning and how this self-made man made it to the top?

It appears, however, that Dr. Sethman had a little help along the way. It didn't come from his wife, who spends her days giving tea parties and playing in the rose gardens at one of their two lovely homes, and who spends her evenings standing at her husband's side playing the gracious wife while he plays the gracious host of several college activities. It didn't come from his parents, who spent their quiet years in some retirement village; and it didn't come from some long lost relative because there aren't any. It came from the following: student tuition, teacher salaries, and alumni contributions. Dr. Sethman cleverly took a little bit from all three of those sources; and like true embezzlement, it was hard to detect at the time but eventually came to the surface.

There has been a new chief accountant for each of the past four years, and all the records for the past four years have been destroyed – or so the president thought. As it turns out, one of those bean counters made some copies; and now those copies are public record. Our source got his hands on those documents and turned them over to us. "For once," our source claims, "somebody beat him to the paper shredder."

Dr. Sethman was not asked to comment about his prosperity, but a representative for the president said that his current opulence was the result of some very sound investments. Indeed, but records indicate that the money invested, wasn't all his.

It's hard to say just how long the president's private slush fund has been in existence, but one thing's for sure. It's been long enough to turn that "ordinary" guy into a very rich man.

Along with the editorial, there were several satirical cartoons that showed the president as a free spending egotist along with an invitation for him to come forward and address the issue. The president continued to speak through a representative and denied all charges levied against him by the school paper. When the newspaper staff demanded documentation, which might prove their allegations to be false, he refused. Furthermore, he insisted that the paper print a retraction and an apology, or all who were connected with the article and its sidebars would suffer the consequences.

On Friday at twelve o'clock, the members of our school's newspaper announced that they would not back down in any way to the president's threats. At one o'clock, they were expelled from school and ordered off campus. The school's newspaper was then officially shut down. At seven o'clock, the sorority sisters held an emergency meeting.

This was the support Kerry had spoken about to me. In less than half a day, phones had rung, people had knocked on doors, and announcements had been made in class – all to insure that sorority members were present at the meeting.

"Fifty students were expelled today!" shouted the chairperson. "Fifty!" The hall was silent with each of us looking at the podium. For thirteen days, most of us had had nothing but contempt for this person, who had barked out orders and devised methods of torture; but now we respected her. This dark haired beauty, who now looked all female, demanded our attention as much as she had that first rush night when she had dressed like something out of a spy novel. There were no sunglasses this time, and her dark brown eyes, which seemed to dance all over the room and stare at each one of us individually, blinked a few times and exposed a tear of emotion. "Five of our sisters were members of that fifty," she said as her voice cracked. "Expelled for printing the truth!" she shouted, no strain in her voice this time. "This is an obvious admission of guilt on the president's part, and we cannot stand by and let this happen. Those students – all fifty – need our support. Tomorrow night at seven o'clock, the Intra-Fraternity and Sorority Council will hold a meeting on the soccer field. Show your support for your school and your classmates by being there."

The noise was deafening as she left the podium. "This could get out of hand!" I shouted to Kerry, trying to be heard over the crowd.

"We can't let that corrupt bastard push us around," she shouted back. "You going back to the dorm?"

"To Keith's," I said. "See you later." I shoved my way through the confusion and made it to the exit. When I arrived at Keith's, I found him asleep on his couch with the headphones from his stereo lying by his side and the television going with the volume all the way down. There were a few empty beer cans strewn about the floor with one half-empty wetting the carpet.

"Jesus Christ," I mumbled to myself as I waded through the refuse to the kitchen. There I poured myself a drink and took a handful of stale pretzels from an open bag on the counter. "What a mess!" I went back to Keith's resting place and kicked him in the side. "Get up, you lazy bum," I said. My voice was just loud enough to help my love tap awake him.

"Well, glad you made it," he said, his words barely audible as his groggy mind tried to operate. He pushed himself up and straightened the cushion behind him. "What time is it?" he asked, searching desperately for his watch, which must have been hidden amongst the rubble.

"It's not even eight o'clock," I responded with disgust.

"You're kidding." He stood up and started scratching his head. "How'd the meeting go?"

"Fine," I said. "It looks like all the fraternities and sororities are joining forces."

Keith yawned. "They have to do better than that."

"What do you mean?" I asked rather unpleasantly.

He started scratching his head again. "You need the support of the entire student body," he said with a certain force in his tone. "If the Greeks try to do it alone, Sethman will just have them dismissed from campus."

"Expel all the Greeks?" I asked with bewilderment.

"No, he wouldn't do that," Keith answered calmly, "but he could outlaw all fraternity functions almost immediately."

"No way," I exasperated.

"With the stroke of a pen," Keith clarified. "Look, Sethman's been looking the other way when it comes to a bunch of things – like drinking on campus for one. If he wants to show his authority, he can do it."

"And it's all legal."

"Every bit of it," Keith declared. "Permits for just about everything go through his office; so if he wants to shut down the frats, he has legal recourse to do it." He pointed his finger at me to illustrate his point. "He giveith and he takeith away."

"What do you suggest?" I asked.

"Before he threatens to shut down operations, the student body should shut down everything *for* him."

"What do you mean?" I asked.

"Think about it. He allows a lot of things to go on because it makes money; and when the money is coming in, everybody is happy. So shut down everything. Have sit-ins, demonstrations, a total student boycott where everyone refuses to go to class." He smiled and raised his eyebrows a touch. "It's not very original, but it's very effective," he said, shrugging his shoulders and flipping his hands with the palms up.

"And how are you going to get the whole school involved?" I asked skeptically.

"Believe me," Keith continued, "that's the only way things will get done. It has to be like a massive strike, the way unions cripple a whole city or even the whole country." He removed his shirt and put his hand up, instructing me to be quiet. "Let's not get uptight about it now," he demanded. "I've got to take a shower, and then we can hit that new club in town."

"You're amazing," I said sarcastically. "You talk about total anarchy for the students, and now you want to go out partying."

"Exactly," he answered.

I just laughed and then waited for him to get ready. By nine, we were at the establishment where we danced and drank till two when my feet got sore, and my head filled with cobwebs. I spent most of Saturday at Keith's by sleeping till noon with a brief copulation before one, and an eternity of television and music. By six, I was back at my room, preparing to meet Kerry and go to the meeting.

By half past seven, the soccer field was already crowded; and we had to force our way to find an open spot. Most of the people were wearing their fraternity or sorority shirts; and for once, it seemed like we were working together instead of against each other.

For nearly forty-five minutes, people talked and shook hands and back patted or hugged. There was camaraderie among the groups because the games were over, and there was no need to prove superiority now – no need at all. We were one, united and working as a whole.

A temporary stage had been set up on the north corner of the field, and one of the college D-jays provided some sound equipment. Suddenly there was some tapping on the microphone, and silence was instantaneous throughout the masses. A tall, well-dressed boy stood before us, and his presence alone commanded our attention. "My name is Christopher Noland," he said, his voice booming everywhere, "and for those of you who don't know me, I'm student council president."

"So that's what he looks like," I thought. I had heard about him and even read articles, which he had written in the now defunct newspaper; but I had never seen him before. I folded my legs to be more comfortable and listened carefully.

"I have been asked to be the spokesman for this assembly and I would like to say that I am honored to be here. I would also like to say that this might be a brief meeting since I'm sure Dr. Sethman will be sending some of his goons to break up this little gathering." That ignited the crowd and the cheering would have been endless if Noland hadn't asked for our attention once more. "I am very pleased to see all those faces out there – both Greek and independent, but it is because of the united efforts of each fraternity and sorority president that this assembly was made possible." Again there was thundering applause and again a plea for silence. "Yesterday when the announcement concerning the staff of our school newspaper was made, I was contacted immediately by the president of the I.F.S.C. It was through the efforts of your individual leaders that you were all contacted and are here tonight when – I am sure – you would rather be someplace else. Everyone should be commended for a job well done." The noise was deafening as we all stood up and gave a rousing ovation. This time Noland waited until the noise cleared and then continued. "The board knows its power and its limitations." He paused and searched for the right words. "A great injustice has been done – not just to the brave members of the staff but to all of us. The I.F.S.C. and all its participants cannot solve this problem without help; therefore, I am asking – no I am pleading that you get others involved." He signaled for two young men to come forward. "Earlier today, these two individuals went into town; and at a private print shop, they had several thousand flyers printed up." He then took the microphone and pointed it toward the crowd. "Your job," he shouted, "is to see that theses flyers are delivered to every student living on or off campus." He put his head down as if in silent prayer. "I was asked to motivate," he said calmly with his head still down, "but I don't think it's necessary. If you would return to your respective houses, you'll be instructed as to what to do." His voice almost cracked as he finished his message, and then – just as we had all expected – the campus police arrived and declared that this was an unlawful assembly. Rather than cause a riot, we managed to leave orderly and get back to our houses.

Each fraternity and sorority had been given a designated area where the flyers were to be delivered, and each area had been broken down even further regarding individuals. I picked up my stack along with a map of my designated deliveries and headed for Keith's – well aware that I had a very busy Sunday ahead of me.

When I arrived at Keith's I began to read the pamphlet more carefully. It not only gave all the sordid details, it asked for a complete student boycott. I smiled as I read the paragraph, which compared the boycott to a union strike; and then stormed recklessly into the Keith's bedroom, slamming the door behind me. "You louse!" I shouted. "You knew all along." Keith was sitting up and looking at one of his textbooks, but I didn't fall for his charade. "Oh, don't act like you can't hear me."

He looked up at me and calmly said, "Sure." Then he started laughing. "Chris Noland and I are friends. He told me about this idea yesterday."

"And you led me on," I said somewhat betrayed.

245

"Yep," he said, laughing through his nose.

"Oh, you creep!" I shouted and then threw a stack of flyers at him. He jumped up, tackled me, and then wrestled me to the bed where he tickled me unmercifully.

"I give up," I said, trying hard to speak between my gasping for air. "I give up!"

Keith stopped and then rolled from the bed to a standing position. I stayed on my back, letting my lungs fill with precious oxygen. Keith kept staring at me, and it didn't take long for me to become self-conscious. "What are you looking at?" I asked with a sinister tone.

"Nothing," he said acting rather aloof suddenly. "Nothing at all."

"We've got a big day ahead of us tomorrow," I said.

"We?" he exclaimed.

"Sure," I said. "You don't expect me to deliver all of these things by myself."

"Then we better get to bed early," he said, staring down at me once more.

"Sounds good," I giggled.

Instantly, he pounced upon me like a wild animal attacking its prey. I gave no resistance as he did to me whatever he desired.

16

It had been a long, tiresome weekend; but when Monday rolled around, it became apparent that more people read the flyers than threw them away; and out of those who had taken the time, the majority did as requested. The classrooms on Monday morning didn't have enough students to make it worth the teachers' while; so by the afternoon, they stopped showing up too.

The president, however, would not be intimidated; and through a spokesperson, delivered a message over the college radio station. He made it clear that he could not be pressured into anything. He would not allow the staff for the school's paper back on campus, and he insisted that all students return to class by the next morning or suffer the consequences academically.

Chris Noland went on the air about two hours later and encouraged the student body to keep the boycott going. He claimed that the pressure was on the president and that sooner or later he would have to back down.

The classrooms remained virtually empty the next day, but the president held his position and declared the radio station off limits to any person involved in the boycott. He then suspended all late afternoon and evening shuttle service in hopes to burden the lines of communication. However, with the aid of private vehicles, enough information reached the right people. The boycott not only continued but it got even stronger.

Later in the week, committees that represented several organizations tried to meet with the president or his staff; and when this failed, a new course of action was taken. It took longer and it was hard work, but the word was spread over the weekend that there would be an assembly on the lawn in front of the administration building. At first, only a small crowd appeared; but as time went on, the numbers grew until the small gathering became an overwhelming mass. The minutes turned into hours, and the hours turned into days, each hosting a greater number than the day before. By day five of the student boycott, the numbers had become so great that temporary lodging was set up. There were tents everywhere; and with the loud music blaring, it reminded me of a rock concert. The school's bar was off limits, and Sethman no longer looked the other way about alcohol on school grounds. This, however, didn't stop certain protesters from smuggling in some goods that helped take off the edge and relieve the boredom. As usual, there was plenty of pot to go around; and most of us indulged. Keith and I shared a tent, some beverage, and even a joint or two; but we remained serious enough to stay focused on the situation at hand and avoided any other pleasant distractions.

Earlier in the week, Sethman got *to* and *from* his office with the aid of a police escort, but never once did he come outside to address the audience. By the end of the week, he stopped coming to his office and was nowhere to be seen.

The mounting pressure started to grow; and on the eighth day, Sethman announced – once again through a spokesperson – that if students did not return to their place of residence, they would be arrested as trespassers. With too many students high on emotion, high with adrenaline, or just plain high; things got out of control. Amidst protest chants and songs for justice, the students took over one of the buildings. Noland tried to diffuse the situation with a plea that order be maintained, but his words went unheard. The students violently charged the science building, set up headquarters, and housed several small armies. All types of furniture were used to barricade the doors and windows; and those of us, who had remained on the outside, watched in anguish as the campus police charged the building in one futile attempt to regain it. A few heads were bashed, some glass was broken, and a student or two were escorted from the building; but – for the most part – the hall remained student property. The mass observers cheered as the enemy troops fell back in retreat.

By the time evening arrived, we had all calmed down and prepared to settle in for the night; but the troops were amassing, and we knew it. When morning came, the campus was surrounded with college police, local police, and any hired guns that Sethman thought necessary to maintain order. This only made matters worse; and those tired, frustrated souls – who originally harbored good intentions only – began to let their tempers flare until all out hostility pursued. Within minutes, the violence began. Police were everywhere, and there wasn't much that the demonstrators could do. The students were outmanned, outgunned, and outmaneuvered. With nowhere to go, people ran in circles, bumping and crashing – done in by security, natural barriers, and their own created holocaust.

The spirit was no longer with me; so I swiftly ran in pursuit of shelter, hoping to escape the chaos when a blunt object struck me in the back of the head. I fell to my knees and tried to shake the dizzy feeling from my head. I got up slowly and started walking again; but things began to get fuzzy, and I hit the ground with a thud. I was still conscious, and I could see feet moving all around me and hear screaming from every direction. My mouth was filled with sandy soil, and my nostrils inhaled the dusty fumes created by the stampede. For a moment, I was lifted and carried but then dropped; and as I crashed to the ground once more, I knew I couldn't get to my feet again. I rolled over and looked straight up. There was nothing but the hazy sky at first, but then there were police and people who looked like giants. The pain was now overwhelming, and I stretched my hand as far as I could, hoping that someone would take it.

Voices seemed to rush by me, and lights flickered – slowly at first, then quickly – but nothing was clear. I tried to reach for the ache in my head; but my arm was heavy, and I couldn't lift it. Yesterday was today, and today became tomorrow.

17

I awoke from a horrible dream and noticed the clean white walls of a hospital room. The distant blur of a figure became clearer until it formed a distant image and then came closer to me. "How do you feel?" Keith asked.

"Oh," I groaned. "How did I get here?"

He smiled and opened the curtains to let a little light in. "College rescue squad," he answered.

"How long have I been here?"

"A few hours," he said with some concern. "We were getting a little worried. You've been in and out of consciousness, and you were delirious at one point."

"When can I get out of here?" I asked impatiently.

"You have a concussion, so you'll have to stay here for a day or two." He gestured like a scolding parent. "They'll also have to make sure that there's no other internal damage."

"Who's going to pay for all this? Me?" I hesitated and then continued, "Or my insurance company, I mean?"

"It'll all be taken care of," Keith guaranteed. "Your sorority has an emergency fund," he said, waving his hand in a sweeping motion, "and this is an emergency."

"And my parents?" I asked.

"No problem there either," Keith said. "They've been contacted and informed about everything."

"Oh God!" I cried. "They're probably worried sick."

"Can't blame them," Keith said, tapping his finger on the bedpost to help make his point. "You can call them from here. Just put it through the front desk."

"Were any others hurt?" I asked with concern.

"A few," Keith said nonchalantly, "but none were any more serious than you."

"What's the campus look like?" I asked, afraid to really know.

"I've been here with you; but when I left, it didn't look too bad," Keith assured me.

"That's good," I said with a sigh of relief. "The boycott's over I presume."

"The boycott's over," Keith said while slowly nodding his head. "But let's not worry about that now. Call your parents." He kissed me softly and then left.

Things were good on the home front, and I convinced my parents that it was completely unnecessary for them to come out to California. We kept in touch for the next few days as I stayed in the hospital to be tested, probed, and tested again. Keith came around often and so did Kerry; but neither wanted to burden me by keeping me informed as to what was going on.

Keith picked me up when I was released from the hospital and finally felt comfortable to tell me what was happening at Citra University.

"It's over, Gerry. It's all over," he said as he pulled out of the parking lot.

"You mean the boycott? I know about that," I said with revulsion.

"He's gone," Keith replied. "Handed in his resignation two days ago."

"And you're just telling me now!" I exclaimed.

"I didn't want you to get all worked up." He paused and then smiled. "Like you're getting right now."

"Fine," I acknowledged grudgingly. "So the boycott worked."

Keith took a deep breath and then exhaled. "I'd love for the boycott to take all the credit, but there were other factors that really did the trick."

"Like what?" I asked, almost bursting at the seams.

"Unbeknownst to us, the union was putting a ton of pressure on Sethman; and this guy Kingsley was digging up stuff from all over the place."

"Wasn't he the one who wrote the article for the school paper?" I asked with confusion.

"He submitted it," Keith said, stumbling over his words. "He works for one of those newspapers back in New York; and according to Chris Noland, most of his early information was delivered or phoned in."

"So what difference does that make?" I asked, even more confused.

"Sethman might have been able to push the school paper around; but when the big shots got involved, he couldn't stop the bleeding." He smiled. "Before too long, Kingsely was everywhere."

"What paper does Kingsley work for?" I asked.

"This one," Keith said as he handed me an old edition. There, in a section all its own, was the story about the rise and fall of Dr. Sethman.

"So what was the purpose of the boycott?"

"Oh, the boycott was legitimate," Keith said convincingly. "Even Chris Noland was unaware of how much this Kingsley guy had on Sethman.

"But what did *he* have that the school paper *didn't*?"

"According to Chris, that source in Sethman's office wasn't about to give it up to a college publication."

"But was willing to hand it over to a national paper," I said, completing Keith's sentence for him.

"None of us can be sure, but some money must have exchanged hands."

"You mean the New York paper paid for the story?" I inquired.

"If not the paper, then someone else. Kind of mysterious; isn't it?"

"Yea," I said, not sure what to think.

"Well, fortunately, whatever means he used, and how he came across the information, it got the job done. He used the school's paper as a catalyst and his own paper to complete the story."

"So the boycott was just a waste of time," I lamented.

"Not entirely," Keith said. "Noland said it was the perfect distraction to throw Sethman off guard. That's why he kept sending his mouthpiece to speak for him. He was fighting an internal battle with the union and with those outsiders."

"Well, that makes me feel a little better," I said graciously.

"We still don't have the whole story," Keith admitted. "Sethman was definitely guilty, but there are a lot of unanswered questions." He patted the steering wheel softly as he made a turn. "It's out of our league, that's for sure."

"Who's going to take Sethman's place," I asked.

"Pressman, the head of the English department – on an interim basis," Keith answered. "He's a good guy, and all the teachers like him."

"Well that's good," I said with a chirp. "And I have to admit that I'm looking forward to getting back to class."

"Me too," Keith agreed as we headed toward his apartment. "Me too."

18

I didn't think my extended hospital stay had put me a behind in my classes, but there were a few missing assignments and some notes to be gathered; yet only Sottlemeyer seemed concerned about my progress. He told me to meet him at his office at three o'clock on Friday, and he would give me some extra help in those areas, which I had missed.

I was prompt, resulting from the apparent necessity of the meeting and from the excitement I was feeling about attending it. I was astounded by the size of his office: walls covered with plaques and degrees, shelves loaded with books on every subject imaginable, and a floor surrounded by all types of recording and filming equipment. In the far corner of the room there was a gray filing cabinet with the word "Films" printed on it.

Sottlemeyer was working at his desk when I walked in and quickly acknowledged my presence with a wave of his hand and a point toward an empty seat. "Okay," he said, not looking up from his desk as he shuffled through paper after paper. "I can give you all the information you need for your film sequence, but I don't have the film you need to watch."

With all that had happened, I didn't realize that my film sequence was due. I also didn't understand the urgency as to why I had to make it up so quickly, but I didn't care because I was getting a cheap, little thrill as I sat in Sottlemeyer's office. "I don't understand," I said.

"We watched it in class," he said, "and I apologize for not having it with me. Another teacher had to borrow it; and if I had known, I wouldn't have made this appointment."

"That's all right," I said, still feeling like a little girl with a crush on her teacher. I pointed to the filing cabinet and asked, "Can I watch one of the other films instead."

He finally looked up and then smiled. "No, I'm afraid not" he said calmly. "Those are some of my personal films." He got up from his chair, walked to the cabinet, and pulled out a chain of keys with which he fumbled until he found the one that fit the lock. "Here," he said politely as he handed me a metal container. On a piece of tape were the words: *The Heart of the Matter* Part 1. "That's one of my favorite films," he said as I handed the can back to him. "I'm a collector. I have some two hundred films and over four hundred movies on video cassettes."

"Wow! That's some collection," I said, "but where do you keep them all?"

"Some are here," he said while closing the cabinet, "and some are home."

"Does your collection include the school's films?" I asked, still showing slight astonishment at his earlier statement.

"A few of the films I use in class come from my private collection, but most are demonstration films that come from the school's library." He sighed. "The film you need to see is a demonstration film, and it's been signed out till five. Again, I apologize. I can't expect you to wait till five."

"I can leave and come back later," I said a little too enthusiastically.

"Do you have a projector?" he asked sarcastically.

"Of course not," I answered, matching his sarcasm.

"Then how do you plan on watching it?"

"Can't I watch it here?"

He frowned. "That would be fine except that I have a meeting from five thirty to six thirty. That and the fact that they lock this place up around six on Fridays."

"I hate to fall behind," I lamented. "Can I watch it at your home or something?" My words almost shocked me with their boldness as I waited for an answer.

When he didn't answer at first, I was positive that I had embarrassed him – along with myself, but then he looked at the clock and then at me. "You've got a deal. Be here at seven, and we'll do just that," he said abruptly. I shook his hand and then left, not quite sure of what I had just done, but more than certain it was too late to change my mind. I went to my room and lay on my bed, continuously thinking about what to wear and how to act. My heart was pacing at an exceptional rate, and my mind was racing with mysterious thoughts of a possible entanglement. I wasn't sure of my feelings at first; but the more I let my mind control me, the more certain I became. There was no sense denying it at this point, and there was no sense in denying myself what I wanted.

At five I called Keith and cancelled our date. My excuse of menstrual cramps convinced him that a night out would not be in his best interest; but when Kerry asked me where I was going, I was somewhat abrupt and even a bit abrasive with my answer. "It's a school related matter," I said.

"On a Friday night," she said suspiciously. "Is Keith involved?"

"No, he's not," I said defensively, "and he wouldn't understand."

"Good luck," she said condescendingly.

"Fuck you!" I shouted and then ran away. I rushed to the cafeteria and grabbed a quick bite, hoping that it would settle my nerves; but it didn't help. Even the three cigarettes that I smoked during the bus ride couldn't calm me down. When I arrived at Sottlemeyer's office and saw him standing by his car, I thought I would melt. His dark curly hair was vibrating in the slight breeze, and his chiseled features seemed to glare out from the shadow of the overhead light under which he was standing. With the Roman nose, the deep-set eyes, and square jaw; he was truly handsome, I thought. As I stepped from the bus, I froze for an instant, not aware if he could see me; but my courage returned as I walked towards him and noticed the smile on his face. He opened the door for me, and my anxiety started to cease as I sat next to him.

"Good evening," he said.

"Hi," I squeaked out, embarrassed by the crack in my voice. I said nothing for what seemed like an eternity, just stared and probably would have continued to do so if not for the sharp movement of the car – a small sports model that seemed to hop along the road.

"Are you all right?" he asked with slight consternation.

"Fine," I responded quickly, followed by a deep swallow. "I really appreciate this."

"Don't worry about it," he replied. "When you're done watching the demonstration film, we can watch a movie from my collection." He paused. "Then you won't feel like you've wasted your Friday night."

"That'll be nice," I said admirably, but I never felt like I would be wasting the evening. Before too long, we pulled into a quaint wooded area, which all but hid a house on stilts. We parked underneath next to a large van and a motorcycle. "They both yours?" I asked as I examined the two vehicles.

"Dirt bike," he answered as he pointed to the motorcycle. "The van is used to haul stuff around." He smiled. "Like the dirt bike."

He grabbed a canister from the back of the car; and together we climbed the wooden stairs, which lead to a huge wooden deck that surrounded the house. "Do you live here alone," I asked, doing my best to mask the real intention of my question.

"Yep," he replied curtly. "I love the solitude that this place provides." We entered the house through the kitchen door where I saw the largest and most immaculate kitchen possible. "I eat out a lot," he said before I could compliment him on his domestic skills. We entered a living room that was equally large and every bit as clean. Beautiful shag carpet seemed to bury my feet, and I almost sank into the chair where he instructed me to sit. The entire place was a tribute to the film industry: paintings, posters, and even sculptures – all related to the movies. A projector sat on a small stand in the center of the room and was aimed at a clear white wall, which obviously acted as a screen. The lights went out, and the movie began before I could even feel settled.

"No need for any introductions," he shouted over the sound of the clicking reels. "This movie speaks for itself." I leaned back as far as I could without hindering my view and watched intently for the complete length of the film: running time – 45 minutes. When it ended, and the lights came back on; Sottlemeyer looked at me and smiled. "Any questions?" he asked.

"None," I answered. "It was very easy to understand." My tone changed, "And you want us to make a short film using those techniques?" I asked, trying to reassure myself.

"That's right," he said as he started the machine on re-wind. "Will there be any problem with that?"

"None that I can think of," I said.

"Great!" he declared with exaggerated enthusiasm. "Be sure to get a copy of the lecture notes, and you'll be fine."

"Is that all there is?" I asked, afraid that he had forgotten about his earlier offer to watch another movie.

"That's it," he said. "Now, if you would like me to take you home; I can do that; but if you want to watch another movie like I suggested earlier, that's fine too."

"I would love to watch another movie with you," I said affectionately. "It sounds like a lot of fun."

He led me to a huge closet, which stored literally hundreds of video cassettes and piles of file canisters. "Take your pick, but I recommend the cassettes." He laughed. "They're easier to load."

I was too overcome to hold back my next statement. "How do you afford all of these movies and a place like this on a teacher's salary?"

"I do more than teach," he answered without hesitation. "I edit film for two or three of the smaller, independent movie companies, and it supplements my income quite nicely."

"Why do you bother to teach at all?" I asked as my eyes searched through title after title.

"I enjoy it," he said evenly. "Besides, it's a good way for me to hone my craft, and it gives me the opportunity to meet people who may prove capable in the field."

"Is that all?" I asked, looking at him and feeling braver now.

He smiled, apparently aware of my innuendo, and answered unashamedly, "It gives me a chance to meet people – period."

"You mean people like me."

"That depends," he retorted. "What kind of a person are you?"

"I'm interested in film," I said seductively.

"Then pick a movie you'd like us to watch," he said a bit rudely.

"Let's watch this one," I said as I handed him a tape.

"That's an adult film and pretty explicit," he said with a calm demeanor.

"I know," I snapped back. "I remember all the controversy this thing caused when it ran in theaters. How'd you get a copy?"

"A lot of the cassettes are bootlegged," he answered with a certain sense of pride.

"You mean they're illegal," I confirmed.

"Sure. You got a problem with that?"

"No," I replied quickly. "Do you have a problem watching it with me?"

"That depends."

"On what?" I asked.

"On where you want to watch it – big screen in the living room, small screen in the bedroom."

"You decide," I said, now confident that he was just as interested in me as I was in him. Rather than saying another word, he took me

267

by the hand and led me to his bedroom, which was equipped with a large waterbed and even more movie memorabilia. I sat on the edge of the bed as he put the tape into the VCR. The two of us then leaned up against the soft headrest and began to watch consenting adults performing all types of sexual acts. In less than twenty minutes, we were embracing; and as the flick rattled on, we wrestled out of our clothes and soon forgot that there was a movie at all. The soft, white light had been replaced with a harsh black one; and it felt kind of eerie as pale specks seemed to glitter everywhere. No drugs had been used, yet it was all rather intoxicating as I responded to each of his movements. My body had become numb with pleasure, and I was higher than I could possibly imagine; for I finally knew what it was like to have sex with a man.

19

My night with Sottlemeyer was fantastic, but I never intended it to be anything more than a one- time thing. I had fulfilled a dream that so many students before me had: I slept with my professor. However, it turned into a full-blown affair that lasted for over a month, and it contained all the excitement usually connected with a back alley romance: stolen moments after class, the occasional rendezvous in a vacant room, and trips to places where we were left alone. Most of the time we made love at his house, but there were weekends at the beach and one time at his office when we violated the sanctity of the campus hallowed ground. It was all happening so fast, and I convinced myself that I was happy. However, I couldn't foresee the disaster that awaited me.

I tried to keep things going with Keith because I didn't want to lose him altogether, but I couldn't keep up the façade and soon admitted that there was someone else. Keith did not take it well at all and allowed his frustration to turn to anger. Although he never became violent with me, he verbally abused me when I told him that things were over.

As my relationship with Sottlemeyer intensified, I allowed more than one friendship to dissolve. I spent less time with my sorority sisters, and Kerry became disappointed with me. She continually warned me that I was being foolish, but I wouldn't listen. "You're setting yourself up for a big fall," she told me one time after a surprise visit to my room. "Besides, isn't there something illegal about a student dating a teacher?"

"Not a thing," I giggled. "Unless I claim that he's giving me a good grade because I'm sleeping with him."

"So is that the case?" she asked insolently.

"I think you're jealous," I shot back.

"I'm just worried about you," she said in a much calmer tone. "We all are."

"Who's we?" I asked impertinently.

"The sorority is worried about you."

I didn't give her a chance to say any more. "The fucking sorority can mind its own fucking business. I'm a big girl, and I can take care of myself."

"Suit yourself," she said as she left the room and never looked back.

At that point, I was convinced that I didn't need her or anybody else because I had *him*; but soon that was *all* I had, and I began to cling to him like a lost soul. I became more and more possessive; and eventually, it took its toll. I cried at first, but then I became angry; and when I became angry, I thought about Keith and how I had lost him as well. Then I thought of all the friends whom I ignored and whose help and advice I refused. I needed someone, but there was no one around. No matter how much I pleaded or how much I promised to change, things with Sottlemeyer were over. For the first time in a very long time, I felt alone. Reconnecting with people seemed impossible, so I wandered and I floundered and I stopped going to my classes. I slept more, ate less, and did very little to improve the situation. People stopped coming by, for I had made it obvious that I didn't need them.

I continued with my abstention and kept up my self-imposed exile for over a week. Eventually, I decided that I had to get out; and when Friday night arrived, I made it to the school bar where I sat alone and drank till I was drunk, and then I kept on drinking. Getting drunk was different than getting high. It was coarse and even a bit crude. The smooth sensual feeling I got when I smoked pot was replaced by irregular pulsations and sloppy awkwardness. I didn't want to feel sensual. I wanted to be vulgar. I could even get sick and then purify my insides with regurgitation on the floor of the bar. Others could follow, and we could empty our systems and start all over again.

No one looked familiar at first; but as the evening wore on, all the faces began to look the same. People had come and gone all night long; but I stayed forever, listening to stories, arguments, and horrible tasteless jokes. The smell of beer was constant, never trailing the pungent clouds of tobacco or the strong scent of one's cologne. By the time twelve rolled around, I saw and smelled things differently and decided that I had gone about it all wrong. I was ready to attack the world now, and there would be no holding me down. The male eyes were all looking at me with desire – yet fear, for I had been taken too many times, knew too many things, had too much experience. They wanted a challenge, needed to feel superior, and had to have young blood to satisfy the conquest. I was too much for them, and they knew it.

I rose from the stool and staggered in the direction of the exit where I could make out the figure of Steve Connolly. His blonde hair was unkempt as usual, and that solemn expression, which he seemed so fond of carrying around, didn't change as I catapulted into his arms. "Where's Mac?" I asked, barely audible. "Where's your little friend, your little companion?" Steve ignored me as he carried me to his car and carefully placed me in the back seat. I noticed flickering lights and shadows forming on the inside roof as we pulled away, and things seemed to be spinning around. The traffic sounds,

272

which were loud at first, became softer and eventually distant with only the hum of the tires hitting the road to break an otherwise absolute silence. The car had been jolting frantically when suddenly it stopped. Again, I was being carried; only this time I was more awake – more aware of what was happening. He carried me into his apartment, to a back room where he placed me gently on his bed. He thought I was asleep, but I wasn't. I was conscious – totally conscious, and nothing would happen without my approval. I tore my clothes from my body and waited for Steve to perform his manly act. I only hoped that I could stay awake the entire time; otherwise, it would be rape, and I would not be raped. I fought the desire to pass out as long as I could, but eventually I had nothing left as I felt myself drift away.

20

When I awoke, I heard the television playing in the other room. I was still naked but not quite sure about what had happened. I had no idea of the time until I noticed a clock radio, which read 11:55. My clothes were neatly folded on the chair next to the bed, and they looked as if they had been washed. The door to the room was shut, and the curtains were closed, which made things slightly dark but very cozy. I still smelled of beer and reeked of tobacco, and I didn't want to put my clothes on because I felt dirty. I noticed a bathrobe by the foot of the bed and assumed that it was left there for my convenience. I put it on and walked out to the living room. Steve was sitting in a comfortable looking chair, and Mac was lying on the couch. They were both watching television and looked up as they heard me approaching.

"Good morning," I said with considerable hoarseness in my voice.

"Good morning to you," Steve said in a manner that was neither pleasant nor angry.

"Good morning," Mac added. "Would you like some breakfast – or lunch?"

"I haven't been eating much lately," I explained, "so I probably should eat something. I just hope I can keep it down."

"Well that explains it," Steve said.

"Explains what?" I asked.

"You drink on an empty stomach and…"

"You don't have to tell me," I interrupted. "Believe me, I know."

"I see you found the robe," Steve said politely. "It was intended for you. You might want to take a shower and freshen up before you put your clothes on. They're clean."

"Yes, thank you," I said. "I think I'll take you up on the offer."

"And breakfast?" Mac added.

"Coffee would be nice for starters," I admitted, "but I would like to shower first." I walked back to the bedroom and entered the adjoining bathroom. A hot shower had never felt so good as I removed last night's remains from my body and then got back into some clean clothes.

When I came out from the bedroom, Mac pointed to the coffee maker and said, "Help yourself." I poured a large cup and then sat down in the living room. I was relaxed but certainly uncomfortable because of my behavior the previous night. Actually, I was uncomfortable because of my behavior for the previous month. "I really appreciate what you did," I said, well aware that nothing inappropriate had occurred between me and Steve. "I'm sorry and a little embarrassed."

"It happens," Steve said abruptly. "Let us get you something to eat, and you might feel better." I sat and watched as Mac prepared a somewhat eloquent breakfast. Two cups of coffee and a bacon and egg sandwich turned out to be the perfect combination, and I was feeling quite a bit stronger.

"Of course," Steve said when I finished my food, "I'll drive you back to your dorm if that's what you want, but you're welcome to stay here as long as you wish." I said nothing, but my expression made it obvious that I had nothing to do and not a friend with whom to do it. A midday movie was being aired – one with all the ghouls of the graveyard and all the demons of the used car lot gracing the screen. No one seemed particularly interested, but it served as nice background noise while we played Scrabble and then some cards. The movie was followed by a basketball game, a sport I usually dreaded, and then by a hockey game, a sport I didn't dread quite so much. However, I watched them both and never complained. Steve grilled some hamburgers during a break in the action and insisted that I join him and Mac for dinner. Hamburgers and potato salad tasted like manna from the gods. It was nice to feel welcomed again

– by anybody, and these two guys were going out of their way to make me comfortable.

I was sure that sooner or later they would ask me about Friday night and why I was behaving so recklessly, but neither ever brought it up and continued to act as if I were a frequent guest of theirs. While Steve was driving me home, I couldn't take it any longer, so I politely asked him, "Why?"

He had a startled look on his face. "Why what?" he asked back.

"Oh please," I said somewhat ungraciously. "Everything you and Mac have done for me today. It's been wonderful, just what I needed; but you've never questioned me about anything."

He curled his lip and rolled his eyes. "It's none of our business," he said spryly.

"None of your business," I retorted. "I just spent a lot of time at your apartment, ate your food, am wearing the clothes you washed," I said tugging on the shirt to emphasis my point. "I think you're entitled to an explanation."

"Fine," he said, "if that'll make you feel better."

"It would," I said. "Forget about getting me home, let's drive some place."

We drove to the edge of an orange grove and parked under one of the trees. Then I told him everything – about Keith, the sorority, Kerry, and Sottlemeyer. Not a single detail was left out. When I finished, I looked deeply into his eyes and said, "Well?"

"Why tell me?" he asked. "I just happened to be there. I didn't know where you lived, and no one in that place was about to tell me—"

"That's not the point," I interrupted. "The both of you have been very kind, and I feel indebted to you."

"Don't!" he said sharply. "We're not looking for anything in return. We would have done the same thing for anybody."

"I believe that you would," I agreed, "but most people would have done nothing – or taken advantage of me."

"That's possible," he conceded, "but once again. Why tell me all that's happened to you?"

I hesitated but only momentarily as I said, "Because I thought you would understand."

He put his finger to his lip. "Mac and I are pretty good students; why don't you let us help you in those areas where you might need it. You can get caught up pretty easily for that week you've missed."

"I haven't been giving that much thought, but you're right. I probably could use some help in a few areas."

"Sure," he said enthusiastically. "I can help you with some compositions, and Mac is pretty good with languages."

I sighed and then bemoaned, "My biggest concern is my film class."

"I wouldn't worry about that!" Steve interjected. "I have a lot of the same notes from when I took the class last semester. They're yours if you want them." He shrugged. "It's easier than going to Sottlemeyer."

"Isn't that like cheating?" I asked sarcastically.

"A little," he concurred, "but we won't tell anyone."

I could hardly get my voice above a whisper as I asked, "Why are you being so nice?"

"We enjoyed your company a lot today, and this would be a good excuse to get you over more often."

"You don't need an excuse," I declared, and with that, Steve started the car and took me back to my dorm. It was late for some and prime time for others on this Saturday night, but I ignored the nonsense and paid little attention to all the noise. I began to feel happy about myself again and fell asleep with no problem.

On Sunday I was back at the boys' apartment, and the two of them bombarded me with information from two directions. The only class in which they couldn't render some assistance was my bowling class, but that didn't bother me. Fortunately, I had not gone over the cut limit for any of my courses, and therefore, would not be issued a failure due to absence. Steve didn't write my overdue compositions for me, but his insight and expertise made it very easy for me to complete them. Mac's hints on how to handle Spanish as well as how to handle the teacher proved to be useful, and Steve's notes from his previous film class made an uncomfortable situation a little less uncomfortable.

21

When I returned to my normal schedule, things appeared to be just that – normal. It was difficult to face Sottlemeyer, but I said as little as possible and tried to act as if nothing had ever happened between us. I also got the impression that he would rather have forgotten the whole thing as well, and that was fine with me. Within a few weeks, things didn't appear to be difficult at all.

I started attending sorority meetings again but avoided most of the parties; and although Kerry and I were back on speaking terms, there was very little for us to say to each other these days. I spent a good deal of my free time at the pool, swimming and getting into shape as well as soaking up enough sun to lighten my hair and keep my body a lush golden brown. However, my greatest joy was visiting my new friends, where I could sharpen my mind and help those two untidy individuals keep their apartment clean.

Being around Steve always put me at ease because he looked with admiration, yet he never touched. He also allowed me to open up on just about every subject; but he never lectured, merely advised and only if I asked him to do so. When I sought his opinion about Keith, he talked about trust issues and how hard it was to get back that trust when one lets it slip away.

"I don't know him," Steve said, "but I can tell you this. He's acting about the way any guy would act when his pride or ego gets crushed. "

"I know that there will never be anything between us," I said despairingly, "but I hate being enemies with him. I mean he won't talk to me or even acknowledge that I exist."

281

"He might get over the hurt and talk to you some day, but it will probably take him some time." He hesitated, took a deep breath, and then carefully said, "And it may never happen. And if that's the case, don't beat yourself up over it." He smiled and then took a sip from the drink in front of him. "I guess I'll never really understand some things. I mean you can wait for a long time and then wait again. But you have to admit things to yourself first, and then go on with your life." He smiled. "I think you're doing a pretty good job of that."

He really did understand things, regardless of what he said; and it was obvious that he spoke from experience. However, I never asked because I was *afraid* to ask. If there was something in his past that brought him a lot of pain, I'd wait for him to talk about it – and only if he wanted to. Knowing him had given me a sense of balance in the world, a new perspective about things. He seemed content with his life, and he was definitely more mature than any student – any person for that matter – that I had met so far; yet this individual, who appeared to have his head on straight, and possessed an air of confidence like none other, remained a mystery to me. Amongst those who had a modicum of brains, he was a genius; and around those, whose only intentions in life were of a selfish nature, he was the most caring and considerate person alive. I didn't know him though. I knew about his passion for hockey and how he put his hands up straight and yelled "score" whenever the puck went into the net, and I was aware of his extreme dislike for insensitive people, whom he attacked with a fierce invective; but I didn't know *him*. I wanted to know all there was to know, but again, I was afraid to ask.

22

Things had gotten to the point where I spent so much time at Steve and Mac's apartment that they gave me a key and a free run of the place. I felt obligated to keep the place clean although no actual duty was required for my liberal visitation rights.

It was a Sunday morning, and both occupants were gone when I arrived to do my customary maintenance. Steve was playing golf, and Mac was at the library where he could work on some research project that was very important to him. As I tried to get the vacuum cleaner out of the closet, I bumped one of the loosely attached shelves. Books, papers, and assorted pictures came tumbling down and almost buried me up to my waist.

"Shit!" I said aloud. "How did they fit this much crap on that little shelf?" Patiently, I started to pick things up, sorting the papers, stacking the books, and looking at every photo, which might prove to be interesting. It was by this intense study that I came across a piece of the puzzle which helped me understand part of Steve's past but clouded his present situation that much more. When he came home from playing golf, I confronted him with it. His eyes studied it briefly, and he tried to force a smile when he put the photo on top of the television. "I knocked it off the shelf in the closet when I was getting the vacuum cleaner," I confessed, "but I wasn't snooping, honest."

"I know you weren't," he reassured me. "So what do you think?"

"Well," I said, my shoulders shrugging to show my bewilderment. "It's a picture of Mac with his class, and the caption reads something about ninth grade. The teacher standing to the left of the group looks a lot like you."

I could tell that he was trying not to smile, but a slight sneer managed to work its way across his lips. "The person in that picture could be my older brother," he said in a most unconvincing manner.

284

"I doubt that," I replied curtly. "Besides, why would you have it?"

"It's Mac's picture," he declared. "You'll have to ask him."

"Nice try," I said unable to contain my amusement. "But that's you." He took the picture from the top of the set and handed it to me, so I could look at it again. "It is you," I said confidently.

"It is," he confirmed.

"So," I said, handing the picture back to him, "you were Mac's ninth grade teacher."

"Actually, I was still in college. That photograph was taken while I was doing my practice teaching or internship, as we liked to call it. Mac's mother was a fellow classmate of mine."

"You mean teacher, don't you?" I said, certain he had misspoken.

"No," he assured me, "she was a classmate. A little older, but a classmate nonetheless."

"I'm lost," I said, shaking my head.

"Like I said, it was a few years ago; but sometimes it seems like yesterday. Mac's mother was a student and eventually became a friend of mine when she discovered that Mac was in my class."

"But Mac said you guys were from New York." My expression was all he needed to know how confused I was.

"We are," Steve said quickly. "After I graduated from college, I got a job at the high school where I interned. Mac, on the other hand, moved back to New York with his mother."

"So how old was Mac's mother at the time?"

"I never asked her," Steve said cynically. "I just knew that she was a widow, who decided to attend school when she was older."

"So you knew her for the four years you attended college."

"Not really," he snapped. "I saw her in some of my classes, but I didn't get to know her until I met Mac."

"So that explains how you met," I said, "but if you're not here to protect Mac, why are you here? Are you even a student?"

"You've seen me attending class," he declared emphatically. "Of course, I'm a student. I am an official student here at Citra University, courtesy of one Dorothy MacIntyre."

"But why?" I asked, still puzzled.

"People *are* permitted to get more than one degree, you know." He stopped, realized how condescending he sounded, but then continued. "To pick up a new major, to be retrained so I can get a better job out in the world."

"It seems like you're going to some extreme just because you don't want to teach anymore."

"Don't want to teach," he said complacently. "Did I say that?"

"Then why else?" I asked.

"All right," he said reluctantly "I do keep an eye on Mac, "but there's more to it. It's a long story."

"I have all day," I said, "unless you don't want to talk about it."

"I haven't talked about it for a very long time," he conceded. "It's not something I'm all that comfortable with, but I'll talk about it. Maybe it'll do me some good."

As I listened to his story, it became obvious as to why he didn't like to talk about it. He spoke of betrayal – and not just about administrators who wanted him to alter grades for some star athlete – but about those who were close to him, about those whom he considered as friends. As I assimilated all that he told me, I realized that my personal problems were so small, so insignificant compared to what he had gone through. His pain was far greater, and I wanted to give him some comfort. "I'm sorry about you and Jillian," was all I could force out, and I hardly believed that I had spoken.

"She was vulnerable," he said flatly, "and he took advantage of her." Suddenly he seemed aloof, momentarily lost in thought until his next sentence shot out like a bullet from a gun. "I honestly think she regretted it, and I will never stop believing that."

"And do you think that's why—"

"I don't know," he interrupted, "and I feel better not knowing."

"And what became of Frank Stewart?" I asked timidly.

"Believe it or not, he's living somewhere in L.A. with his sister."

"No way," I said skeptically. "Have you ever tried to look him up?"

"To do what?" he said indignantly.

"I didn't mean it like that," I said somewhat apologetically. "I just meant have you ever thought about where he lives."

"Oh sure," he admitted, using a much softer tone. "But I've never wanted to make the effort. Besides, we have nothing to say to each other."

"Well, I can certainly understand that," I said with compunction. "So you've explained why you aren't teaching in Florida, but you haven't explained how you ended up here – with Mac."

"That's simple," he said. "I ran into Mac's mother while I was living in New York, and she made me an offer that was too good to turn down."

"Keep an eye on Mac, and she'll pay your tuition," I responded with a certain level of authority.

"Something like that," he conceded, "but it's more about *me* than it is about *Mac*. If push came to shove, he'd be fine. His mother is doing this because she wants to help *me*."

"Were you a teacher in New York?" I asked.

"No," he replied quickly, "the higher authority in Florida made it next to impossible for me to ever teach again. I was a reporter, but," he said slowly, "that didn't work out so well either."

"What happened?"

"There were a number of things that went wrong," he confessed, "and not all of them were job related."

"Like what?" I asked, trying not to appear so nosey.

"Let's just say that some of my inner demons surfaced, and overindulgence got the better of me."

"You mean drinking," I said.

"Among other things," he answered frankly.

"I find that hard to believe," I said.

"Believe it," he shot back. "I was on the fast track to nowhere."

"Did you get fired?"

"Not exactly, but I needed to move on; and thanks to a chance meeting with Dottie MacIntyre, I got to do that."

"So the two of you had lost touch?"

"Yea," he complied. "In fact, we hadn't spoken since our graduation." He curled his lip and titled his head. "Things like that happen sometimes."

"Does Mac know what happened to you in Florida?" I asked with trepidation.

"Mac knows everything about everything," he responded with no apathy at all. "And before you even think about asking – no, he is not keeping an eye on me. There are no stipulations, no rules or regulations whatsoever. This is nothing more than an agreement between friends." His tone had turned slightly defensive, and I knew better than to press him further on certain details. For the first time I really began to understand this person – this person who had always looked just a little older and acted a little older as well, this person who impressed me with what he knew and with what he said, and this person who now revealed some glaring weaknesses and drastic insecurities about himself. I took a good look at his face and noticed the crow's feet around his eyes – a sign of weariness more than age. The spots of gray in his hair were now more obvious although the bleached mop still made him look younger, and I took a strong notice of the imperfect nose – the result of too many Sunday afternoon football games in the park or maybe the lasting effects of a brawl or two. It was as if he had aged right before my eyes.

"I've got to pick Mac up at the library. Wanna take a ride." His words were curt but polite.

"You go," I said. "By the time you get back, I'll have the vacuuming done." He nodded graciously and went on his way.

I finished my unassigned chores and waited impatiently for the boys' return. When they finally arrived, Steve announced that he had several errands to run and that he would be gone for over an hour. Apparently, he had told Mac about my discovery; and now he was willing to leave me alone with his young protégé, who would tell me more and answer all my questions.

"Was she pretty?" I asked, making no apologies about going to a rather frivolous detail.

"I only saw her a few times," he said, trying hard not to laugh, "but she was a knock out. Unfortunately," he added, "she was very Southern and very much daddy's little girl."

"So she approved of the grade manipulation?" I asked.

"To some extent," he replied. "I'm sure Steve told you that sports – especially football – is very important in the state of Florida."

"He did indeed," I concurred. "Was he a good teacher?" I asked abruptly.

"I probably learned more when he took the class over from the regular teacher." He smiled and nodded his head slightly. "He was relentless," he said in a loud whisper. "We worked very hard, outlining chapters and taking notes; but it was worth it. You never get more by asking for less."

"That's very true," I agreed.

"That was his favorite saying," Mac interjected. "Claims one of his favorite teachers used to say it all the time."

"Why didn't you stay in Florida?"

"My mother had allusions of grandeur and wanted to become an art teacher." He hesitated and then continued. "No jobs."

"Is she a teacher in New York?"

"She gives lessons on the side – and does pretty well. But I'm sure Steve told you that it isn't about money."

"He implied that," I said, "but I would have figured it out myself."

"Steve's pretty modest when it comes to most things," Mac stated with affirmation. "He probably said nothing about his athletic skills."

"No, he didn't," I concurred.

"He had a track scholarship when he was in college, and he was pretty damn good – until he got hurt. Torn meniscus. He never recovered."

"So is that why he went into teaching?" I asked.

"I never asked him," Mac replied. "It never seemed important."

"He told me that he was a reporter in New York."

"A sports reporter," Mac confirmed. "But he broke a really big story – quite by accident. It was pretty controversial, and they wanted him to sit on it."

"But he wouldn't back down," I declared.

"Not Steve," Mac agreed. "It just wasn't his nature."

"So they let him go."

"Not really," Mac corrected. "Things just got too hot for him to handle, and he had to get away."

"So he came here."

"No, this has nothing to do with any of that," he said tersely. "This is nothing more than an opportunity for him to get a fresh start on things."

I laughed. "That's what he told me at first. Just getting a second degree."

"And a new name," Mac said. "I know he didn't tell you about that."

"A new name!" I exclaimed.

"Yea, I'm finally getting used to Connolly."

"So what is his real name?" I asked.

"Oh, it's Connolly," Mac said assuredly. "He had it legally changed."

"From what?" I asked.

"Does it really matter?" Mac asked. "It's not like he was famous or anything."

"Probably not," I agreed. "But why?"

"To complete the process," Mac declared. "This way he could bury his past." Mac began to laugh. "Thank goodness he kept the same first name, or I'd never know what to call him."

"Steve was pretty open about some of his personal problems," I avowed.

"He never tried to make excuses for his behavior," Mac confirmed. "But he's never actually apologized for them either. He doesn't come right out and say it, but I think he feels that some of those deeply buried emotions can surface at any time."

"Does he still love her?" I asked.

"Back on that again." Mac lamented.

"Well, does he?" I asked once more.

"Yea, and I don't think he'll ever stop loving her," Mac said. "People go through different types of heartache: break-ups, death. Steve got to experience them both."

"Does he talk about her? I mean to you. Does he talk about her to *you*."

"He did, but he hasn't spoken about her for a very long time," Mac said. "Maybe he's trying to forget. I've never gone through it, so I don't know." He hesitated, then continued. "Frank Stewart is another story. He may not talk about him that much, but believe me. He will never forget him."

"Steve told me they were friends," I acknowledged.

"They were *very* good friends, and Steve could never understand how a good friend could betray him with such intensity. That's why he'll never get over it."

"Would you?" I asked seriously.

Mac didn't say a word. He just looked at me, pursed his lips, and then sighed.

I heard the car pull up and then the apartment door open. Mac moved to the kitchen, so I was alone in the living room. Steve just looked at me and smiled. "So did Mac fill you in on all the details I left out?"

"He told me enough," I said.

"I'm sorry if I misled you," he said regretfully.

"Don't be," I demanded. "In many ways I wish that *I* could just start all over again."

"But you have," he said softly. "You have."

I never told Steve that Mac had informed me about the name change; therefore, I never asked him what his former name *was*. I just knew that this man had rescued me, and now I truly understood why. I didn't care at all about who he had been, just who he was now. To me, he was Steve Connolly, and he would always be Steve Connolly.

Part Six
The Rooster

The smog was heavy, so most of the local residents were inside where it was safe – or at least safer from the toxic fumes that the factories continued to belch out on a regular basis. Traffic was light, but that was expected since it was Sunday morning. However, on this Sunday morning, the traffic was exceptionally light; and that was a good thing. Too much traffic made him nervous, and he still wasn't sure if this was the best thing to do. "Confront your demons," she had told him, "and this is the biggest demon of all."

He had beaten them. It wasn't always easy, but he had done it. He may have had help, but he had beaten them all but one, and this was the biggest challenge out there. As much as he tried to deny it, this trip was necessary. If he was ever going to have total peace of mind, he had to make this trip.

He pulled into a gas station, filled the car, and bought a newspaper. "It looks like the Dodgers won again," he said as he climbed back into the vehicle and sat behind the wheel.

"I don't care," she said. "You're stalling."

"You're right," he said with aplomb. "I am stalling. Part of me wants to go through with this, part of me wants this to be over, and part of me doesn't want him to be there."

"You could have called," she told him in a scolding manner. "If we were able to find the address, finding the phone number would not have been a problem."

"I know," he admitted, "but if I'm going to confront this demon as we call it, I need to do it face to face. A phone call may have scared him away, and if I'm going to go through with this, I've got to see him."

***

The apartment complex had the standard Western motif and looked more like a motel than tenements for those on fixed income. There were a few scattered items, which gave the place that "lower class" look as one person called it; but otherwise, it was very neat and clean. A few walls might have been in need of some paint, but all buildings suffered from a little wear and tear over time.

They called him El Gallo – the rooster. He was not fond of the moniker, for unlike the cock of the barnyard, he was not awarded the same privileges. He was just the male that the women saw most often – not the lone male of the complex, just the one who stayed behind while the others went off to work.

His main provider was gone for the day, so he had the place to himself. He loved her; he truly loved her, but he tired of the pressure she put on him. Things had not fallen his way, but they would – and soon. He knew it would happen when he made the right connection. Clubs were always looking for people like him, and he could perform in more than one language. That had to work in his favor.

He took his usual stroll along the top balcony and down the stairs that led to the pool. There he took the long net and skimmed off any palm leaves or dead bugs that may have been floating on the surface. If only they would pay him for his services. He could keep the area clean and watch the kids swim and be nice to the ladies who sat around all day. After all, he was part of their culture, and he spoke their language. A quick dip not only cooled him off, but it helped wake him up. The air conditioner in the apartment was broken again, and they didn't have the money to fix it. How unfair was that, he thought. Shouldn't those repairs be covered in the rent?

On a patio table sat yesterday's paper, so he picked it up. Old news was better than no news at all, so he sat down and began to read it diligently. He scoured the editorial page, ignored the sports section, and ended up with the want ads. As usual, there was nothing – nothing that would please him, nothing that would make travel easy or non-existent, nothing that he would accept. If gas prices got any higher, nobody would be able to travel. At least, that's what he believed; and by believing that, he never felt guilty when he just lay around all day.

By eight o'clock, El Gallo had fixed himself some breakfast. It was adequate, but not as good as when she was around. She fixed him a wonderful breakfast whenever she could, and he loved her even more for that. Sunday morning television was filled with evangelist propaganda, news programs, or reruns of shows that should never have aired in the first place. He could always go back to the pool. At least it was cooler, but he didn't. He just sat and listened to some music to calm his unsteady demeanor.

***

"I could use another cup of coffee," he said as they stopped for a red light.

"You should have picked one up when we stopped for gas. Besides," she snapped like a mother scolding a young child, "you drink too much coffee."

"Maybe," he admitted. "It's one of my remaining vices."

"Coffee is far from a vice," she declared. "I just worry about your health. Too much caffeine can't be good for you."

"You're right," he agreed. "I'll pass."

She pulled down the sun visor, then shielded her eyes as the light reflected off the front of the car and caused an enormous glare. "It's hard to see where you're going," she cautioned.

"I'm not sure if I even *know* where I'm going, so seeing is not an issue," he joked.

"The directions are pretty precise," she remarked as she picked up the handwritten copy. "And traffic seems good."

"I hate traffic," he grumbled.

"You've told me," she said. "How have you survived this long dealing with it?"

302

"I guess I'm just a survivor," he boasted.

She smiled. Although she would never come right out and say it, she loved him – loved him more than anything, and someday he might even love her. It didn't matter though because things in her life were different now – very different, and if friendship was all that developed between them, friendship was good enough. "We've still got a little ways yet," she reminded him. He nodded but said nothing as he continued to focus on his driving. Within moments, they were on that long stretch of road, which would take them to their destination.

"I'll drive some if you want me to," she offered. "That way you can read the newspaper."

"It'll keep," he said.

"Don't trust me behind the wheel," she challenged.

"I don't trust *any* female drivers," he said condescendingly.

"You're a chauvinist," she replied. "You know that?"

"That's what they tell me," he said proudly. "And I'm never going to change."

She laughed at the irony of his statement. He had buried so many things before and left so much behind. She was convinced that this would give him closure and allow him – once and for all – to end that chapter of his life. This would prove him to be the better person, to show this old friend – this person who had caused him so much pain – that he had moved on.

***

By nine o'clock, El Gallo was getting bored with listening to music. "I can sing better than those assholes," he said aloud. "When is everyone gonna know that?" He picked up the phone and told the operator to put through his long distance call. "When are the rates cheaper again?" he asked himself. He could never remember, but it wasn't important because he never paid for his calls. She did. It was noon on the East coast, so everyone was up; and his contact would be available. "It's me," he chanted into the phone when the other party picked up. "I need more money." The response was negative as usual, but his promise of "You know she's good for it," always reversed the initial refusal.

She may have been older than he was, but she wasn't that smart. She didn't keep very good records; so when the bill was sent in the guise of a Florida realtor, she thought it was another down payment

304

for some property she would eventually own. This had been going on for some time; and if she ever tried to cash in on her dreamland, he would convince her that she had been the victim of an elaborate scam.

He should have felt guilty, but he didn't. When he finally hit the big time, he would pay her everything he owed. Quite often he actually tried to believe this but quickly dismissed it since he knew it wasn't true. He was talented, and the world owed him – owed him plenty, so why should El Gallo feel guilty. He was content for the moment. The money was on its way, and with it he could buy a few more months – precious months to pursue his dream. All they had to do was listen, just listen once, and they would know.

***

"This must be the place," he said as he pulled into one of the visitor spots. "It matches the number we wrote down on the paper."

"If he isn't here, we can go to a movie or something and come back later," she suggested.

"Whatever," he grumbled. "I would like you to come with me."

"Are you sure?" she asked.

"Positive," he said as he slid out from under the wheel. He opened her door, took her hand, and started toward the second level. His heart was racing with each step he took, and by the time they reached the apartment, he thought it would explode. He gave the door four hard raps and then waited patiently – part of him hoping that no one would answer. He heard the sound of the chain lock being released, and suddenly the door was open.

El Gallo nearly fainted when he saw him standing in the doorway and said nothing as the man and his companion walked in. They both looked around before she whispered, "I assume this is the right place."

"This is it," her partner said. "This is it."

"I can't believe my eyes," El Gallo said. "What's it been?"

"Too long," his adversary said. "Too long."

"Are you here looking for an apology or here to give *me* one?" El Gallo said with contempt

The uninvited guest laughed, but it amused no one. His companion looked at him and saw something that she had not seen before – anger, and for the moment it frightened her. "I'm not sure why I came," he said with conviction.

"We were hoping you two could clear the air," she interjected.

"Clear the air!" El Gallo shouted. "Who is she? Somebody you just picked up?"

"She's a friend of mine – a very good friend of mine." He pointed to a chair and instructed her to have a seat. "Do you mind if we stay a while."

"You're not welcomed," El Gallo said. "This is my place, not yours; and you have no hold over me here."

"I never had a hold over you," he corrected. "We were friends, and friends help each other out."

"Yea, right," El Gallo said sarcastically. "When things got too tough for you to handle, you just tossed me out."

"You made me pay for that."

El Gallo stuttered a bit. "I did what I did – because it was the right thing to do. Jill told me what you were doing. She told me that you were buying beer for those students. I had to do something. I had to do the right thing." Then he looked at the girl who was now sitting in one of his chairs. "Why is she here?"

307

"It was my idea," she said calmly. "I thought you guys could talk. I'll leave and give you two some privacy."

"Take him with you!" El Gallo shouted, even louder than before. "I don't know why you came here."

"I'm not sure why I came either," he said, "but now that I'm here, I think I know what I want – a piece of you."

It wasn't much of a fight. Two quick blows to the stomach, one across the jaw, and the rooster was down and out for the count. "Did you enjoy that?" she asked.

"I did," he said. "I really did. Maybe that's what I needed – instead of talking, I needed the opportunity to beat the crap out of him."

"Well, you certainly did that," she concurred. "I guess we can we go now?"

"Hey!" he shouted defensively. "This was your idea, remember."

"To *face* him," she corrected, "not punch his lights out."

"You wanted me to conquer my demon, and I did just that." He looked down at his fallen adversary. "I'm finished here," he said.

They stepped out of the apartment and closed the door behind them. However, they hadn't gone very far before he stopped and ran back. She watched from a distance as he opened the door, looked in for a moment, and then closed it again. "What was that all about?" she asked.

He pulled a crumpled paper from his pocket and waved it in her direction. "I wanted to give him a copy of the poem I once wrote – the one about him. He isn't worth it though. He just isn't worth it."

By the time they got back to the car, the heat had become stifling. He turned the air conditioning on and cracked the windows to speed up the process. Before they drove away from the complex, he turned on the radio. It was the news, and they were giving the sports scores. "Sounds like the Dodgers won again," he said cheerfully.

"I don't care. Remember? I don't care."

"Come to think of it," he said, "I don't either."

Part Seven:
The Detective

Robert Johnson hated cases like this. He had been on the force too long, no doubt; but regardless of his experience and underappreciated longevity, Robert Johnson hated cases like this. He was one of the better homicide detectives on the force, and when he was handed an assignment, which may not have been a homicide at all, he was overtly displeased.

Geralyn Garr was not comfortable as she spoke to the detective, despite his courteous manner and sincere attempt to put her at ease. Johnson was also a bit uncomfortable, but he didn't show it. Geralyn noticed that Johnson's desk was cluttered with the usual things that one associated with a person in his line of work. There were empty coffee cups, which were indicative of more than one tedious night when Johnson had to stay up way past his bedtime, and an assortment of memorabilia displaying one accomplishment or another – many, not job related; and Johnson kept them, not as a reminder, but simply as a courtesy to those who so graciously rewarded him with these hollow honors. There was also a family picture, and Geralyn examined it closely. It looked enough like

Johnson that it was obviously a recent photo, and she couldn't help but notice how attractive the other three people (who shared the space with him) were.

Johnson was showing some signs of age; but at fifty, he was entitled. His hair had spots of gray, and the body, which used to be so rigid and taught, had a few soft places. Like so many others who did what Johnson did, he looked tired – tired for a number of reasons, but he always put his fatigue along with his frustration aside; and he never lost focus as to what had to be done. Geralyn wondered if he had a bottle of hooch in his bottom drawer like several of those celluloid private eyes that she learned to love by watching too many old movies – but he didn't, for Robert Johnson was the consummate professional in every sense of the word. He certainly wasn't perfect; he would be the first to acknowledge that, but he was a good person and never ashamed of anything he did.

He was working alone these days for no particular reason – at least none he would admit to – and it suited him. He had worked with several partners over the years, and there had never been any public problems; but Robert Johnson was a man of convictions and would never compromise his beliefs under any circumstances. To several outsiders and to a few at the top, Johnson was never seen as a team player; and this became a problem. Johnson also refused to get very close to most of those with whom he had shared a patrol car or a criminal investigation. The only exception was his first partner, a guy who was not only easy to take but extremely efficient to boot. Together, they were the perfect salt and pepper combination that granted them access to those areas usually off limits for one reason or another. Johnson frequently spoke like the college graduate he was, but when necessary could drop to a ghetto slang which was beyond convincing. When things came to an abrupt ending – something about which Johnson never spoke – he refused to get close to a partner again.

Thankfully, those days of patrol work, which often required Johnson to role play his lack of sophistication, were far behind him; and he could do the thing he did best – be himself. He often wondered what his life would be like if he had fulfilled that initial dream, but those reflections always vanished when he thought about his family and how lucky he truly was.

"Have a seat, Miss Garr," he offered while pointing to the empty chair in front of his desk. Geralyn did as instructed and made herself as comfortable as possible. "This won't take very long," Johnson added as he positioned himself. "Would you care for a cup of coffee?" he asked.

"No thank-you," she answered.

"Fine," he said. "Let's get started. I'm sure you know why we asked you to come in." Geralyn nodded but said nothing. "Miss Garr," Johnson spoke softly, "you have nothing to be nervous about. No one is accusing you of anything. We just want to get all the necessary details."

"I understand," Geralyn responded timidly. "This has been very difficult for me."

"Of course," Johnson agreed. "It would be difficult for anybody." Johnson gestured with open palms and requested politely. "Tell me what happened."

For the next twenty minutes to the best of her recollection, Geralyn described everything that had happened. Johnson listened intently and never interrupted her once. When she was done, he was completely convinced that she in no way had participated in anything illegal. In fact, he wasn't sure if anything other than a minor assault had actually happened. There had been a fight, and by her description, not a very long one; but there had also been a death, and she was not aware of that. Johnson believed her when she told him that, and he saw no reason to press her further on the issue.

"You were aware that Steve Connolly had gone through an identity change."

"Yes," Geralyn responded sheepishly. "A mutual friend tried to explain that to me."

"What reasons did he give you?" Johnson shot bluntly.

"He just wanted to get a fresh start," Geralyn said, not sure if she was trying to convince the detective or herself.

"You can understand how and why this looks a little mysterious." Johnson didn't wait for a response. "We need to determine if Frank Stewart's death was an accident or deliberately provoked by Mr. Connolly."

"I don't understand," Geralyn said. "I thought he died from a heart attack."

"He did," Johnson concurred. "However, if Connolly did everything he could to bring about that attack and then left him there to die..." He took a deep sigh and looked at her very cautiously.

"Then there could be a problem with intent and even premeditation," he said, completing his thought.

"When we left, Frank was alive," Geralyn said quickly.

"That's what you said, and I don't doubt your statement." Johnson sighed again, only more deeply than previously. "But Connolly went back – just for a brief moment like you said, but a lot can happen in a brief moment."

"So what happens now?" Geralyn inquired as her voice clearly shook.

"Well," Johnson said calmly. "If motive can be established, and I think it already has, there will be a push to prove that Connolly planned this operation right from the get go."

"He just wanted to beat him up," Geralyn declared, "not kill him."

"Unfortunately," Johnson added, "it doesn't matter what you think or even what I think." He shrugged his shoulders and extended his hand in appreciation for all her cooperation. "The people who charged Connolly are going to have me go out and talk to several others – people who knew Connolly when he went by a different name. It's the name change that has our young assistant D.A.

315

convinced that this was all some kind of mysterious plot or conspiracy dreamed up by Connolly -- or whoever he is." Geralyn just shook her head in disbelief. There was no way that Steve Connolly could do such a thing. He was a tortured soul. She knew that, but he couldn't deliberately watch another human being die – regardless of who that human being might be. She shook Johnson's hand and then left the police station, well aware that a horrible nightmare awaited her – and Steve – and even Mac.

***

If he wasn't convinced before, he was convinced now. Robert Johnson hated cases like this. This would mean making trips to New York and to Florida as well. Johnson had been to New York on more than one occasion, and a visit to the land, which used to be home for his beloved Dodgers, was never a hardship he grew too tired to endure; but a trip to Florida – even if it was miles from his old stomping ground in Tallahassee – was always an interesting endeavor. He didn't miss the high humidity or the less than subtle racism, which the Sunshine State claimed never existed, but there was something about a return visit to his home state as it rapidly grew from a glorified retirement home to an overly developed and overly populated peninsula.

The air conditioner in the rental car – thankfully – worked perfectly as it blew cool air from the upward placed position and hit Johnson squarely in the face. Although it wasn't part of this investigative journey, he took a quick detour and sneaked a peek at the college campus where the lead suspect had attended. It had grown considerably since his last visit when he was a running back at A&M and prepping for a Saturday afternoon contest. "We killed them," he told himself as he made the necessary U-turn and drove to his intended destination.

The high school still had that look of the solid South: a parking lot of pick-up trucks with gun racks and designer license plates that displayed the stars and bars; but the separate bathrooms were gone, and the Confederate flag that used to fly so high was no longer flapping in the breeze. There were no more segregated schools or establishments that refused his entry, but there were still the attitudes and the unwritten laws which conveyed the true beliefs of a culture that was still living in the dark ages.

"My name is Robert Johnson from California, and I have an appointment to meet the principal." Johnson showed his badge as he stood by the desk in the front office and waited patiently while the secretary went back to the adjoining office.

"Mr. Carter is on the phone," the secretary said in a pleasant but certainly strained manner. "If you would have a seat."

Johnson sat in a comfortable chair that backed up to a huge window, which served as the front for the main office. With a slight adjustment, he was able to look out the window and observe the rustling students who were scurrying to get to class on time. There was a bang on a locker here and there and the occasional shout that would never have been tolerated back in his day; but for the most part, not a lot had really changed. The faces were different, and the styles – clothes and hair – were part of the new modern era; but it was still high school: filled with expressions of several who really didn't want to be there and too many who had no clue as to what awaited them out there in the big, bad world. Johnson just smiled and patiently waited for the school's top administrator to make his appearance.

"Right this way," the secretary chirped in an overly polite melody. "Mr. Carter will see you now." Johnson nodded as he walked into the office and immediately noticed that it was adorned with commemorative material. The wall was covered with elaborately framed photographs of former students signing with one major university after another. Some, Johnson recognized; others were made apparent by the caption that emblazoned the bottom portion of each picture. A few other items that caught his attention were the basketball, which sat on a perch in the corner, and the baseball bat that leaned against the outer side of a huge filing cabinet. However, there was one item that stood out the most – a collegiate style football that was literally covered in autographs of several famous college athletes. Johnson was impressed but only mildly impressed. He also noticed the pen holder which sat on Carter's desk: his nameplate took up the front, and crossed flags that represented the rebel army filled out the back. He tried to divert his eyes from the offending symbols and mask the instant disgust he had for the grand sizing buffoon that stood before him.

"Have a seat, Mr. Johnson," Carter said as he extended his hand.

"It's Detective," Johnson said upon acceptance of Carter's greeting. Usually, he was not so curt and could really care less about what people called him, but he wanted to put a little barb into the side of this egotistical giant and make him feel a bit uneasy.

"Whatever you say," Carter responded in a tone which made it obvious that Johnson had succeeded. When Johnson seated himself, Carter remarked defensively, "You've come a long way, Detective, to ask me some questions which could have been done over the phone."

"That's true," Johnson conceded, "but I prefer to conduct interviews in person whenever it's possible." He smiled. "You can learn quite a bit about a person when you look at him and his surroundings." He hesitated and then increased his smile. "Besides, I'm originally from Florida, so I thought I'd take some time to visit some old friends along the way."

Carter smiled back, but his smile was one of contempt; and he did nothing to disguise that as he asked, "What do you want, Detective Johnson?"

"Do you know this man?" Johnson asked as he slid a photograph of Steve Connolly across the desk.

Carter picked the photo up, studied it for a moment, and then nodded his head affirmatively. "Yea, I know him. He used to work here a while back. What did he do?"

"We don't know if he did anything, but he goes by the name Connolly," Johnson said. "I believe that when he worked here, he went by a different name."

"That's right," Carter agreed. "He didn't go by Connolly." He gave Johnson a bewildered look. "Is that his real name?"

"It is now," Johnson confirmed. "He had it legally changed, so don't worry. When you hired him, he wasn't using an alias or anything like that."

"Well, that's good to know," Carter said with feigned relief, "but let's get one thing straight. *I* didn't hire him. A man named Ed Stansky did; and when Ed got sick and had to step down from his position, I merely honored the original agreement that the two of them made."

"I take it you didn't care much for – let's just call him Steve to avoid confusion."

"No, I didn't care for him all that much," Carter declared, "but what's that got to do with anything? Is it against the law now to change your name?"

"Not at all," Johnson assured him, "but when a person does change his name, it appears that he has something to hide. We just want to learn more about him. So tell me. Why didn't you like him?"

"He wasn't a team player," Carter snapped without hesitation. "That's the problem with these track people. They perform as individuals and never really establish what it's like to work with others. Did you play sports, detective?"

"Football at A&M," Johnson answered.

"My point exactly, a real sport that demands dedication and teamwork." Carter clasped his hands together and leaned back with an expression to show that he was quite proud of himself.

"I ran track too," Johnson added. "The mile relay. I was the anchor, but without my teammates, we wouldn't have been very good?"

Carter unclasped his hands and leaned forward. "What else do you want to know about – Steve?"

322

"For one thing, why did he leave?"

"There was a problem," Carter answered, "and in everybody's best interest – including his – he just moved on."

"Was he ever charged with anything?" Johnson inquired.

"Not officially," Carter said.

"But he was accused of things," Johnson concluded.

"A number of things," Carter replied quickly. "A number of things."

"Like what?" Johnson asked casually.

"I'm not sure that I'm at liberty to say," Carter said indignantly.

"Was there a cover-up?" Johnson implied.

"Mr. Johnson," Carter spat out with an emphasis on mister to qualify his disrespect, "I don't appreciate your implications one bit."

"I have two children," Johnson interrupted. "My daughter is a teacher in Arizona, and my son is a student at UCLA. I've spent a lot of time dealing with school related issues – both as a parent and as a police officer. I'm more than familiar with how things are done."

"UCLA," Carter said approvingly as he tried to divert Johnson's attention. "Does he play basketball?"

"Medical student," Johnson retorted with resentment for Carter's assumption that all blacks are good at basketball.

"Anyway," Carter continued unwillingly, "sometimes it's just best to remove the problem and avoid all the unnecessary hassle."

"So you just swept things under the carpet and sent Steve packing," Johnson said bluntly.

"If that's what you want to call it, fine. We just felt that it was the right thing to do."

"Since there were a number of accusations," Johnson reminded Carter, "and no formal charges, there's no reason not to tell me." He gave a big toothy grin and put his elbows on the desk. "If you don't tell me, I'll just find someone who will."

"Suit yourself," Carter said dejectedly. "There was some petty stuff which dealt with his lessons plans and how he conducted himself in the classroom, and that's bad enough; but he was also accused of buying alcohol for minors – for students. I don't have to tell you. That's not a petty problem."

"And you had proof of this?" Johnson inquired politely.

"All the petty stuff was documented," Carter responded quickly. "As for buying alcohol for students, we had witnesses."

"And they were reliable?"

"Very reliable. One witness was a close, personal friend."

"I see," Johnson said. "And that close friend's name?"

"I can't really remember," Carter answered honestly. "It was Frank something."

"Stewart?" Johnson added.

"Yea," Carter answered, "that sounds about right, but he wasn't the only witness."

"Of course," Johnson agreed, "but he must have been your primary witness?"

"He was just a witness. That's all," Carter said defensively. "He volunteered information, and we appreciated his cooperation."

"So," Johnson added with skepticism, "you can remember the details but the name slipped your mind."

"Exactly," Carter said very deliberately. "Is this investigation of yours about Steve or about Frank?" he asked harshly.

Johnson completely ignored Carter as he stated emphatically, "Providing alcohol to minors is a pretty serious offense; shouldn't the perpetrator have been fired?"

"I can't argue with that, but the school board didn't want any negative publicity," Carter said almost apologetically.

"Hmm," Johnson mused. "I know how those things can be." He stood up and pushed his chair in. "I'll need to talk to some other staff members – members who knew Steve of course." He paused but just slightly. "Are there any around?"

Carter was observant enough to catch Johnson's signals. If he didn't provide him with a list of names, Johnson would question everyone on staff and cause a great deal of embarrassment to the school. "Let me go through my files," Carter said reluctantly, "and I'll come up with some names. But I must warn you. People are very reluctant to talk about things."

"And you'll provide me with the names of those who knew Steve but no longer work here as well?" It was more of a statement than a question.

"I'll do my best," Carter replied unable to hide just how annoyed he had become.

Before the day was over, Johnson had spoken to over a dozen people or more, all claiming that Steve's departure had been a mystery to them. Only one, a young man named Henry, had anything of interest to say.

"I knew Steve pretty well," Henry said as he stirred the coffee which sat before him. They had retired to an unoccupied office to insure total privacy, and Henry's voice trembled slightly as he spoke. "I never knew what happened either. It wasn't until Steve came back that I got the whole story."

"He came back?" Johnson asked as he reared his head to indicate his surprise.

"For a funeral," Henry quickly added. "He tried to stay low key, but I caught up to him." Henry smiled and then set his hands as if they were pistols and fired in Johnson's direction. "And I pressed him. He didn't want to talk about things, but I got him to open up."

"I'm interested," Johnson said. "What did he have to say?"

"This has to be between you and me, Mr. Johnson. No one else can know that I've told you this."

"It'll be off the record," Johnson assured him.

"I'll give you the short version, and you'll get the gist of the story," Henry said while looking around and checking for imaginary spies. "There was grade tampering; and when Steve found out about it, he threatened to go public."

"So he was set up," Johnson reacted with alacrity.

"It concerned a football player," Henry continued. "They take sports very seriously in this state, Mr. Johnson, especially football."

"I know," Johnson granted. "I went to school in this state."

"No kidding," Henry said with legitimate interest. "Where abouts?"

"Tallahassee. I'm a graduate from Florida A&M," Johnson volunteered.

"Wow!" Henry exclaimed. "How'd you end up in California?"

"My wife is from California," Johnson answered. "We met in college, and things just seemed to lean towards the West."

"And you're still married?" Henry asked unashamedly.

"For a very long time," Johnson said proudly. "And I have two kids. In fact, one is currently attending UCLA."

"Impressive," Henry said pleasantly. "What's he taking up?"

"Besides space?" Johnson joked. "He's a medical student."

"And the other one," Henry asked, "older or younger?"

"Older," Johnson answered with pleasure, "and teaching out in Phoenix."

Henry shook his head approvingly. "You must be very proud."

"Oh sure," Johnson answered casually. "They're good kids."

"I meant of yourself," Henry said emphatically.

Johnson just nodded to show his appreciation and then gave a slight smile. "Did you know a Frank Stewart?"

Henry sighed and then answered. "I knew who he was, but he wasn't a friend." He pursed his lips and then took a deep breath. "From what Steve told me, they used to be good friends."

"But something happened," Johnson prodded.

"I never got the full story as to why he came forward to testify against Steve, but I learned that he was one incredible backstabber."

"In what way?" Johnson inquired.

"Turns out that he slept with Steve's girlfriend," Henry replied. "That's pretty low."

"I agree," Johnson conceded, "but it takes two to Tango."

"Well, needless to say," Henry continued as if he had ignored Johnson's most recent statement, "Steve didn't have a lot of nice things to say about his old pal."

"I'm sure he didn't," Johnson whispered more to himself than to his partner in conversation. "Well, Henry," Johnson said as he stood up and extended his hand, "you've been a great help. Thank you."

"So is Steve in some kind of trouble?" Henry asked as Johnson headed for the door.

"This is all background information," Johnson said as he stopped and turned to face Henry. "I just put the notes together and let the higher authority decide." He left the room rather abruptly and left the building even faster. He saw no need to seek out those who no longer worked at the school, so he started for a more familiar location. It was a three-hour drive to Tallahassee, and he was anxious to find a place for the night, call his wife on the phone, and look up an old friend.

***

There were only a few areas where traffic could match the gridlock of California; therefore, the trip went even faster than expected. His flight to New York did not leave till noon the next day, so he felt no urgency as he settled down at the local Holiday Inn.

He wanted to talk longer with his wife when the call finally got through, but both agreed to keep it brief to save on expenses. His per diem covered only food and travel with all personal calls coming out of his own pocket. This entire journey seemed all too unnecessary, and like that pompous ass of a principal had said, could have been handled by phone. His comments about person to person interviews may have had a ring of truth about them, but they served as a ruse to cover the indignity that he was forced to endure by an overzealous D.A. and a captain who really had it out for him.

A light dinner helped settle his stomach, and a drink with an old friend helped settle his nerves. "How's it going, Larry?" Johnson graciously asked as his friend took up the seat next to him. "Still drink bourbon?"

"On the rocks," Larry acknowledged as he shook his old friend's hand. "I see that affirmative action is still working in your favor," he said with a smile. "You're a detective who gets to take cross country trips."

"Still an asshole," Johnson blurted out with no fear of offending the other patrons at the bar.

"Things will never change, Bob." He held his freshly poured drink forward and prompted Johnson to do the same. "Seriously, it's great to see you. It's been too long." He took a healthy sip and wiped his tongue across his upper lip. "How's that lovely wife of yours and those two great kids?"

Johnson showed his appreciation with a slight glance and then a drag from his drink as well. "Everybody is doing just fine, and you?"

"Hanging on to wife number three," Larry replied earnestly. "I think this one's gonna work out."

"I hope so," Johnson agreed. "Those alimony checks have to cut into those hefty fees that you big shot lawyers make."

"You ain't lying, but forget about me. What's this trip all about?"

Johnson took another swig from his cocktail and then gently put his glass on the bar. "I can't be sure," he said with total uncertainty. "Some college kid decks this guy, and the guy dies from a heart attack."

"Manslaughter," Larry interjected.

332

"Normally," Johnson answered, "or maybe even nothing at all. As it turns out, however, the college student has a bit of a mysterious past – even a name change; so this has our new D.A. throwing around terminology like 'elaborate plot' or 'conspiracy.'"

"Guy sounds like a real tool," Larry declared before taking another manly sized gulp of his bourbon. "But we've got em everywhere, youngsters looking to make a mountain out of a mole hill and in the process a name for themselves."

"Yea, I just came from that high school down in Palmetto where this guy Connelly used to be a teacher."

"Connelly is the suspect's name?" Larry asked to verify his understanding of the situation.

"That's his name now; it was different when he was a high school teacher," Johnson stated politely.

"Wait a minute," Larry said as he put his palms forward. "You said he was a college student."

"And he was," Johnson continued. "But before that he was a teacher under a different name."

"It does make him appear a little suspicious," Larry contended. "What does Connelly have to say about all this?"

"Claims the name change was nothing more than a way to get a fresh start on things. He also claims that he's being backed by the mother of some kid he used to teach."

"While using the other name," Larry interrupted.

"You can see why things are confusing," Johnson stated while moving his head from side to side.

"What do you think, Bob?" Larry asked very slowly.

"I'm not sure what I think," Johnson admitted. "I talked with the redneck principal who claimed that Connelly was let go for a series of violations that the school kept quiet, and most of the other people I interviewed were pretty much in the dark about everything. But there was this one guy. This one guy who said Connelly was set up because he was about to go public about grade tampering."

"So they blackmailed this guy with some trumped up charge."

"Perhaps," Johnson said, "but here's another interesting thing. The guy who testified against Connelly just happens to be –"

"The dead guy," Larry said, finishing the sentence.

"The dead guy," Johnson repeated.

"It's pretty convoluted," Larry declared, "and it's still kinda weak, but I can see some upstart using this to jumpstart his career."

He drained his drink and signaled for another. "All that aside, why do they have you doing all the bullshit leg work?"

Johnson sneered as he took another strong pull on his drink. "What do you think?"

"You pissed somebody off; that's for sure."

"For sure," Johnson added. "It's the story of my life."

"Just think," Larry stated as he grabbed his new drink, "if you had finished law school, you could be pissing off judges and politicians."

"Oh, I've pissed off a few of them too," Johnson concurred. "There's no boundary to whom I offend."

"To equal opportunity offenders," Larry shouted as he hoisted his glass into the air.

"Here, here," Johnson sang out as he glanged his friend's glass.

The rest of the evening was filled with idle chatter about how the Southern universities were on the brink of dominating college football because of the acceptance of once forbidden black players. Although Johnson agreed with this assertion, he expressed his new allegiance for the West coast teams – with the exception of the Southern California Trojans who rivaled his son's UCLA Bruins.

Johnson dropped off the rental car at the airport and boarded his flight in plenty of time for his next stop on the East coast. By three o'clock, he had passed through the gates of Kennedy Airport and hailed a cab to take him to his next destination. When seven o'clock rolled around, Johnson had showered and dressed in more casual attire. His cab dropped him off at a quaint little bar and grill where he sat down and waited for his prearranged appointment to arrive. By half past the hour, he was drinking his second cup of coffee and conducting an informal interview with a fellow citizen of peace, who immediately insisted that they get on a first name basis.

"So how long have you been doing this, Jack?" Johnson was reluctant to dive into any type of interrogation without showing some respect for a colleague by indulging himself with some casual conversation.

"Too long," Jack said as he sipped his beer. "Are you sure, I can't get you something, Bob?"

"Maybe later," Johnson said sincerely. "Right now, coffee is fine."

"Suit yourself," Jack complied, "but if you change your mind, don't hesitate to ask."

Johnson nodded and then slid a photo of Steve Connolly across the table. "Do you recognize this guy?" he asked softly.

"Yes I do," Jack answered quickly. "Is he in some kind of trouble?"

"He might be," Johnson replied. "He's been accused of beating up some guy and then allowing him to die."

"Allowing him to die," Jack said with no attempt to hide his confusion.

Johnson smiled. "This could turn out to be a whole lot of nothing, but the guy had a bad heart and died from a massive coronary."

"And you're trying to establish a motive," Jack added confidently

"Exactly," Johnson concurred.

"So this is what it's all about," Jack decided. "You could have done this over the phone and saved yourself a trip." He sat forward in his chair and took a long sip on his beer.

"It gets a little complicated," Johnson interjected. "First of all, there's a problem with his name."

"His name?" Jack asked, once again unable to hide his confusion.

"Out by us," Johnson answered slowly, "we know him as Steve Connolly." He hesitated. "I believe he went by a different name when you knew him."

"Yes, he did," Jack conceded. "Why the alias?"

"We're not sure," Johnson said as he reached for his coffee, "but it might be important. For now, let's just refer to him as Steve and make it easier on ourselves."

"Fine," Jack agreed. "So what do you want to know about Steve?"

Johnson smiled and placed his hands – palms flat – onto the table. "Just tell me anything that you might think is relevant."

"Relevant?" Jack said, slightly taken aback. "Relevant to what he did?"

"Just tell me anything you can," Johnson retorted with remorse in his tone, "and I'll decide what's relevant."

Jack made his comments short but precise. Steve was a good reporter, who – according to Jack – had tried to give legs to a story when there were none. According to Jack, Steve drank too much, whored around, and too often allowed his big mouth to get the best of him. And according to Jack, Steve Connolly had gotten in way over his head and refused to back down when he should have.

"You know what it's like to get caught up in things," Jack said, doing his best not to sound condescending. "Sometimes you have to compromise."

Johnson smiled. "I've been caught up in things myself from time to time." He pursed his lips and then took a deep breath. "But I've never compromised."

Jack gave nothing in response, but his expression made it clear that he did not like Johnson's implications. "I'm a good cop," he finally said. "I had nothing to do with all that …" He paused and searched for the appropriate word. "Controversy," he stated very slowly. "I had nothing to do with any of it."

"But you might have known some who did," Johnson said in the form of a statement and not a question.

Jack swallowed and then answered in a somewhat hoarse whisper. "Perhaps."

"And like a good cop, you wouldn't turn on your fellow officers – on those officers who did get involved," Johnson let these words sink in and then took another sip of coffee.

"That's right," Jack stated very slowly. "The evidence was pretty weak, and I wasn't about to get my ass in a sling."

"And how long have you been a sergeant?" Johnson added.

"If you're saying that I traded testimony for a promotion…"

"I'm sorry," Johnson interrupted, now realizing that he was drifting a little too far from the topic. "Sometimes I get carried away."

Jack shook his head to indicate an acceptance to Johnson's apology and then lifted his empty glass to indicate that he wanted another.

"Did Steve ever talk about a guy named Frank Stewart?"

"Don't tell me," Jack said somewhat sarcastically, "let me guess. That's the dead guy?" Johnson shook his head affirmatively. "Not favorably," Jack said, "but I can't believe that Steve would do anything to the guy."

"Did he ever make any threatening comments?" Johnson asked calmly.

"Oh sure," Jack answered with equal calm. "But I never took him serious. Besides, he usually made those comments after a few belts."

"Hmm," Johnson muttered, "and you said that Steve drank a lot."

"I did," Jack responded curtly.

"So you're saying that Steve had a drinking problem."

"No worse than mine," Jack said abruptly. He regretted these words the instant he had let them roll off his tongue since his own indiscretions should have remained private. He put his glass down, looked directly at Johnson, and very slowly said, "He may have kept a few late nights which made him late for work sometimes, but he never drank on the job."

"And stuff like that doesn't relate to motive," Johnson said assuredly.

"Unless he killed this guy in a drunken rage," Jack added, well aware that this was not the case.

"We have a witness to the contrary," Johnson said, sounding too much like a lawyer. He leaned back in his chair and put his hands behind his head. "I'll be honest with you, Sergeant," he stated in a feigned attempt to appear formal. "This whole thing is the result of some overzealous ADA who would love nothing more than to make a name for himself."

"So you don't think Steve did anything wrong."

"I think he wanted to put one major hurtin' on Frank Stewart," Johnson said with sincere confidence, "but I don't think he really wanted him to die."

"I don't either," Jack agreed. "But if he caused the heart attack…"

"That's where it gets tricky," Johnson surmised. "If he was torturing Stewart, or if he kept on hitting him after Stewart pleaded for him to stop, then you might have something."

"But you have a witness who says otherwise." Jack grinned salaciously, well aware that Johnson was about to make that exact statement.

"Yea, we do," Johnson replied, "and there's no reason not to believe her, but there's a gap in her story – a few minutes when something else could have happened."

Jack folded his arms and then said with authority, "There's another way to look at this. If Steve knew about the victim's condition, and he went there with full intention of provoking a heart attack, then …"

"Then it's premeditated," Johnson agreed with an affirmative nod of the head. "And that is exactly what our ADA is trying to prove."

"And that gap in the witness's story can prove to be harmful," Jack responded like a first year law student.

"Could be," Johnson concurred.

"I find it all rather ironic," Jack announced with a bit of satisfaction in his tone.

"How so?" Johnson inquired.

"When Steve ran with that story about Valentine, he was trying to make a name for himself by making a mountain out of a molehill."

"But that story did turn out to be a big thing," Johnson corrected.

"It sure did," Jack said, unable to conceal his laughter, "but he didn't know that at the time."

"And if he had just held back, he'd still be working for the newspaper." Johnson did nothing to mask his condescending tone, and Jack did nothing to display his resentment. A full minute passed without either man speaking. "Did he piss off any cops out in California?" Jack asked, finally breaking the reticent stalemate.

"None that I know of," Johnson replied quickly, "but he wasn't a reporter. He was a college student."

"Yea, that's what you told me." Jack pressed his hands to make a steeple and propped the structure under his chin. "Anything else you want to know?"

Johnson took a long sip of his coffee and pushed the mug aside as he set it on the table. "Did you ever see him lose his temper?"

"Other than throwing something at the television set when his team was getting beat – I never saw him lose it. But he was pretty passionate when it came to things – especially things he believed in."

"Like that story he pursued when he was warned to back off," Johnson added stiffly.

Jack said nothing at first but then let a guttural "Yea," leak out. "Look," he said trying to dismiss the earlier implication, "he was really hired to be a sports writer, and to be honest with you, he was pretty damn good at it. That's where his real passion was, and I wish he had kept it there."

Johnson may not have cared for the corpulent officer, but he did find him to be helpful – in more ways than one. He not only had a better insight on Steve Connolly, but he realized – once again – that a decision he had made some time ago – a decision that pushed him down the chain of command, and a decision that gave his superiors

the incentive to send him on meaningless assignments like this one –
had been the correct decision, and he never regretted the choice
which he had made.

"Are you going to talk to anybody at the paper?" Jack asked.

"Do you think there's anyone who can give me anything I need?
Johnson countered politely.

"Probably not," Jack said. "He didn't get close to many people at
the paper. He did take some college kid under his wing, but Steve
was gone before the two really got to know each other."

Johnson smiled and even chortled slightly. "I think that kid
you're referring to, did all right."

"How so?" Jack inquired.

"Do you remember about the trouble they had out at Citra
University?" Johnson asked.

"It was pretty hard not to," Jack answered. "They were one step
away from the National Guard..." He paused and then sighed. "You
know like Kent State and everything."

"Yea," Johnson said and then sighed. "Things can get pretty
ugly."

"I didn't know that Steve was out there at the time. Did he have anything to do with it?"

"He had nothing to do with the demonstrations, but he might have helped with the investigations into the college president's embezzlement."

"Yea, that sounds like something he would do."

"Well, he turned everything over to some young reporter."

"T.J.Kingsley," Jack said enthusiastically.

"So you know him?" Johnson asked.

"I know *of* him," Jack answered. "But I never put it together till now. Whenever Steve mentioned this guy, he called him Tommy; and he never used his last name." He nodded his approval. "You gonna talk to him."

"I've made an appointment," Johnson said. With that, Johnson bid his farewell and returned to his temporary quarters. He thought about cancelling his meeting with Kingsley, for he was sure that nothing more could be added. When an earlier flight proved to be impossible, he kept his appointment – more out of courtesy than importance.

Kingsley's office had the standard clutter, which offices of hard workers usually had; and as Johnson looked around, he couldn't help but be amused. "I know that you're a busy man, Mr. Kingsley," Johnson said, slightly uncomfortable to address one so young as mister.

"Call me T.J.," the young reporter interrupted, putting Johnson at ease.

"Thank you," Johnson said. "I have a daughter older than you."

"Look, detective, I know why you're here. Ever since that debacle out in California, the school's student body president has been in touch with me; so I know what happened to Frank Stewart, but couldn't this have been handled over the phone?"

Johnson laughed. "That seems to be everyone's point of view, but let's not worry about it. I'm here to talk about Steve Connolly."

"Yea, I heard he was charged," Kingsley said. "What do you want to know?

"You're one of the few people who knows Steve Connolly by more than one name."

"That's true," T.J. replied, "but I got to know him a lot better when he was using Connolly as his last name."

347

"Because of the situation out at Citra."

"Absolutely," T.J. concurred. "Before Steve left this place, he said he would help me anyway he could." He stopped, thought for a moment, then continued. "I just didn't expect it to be in the manner that it was."

"So you guys weren't that close."

"We would have been," T.J. declared, "if he had stayed around."

"But you kept in touch after he left."

"Nope," T.J. corrected. "I hadn't heard from him at all until he contacted me about what was going on at the school."

"I see," Johnson said, more to himself than to Kingsley.

"I don't know what you're looking for, detective, but I can tell you this. Steve – Steve Connolly that is – was at peace with himself when I saw him. He was never at peace when he worked here."

"Did you guys talk about things when you were out there?"

"Nothing personal," Kingsley responded quickly. "We were way too busy for that."

"So he never mentioned Frank Stewart."

"I have to admit that I didn't know who Frank Stewart was until I found out about his death." T.J. leaned back in his chair. "I wish I could tell you more about Steve as a person, but I didn't know him that well. But I'll say this: when he put his mind towards something, he was relentless about it."

"Like the story that got him fired."

"And the one that jump started my career," Kingsley added. "I'm going to let you in on a secret. That whole thing out there in California was all his. The person who came forward with the incriminating evidence wouldn't have done so without substantial compensation."

"So you're saying that the source was being paid."

"Exactly," Kingsley replied.

"So who put the money out – the paper, Connolly?"

"It certainly wasn't the paper. They would barely cover *my* expenses, and it couldn't have been Steve. He didn't have that kind of money." He leaned forward like a small child about to tattle-tell on a friend. "But he must have known somebody who did."

"So where did you come in?" Johnson asked.

"Steve needed credibility, and he believed that I could give it to him."

"So you were nothing more than a front," Johnson conjectured.

"At first," Kingsley admitted, "but when things started to get heated on the campus, I was always the first reporter on the scene."

"Thanks to Steve Connolly."

"For sure, but I still wrote the articles – the ones that made it back to this paper, and it was this paper that thought the story had legs."

"So they ran with it, and you got some notoriety," Johnson said curtly.

"And thanks to me, the story had credibility as well," Kingsley responded somewhat arrogantly.

"That it did," Johnson concurred. "And Connolly just stayed behind the scenes."

"He wasn't looking for notoriety – even though I offered to give it to him. He said that he already had his chance, and that ship had sailed." Kingsley took a deep breath and then let it out. "It could have been a way to get back in, but he wanted no part of it."

"Do you think he murdered Frank Stewart?" Johnson asked so abruptly that it caught Kingsley off guard.

"I don't know," T.J. said calmly. "I've learned one thing with this job and it's that you never really know someone – not completely anyway."

Johnson stood, shook the young reporter's hand, and went on his way. He was glad to have met him, but what little they talked about didn't add much to what he already knew. Steve Connolly was an enigma: a person who did what he believed in, regardless of the consequence; but a person who was possessed by personal demons, which may have proved disastrous.

The flight back to California was a peaceful one, and Robert Johnson was glad to be home. Dinner with his wife and a phone call to each of his children rounded out a perfect day. His report was truthful and accurate, void of any spin that might be swayed, based upon his opinion. As a former student of the law, he knew how he would handle things; but those days were long gone, and the fate of a young man fell into somebody else's hands. Robert Johnson had done his job, and like always, it was a job well done.

Part 8

The Rookie

As he stepped off the bus and had the shackles removed from his hands and legs, he could feel the eyes watching him before he slowly ambled across the yard. His trial had had some notoriety; and since these men were not cut off from the world entirely, it was clearly possible that they all knew who he was. He had felt violated by the fetters which restricted him on his journey, but he did not feel violated by the gawps that measured his every move.

His first stop was at the clinic, where he was given the mandatory physical exam and dental check-up. After a brief orientation, he was taken to his living quarters; and with a mandatory twenty-five years as part of his life sentence, he expected these living quarters to be his home for quite some time. He stood in line with the others when he went to eat dinner, and he stayed in line as he was marched back to his dorm. He said very little that first night and only spoke if someone spoke to him. The next morning he reported to his classification officer. After his records had been reviewed, he was told to report to the prison library and begin his work detail.

Although the assignment suited him nicely, it could not remove the disgrace of imprisonment. The others didn't show any resentment because the choice of assignment was clearly not his own. Besides, he could help them in certain areas, and that wasn't a bad thing.

Every place had to have a rookie; and until somebody else came along, he was it. They all called him rookie, even the ones who weren't the typical hard-timers. It didn't bother him; and he knew that if he wanted to get along – to survive – he would have to answer to that name and accept any stigma associated with the title.

"It's rather ironic," he said as he spoke to his friend over the phone. "They've actually got me doing what I was trained to do."

"When can we come and visit you?" she asked.

"Saturday and Sunday are the visiting days, but you would need to make it in the afternoon. Since the library is open on the weekends, they need me to run the place in the mornings."

"So you work every day," she said with aghast.

"Yea," he lamented slightly, "but my work is pretty easy compared to what some of these guys have to do."

"Is it scary?" she asked, not masking her concern.

"Sometimes," he admitted, "but I see things in a different light during the day. Most of the guys really do wanna learn, so they're pretty cool about stuff. At night, I try to stay to myself. I avoid all card games or anything that might cause confrontation."

"I'm glad to hear that," she exulted.

"So how's our boy doing?" he asked, tersely changing the subject.

"He's good," she replied with alacrity. "If he were here, I'd put him on."

"They have a phone log we have to sign," he said flatly, "so I can make only one call a night – and we can talk for only so long. When you speak to him, tell him I'll try to call tomorrow – if the line isn't too long."

"I'll take care of it," she promised, "and we'll both try to make it on Sunday, if that works for you."

"You can be sure of one thing," he said facetiously.

"What's that?" she asked warily.

"I'll be here."

She laughed and then whispered, "Take care,"

***

The sun was high in the sky, beaming down on the coal black pavement; and steam from an earlier rainstorm could still be seen rising into the air as a yellow bus pulled up and parked by the curb. Its roof was rusted, the sides were dented, and the stench of perspiration reeked throughout the seats. Shoulder to shoulder, blue-shirted convicts sat in quiet anticipation of the day's labor and looked at the floor, which was covered with cigarette butts and blotches of tobacco juice. The rain had delayed their morning's work, and now it would be more humid because of it. Each man, who sat awaiting the orders to depart, was well aware of the conditions.

One by one each person stepped off the bus and grabbed a broom or a shovel from the temporary rack which sat by the right of the door. In groups of two, they set out to clean the sidewalks and remove any other roadside debris. One swept while the other used a make shift dustpan to clear the area of any accumulated trash. Papers and crushed cans were picked out of the gutter, and the wayside litter baskets were emptied and readied for the next day's use by the few conscientious passersby who cared about the environment.

355

Several people had walked by while the prisoners were working, and despite the fear, which these detainees innately instilled in everyone, the locals were all pleased with the work that was being done. An elderly woman got close enough for her favorable comments about cleaner streets to be heard; however, a younger woman with her son in hand stopped twenty feet short of the work detail and crossed the street. A few of the inmates started to wave and smile, but a sharp stare by one of the guards and a quick reappearance of his shotgun sent them back to their assignments. Only those who were classified as "minimum security" were allowed outside the fence with the exception of a few "medium security" inmates when the number of workers had gotten too low. Regardless of the prisoners' status, the guards had to show alert security measures to keep their minds and the minds of the spectators at ease. This job was usually done early in the morning before any crowds could gather, but the rain had spoiled that and allowed the civilian paparazzi access to the captive zone.

Within two hours, there wasn't a speck of dirt to be seen. All tools were returned to their proper places and accounted for as the work squad climbed aboard the bus. The stench of new perspiration would have been even more sickening if not for the lit cigarettes that acted as air fresheners, and each man indulged himself in a tobacco-filled paradise as the wagon made its way through the steamy atmosphere. When the bus jolted to a stop, the men jumped off one by one and grabbed a scythe or a rake from the rack. They chopped weeds and raked the dead grass as the heat started to become more intense. Occasionally a cloud would cover the sun and bring a moment of relief to the unprotected skin. Each time it happened, a small grin could be seen on the face of most, but soon followed by a frown with the event diminishing. The men were never denied water, and there was plenty of it; but it was never very cold and often smelled of sulfur.

In schools, it was called busy work – just something to keep the children occupied while the teacher was doing something else. Here it was called punishment, and the state made no apologies for it. Machines could have done everything so much easier, but the inmates had to have something to do. Sun and sweat were all part of their rehabilitation.

Lunchtime arrived at one o'clock when tuna sandwiches and lukewarm lemonade were served. Although the taste was most improper, the pangs of hunger overcame it. Some ate a half a sandwich at best, and others swallowed two. Many had severely chapped lips, and the lemonade made them sting.

The afternoon went slowly, more slowly than the morning; and the sun was at its brightest. As the cars drove along the road, the people within could see half-dressed bodies gleaming in the sunlight. Every muscle in their physiques was shown off, and a group of health food faddists smeared with mineral oil wouldn't look as good.

By four o'clock, a breeze picked up, and the high weeds that hadn't met an earlier death by the blade of a scythe or a sickle started to sway with the wind. They would be granted asylum for another day because the workday was over. Just as the temperature was becoming moderate, it was time to leave. The bus was loaded in the slowest manner possible as a few men stumbled up the steps; and the seats, which had been broiled by the sun, stuck to the men's perspiring bodies. The return trip always seemed faster, and soon the men would be back to start their routine for the evening.

Rain had not affected those who stayed inside the compound – at least not on this day. Before the early morning deluge, they had lined up two by two and marched without saying a word; for talking was not permitted while they were heading to work. These men may have been sheltered from the sun, but their jobs were no less tedious than and just as mundane as those on the road crew. As the huge doors opened and then slammed after the last person entered, it gave them all the eerie sensation that they were confined even more. Once they were inside and once their positions had been established, they were allowed to speak. The sounds echoed everywhere. The voices blended from individual speeches into a collage of confusion. There was no real conversation, only enough communication that dictated the task, which had to be done. It was no different from any other garment factory. It was hot, and the large exhaust fans kept it bearable at best. There were sewing machines, fabric cutters, and conveyor belts. The process was simple, and each man was assigned a particular duty. The hum of machinery became monotonous, and the heat became overwhelming; but the day was just beginning. This was more than a routine to fill the endless hours for those who had committed the more violent crimes. Theirs was a job that had to be done, and there were deadlines to meet and quotas to fill.

They had breaks, of course, where they could grab a smoke and chat for a moment or two with a fellow inmate or even with a very bored guard. However, nothing made the day go any faster.

Unlike the guards with the road crew, none of the guards inside the prison were armed. However, those who watched the perimeter were fully armed, and were more than happy to shoot an inmate if he got too close to the fence. Inside, there was no place to run, so the inmates just did their work.

For those convicts – inside or out – who did not meet the standards expected of them, they were sent to solitary. The prisoners and the guards alike called it the box, but those days of spending the night in a narrow wooden structure were a thing of the past. Modern confinement may have been more humane, but it was still solitary; and the inmates hated it. It made the day go by even more slowly, and soon it was the equivalent of the Chinese water torture. Confinement also meant a lack of privileges, and those incarcerated never wanted to lose a privilege.

At twelve, the factory workers were given their usual half hour for lunch, but it didn't seem to last that long. First, they stood in line and then squeezed eight at a table that was suited for six. When they finished eating some rather bland spaghetti, they stood outside the cafeteria and grabbed what fresh air they could before returning to the afternoon's work detail.

While some returned to the assembly lines, others were reassigned to the laundry room. It was even hotter there than in the garment factory, and the stench of dirty uniforms, rancid towels and soiled sheets – which had been piling up from the day before – made the air heavy and hard to breathe. The industrial strength washers purred with efficiency, and the driers bumped and bounced if any wet textiles knotted or clumped together.

No job at either location had been started that wasn't finished by the end of the shift, so the last hour was the busiest. At the factory, there was packaging to be done and materials to be put away. Everything was accounted for, from the biggest machine down to the smallest pair of scissors. One by one, each inmate walked past an assigned area and handed in the appropriate tool. In the laundry room, everything was folded neatly and ready for distribution to the general population before the next mountain of clothes and linens were brought in and dumped in a waiting bin.

The sun had been setting by the time the bus arrived back at the prison, and each passenger jumped from the vehicle and made his way to the barracks. There they collided with those who had spent the day manufacturing prison attire or sorting socks. It had been an easier day than usual since no one was exhausted, sunburned, or sick; but the stench of a day's work still clung to them.

Sanitary conditions were not at a premium, but each participant did his best to remove the grime that all members had become so used to accumulating. Clothes were gathered and sent to the laundry while "new" shirts were donned just in time for dinner. The men played their usual game of chance where names were thrown into a hat and a winner selected. The coveted prize of some extra dessert resulted from contributions by the losing participants. The choice cuisine was either smuggled out for later consumption or hoarded and used to buy favors whenever a favor was necessary.

Supper was always served promptly at half past six and completed no later than seven o'clock when all eating utensils were returned and counted before anyone was allowed to leave the cafeteria. When the entire process was completed, the men marched back to their bunkhouses and tried to have some form of entertainment for three hours before the lights were turned off. Radios were permitted as long as headphones or earpieces were used; and books, cards, and even an assortment of dirty magazines were always available. Television privileges were held to a minimum because the captive audience argued so much, but the occasional sporting event always managed to make it to the dorm. The guards often used television as a motivational tool to keep the inmates in check. If a game ran past lights out, lights would stay on, as long as there had been good behavior throughout the day. Of course, gambling was strictly forbidden; but the guards would often look the other way when a friendly wager was placed. Even a few guards partook in the practice themselves.

With everything being more out in the open, it was difficult for the inmates to sneak in drugs from the visitors' park or to build a still and create some jailhouse hooch. However, there were some, who were creative enough to obtain illegal substances; and several, who were willing to pay for the privilege. Most of the guards could be bribed with cigarettes, candy bars, or any loose cash that might float around. The inmates were well aware of the benefits they could receive by greasing a selfish palm or two and easily established the right relationships with the right people.

When the lights did go out, there were no complaints since the men needed enough sleep for an early morning rise. Specific jobs for all work details were selected at random, and the men never knew which job they would be given for the day. The only jobs which remained consistent were those jobs in the skilled areas. Many of the inmates had been trained in the culinary arts and were pressed to put those skills into practice. Highly educated inmates would be given the assignment to run the prison's library or to educate those who were uneducated. School was one of the few programs that remained non-compulsory, and there were many inmates who preferred a math lecture to swinging an ax or pushing a broom. School was only half a day, however, so those looking for higher education still had to put in a few hours on the manual labor force. Part time duties consisted of washing dishes, keeping the grounds clean, or gathering the garments from those who had put in a full day of toil.

This was their routine – day in and day out. They dressed the same, kept their hair short, and stayed clean-shaven. There was no sense of individuality, and the prisoners were discouraged from establishing any kind of unity or camaraderie. Those in charge believed that this dissuaded them from anything which might prove dangerous.

Things, however, were different on the weekends. All but a few of the jobs were suspended, and the men stayed up as late as they wanted. Some watched TV till the wee hours of the morning, and others played cards for the duration. Breakfast was provided at the usual time; but inmates, who elected to sleep rather than indulge in some gooey eggs and rubbery bacon, were permitted to do so.

It was during the weekends when visitors were allowed; and to the general population, this was the most important privilege of all. Along with visitation rights, the weekends provided a kind of solace since certain restrictions were lifted; and the guards were a bit more tolerant. If the inmates weren't spending time with those who came to see them, they were relaxing on the grounds through one method or another. There were plenty of radios blasting, and even a guitar or two could be heard. Guys shot baskets, threw the football around, and even organized a pick-up game or two. Some took the time to write letters while others waited to use the telephones. Since phone privileges were at a premium on the weekend, the early risers always got to the head of the line. It was more convenient to have religious services on Saturday afternoon, so services were provided with the assistance of outside clergymen; and attendance to the denomination of one's choice was accommodated. All this provided the inmates with a momentary reprieve from the bitterness of confinement.

Each of the barracks had a name, and each one represented a particular type of criminal. Since the assignments were usually based on custody, some dorms had factory workers only while others were filled with nothing but road-crew members. There was one exception, however. The smallest barrack on the compound – simply called H Dorm – was a mixed bag of all kinds. It housed only fourteen men, and each one had his own story.

Arthur Wesphol (known as Wes) had been convicted of premeditated murder and sentenced to life in prison. Wes had already spent twenty years in one reformatory or another and would probably die while incarcerated. Sunday was the most important day for him, and he always took a shower on Sunday. He was never sure if he smelled any better, but psychologically he always felt refreshed. He not only wore the cleanest outfit he could find but he sprinkled his hair with a bottle of cologne that he kept hidden under his mattress. Cologne was forbidden because it contained alcohol, and many inmates strained cologne through a loaf of bread and then drank it. Arthur Wesphol knew better than to consume that kind of poison; and because of that, the guards never confiscated his contraband. The lotion, combined with his normal stench and the odor of sulfur water, gave off a rather mechanical scent, like a well-oiled machine. Each wrinkle on his face represented a year he had spent behind bars; and the scars on his back recorded all the fights in which he'd been involved.

Wesphol had no family, so there were no visitors on the weekend; and his ritual was intended to please no one but himself. He never went very far without his cigarettes, and on this particular Sunday, he had a fresh, uncrushed pack in his top pocket. He flexed his shoulders and walked out to the yard where he met several of the convicts from other bunkhouses. They talked about the usual things but didn't talk for very long. Prison had been his home for quite a while, and he wondered if he could survive on the outside. He wouldn't know what it felt like to walk around without someone watching him. He could no longer remember. He put his hands over his face, but the dust still penetrated his nose; so he leaned back against a tree, hunched to the ground, and fell into a trance.

Stephen Stromsoe was a car thief, but not a very good one. He was caught after his second carjacking and sentenced to one year in prison. Each day, while he was out on the road, he admired all the lovely vehicles that sped by and longed for the time when he would be riding in one again.

His mother always came to visit him on Saturday or Sunday – but never on both days because it was too long of a trip. This week her visit was on Sunday; and as usual, she asked him if he had been eating well and that she had a place for him to stay when he got out. He lamented about how they treated him as though he didn't exist, and devoured the chocolate bar that his mother gave him. Stephen was afraid – afraid that one of the other inmates would hurt him, but he didn't tell his mother since he didn't want her to worry. In that respect – and in that respect only – Stephen Stromsoe was a decent individual.

He handed his mother a cup of coffee accompanied with a doughnut and got the impression that it was she who had not been eating well. "How's Dad?" he asked as they sat down on some wobbly bench.

"He's good," she lied. Her husband was very sick, and according to the doctors would not make it for the rest of the year. She couldn't tell him this because if she did, he would blame himself for his father's inevitable death. She couldn't afford to lose anyone else, so she didn't feel guilty about her falsehood. "He's sorry that he couldn't make it, but it's tough for him to get around."

"I understand," Stephen said. "How's the money holding out?"

"We'll make it," she answered, once again lying. "We've sold a few things, but nothing we couldn't live without."

Stephen knew that things were not as she described, but rather than press her, he let her go. He had already hurt her, and he didn't want to hurt her anymore.

Thomas Andrews and Hank Charles had it made. Whether it was Saturday or Sunday, they could always be found back at the bunkhouse playing with each other or with somebody else. On the

369

outside, they had been labeled as sex deviates. Andrews had raped a boy of fifteen, and Charles had masturbated in front of a large audience. On the inside, they were a commodity for several other inmates who needed to fulfill their sexual desires. Andrews loved to tell the story about his deflowering of that teenager, and his eyes would glare each time he described how his "cock swelled while in the boy's ass." Since the boy had been fifteen, Andrews was able to convince others – as well as himself – that he wasn't a child molester. Not many of the inmates liked Andrews, but they were happy to take advantage of his services. Charles was also disliked to some degree, but most of the population viewed him as a harmless little pervert and left him alone. The only person he seemed comfortable around was Andrews, and he was by his side constantly. The guards treated it all as some sick form of amusement and laughed about it rather than do anything to stop it. Each was given a ten-year sentence, and ten years in prison would be a pleasant punishment for both of them.

When one of the guards walked in and saw Andrews and Charles, he just turned and walked away. "Fucking faggots," he blurted to himself. "How can they live with themselves?" He stopped any other inmates from entering the barracks. "Don't go in there," he demanded. "There's nothing in there you wanna see." This was one of the perks that supervision granted the inmates on the weekend; but this one made the old guard sick, and he wanted to throw up.

The weekend was no better for Morgan Stone than any other day of the week. He tried to bother as few people as possible and serve his time the best way he could. Morgan Stone was considered to be a dangerous militant, and innocent people were hurt because of his beliefs. He didn't mean to hurt anyone; that was never his intention. He just wanted to wake some people up, to make them aware of all the bad stuff that was going on. There were people in the organization who called it collateral damage, but he wasn't one of them. However, he got the label, and he would serve the time.

"Whatcha looking at, Stone?" one of the younger guards asked.

"It probably wouldn't interest you," he said politely. "It's just something to help me pass the time."

"You need to try and get along with the others," the guard suggested. "I know this is no summer camp, but at least you're alive."

"I know," Morgan replied, "and I appreciate it. But it's not just this place, it's the whole planet."

"Still on that kick, huh," the guard insisted. "Get a hobby or take up basketball or something. That'll help pass the time."

"I shoot some hoops on occasion," Stone confessed, "but there are more important things to do."

"Like reading that book?" the guard asked.

"Like reading any book," Stone corrected.

The guard tipped his cap and then walked over to check on somebody else.

It all made perfect sense to Morgan Stone. While the other inmates were passing the time through recreational means on a calm Sunday, he was reading a book. Books meant a great deal to him because he was a thinker, and books made him think. He was also a dreamer, and books helped him dream. He kept thinking about what a lousy world it was, and he was dreaming of a better place – a better way. Things could change, and he could change them. He had to. It was his mission. Morgan Stone wanted freedom – not just freedom from his present situation, but freedom from the suppression of his beliefs and freedom from the inevitable problems that faced all forms of life. Morgan Stone was definitely a dreamer, and he would have fifteen years to envisage.

Milo Sternway was twenty-six years old, a graduate from college, and one very good football player. He had been selected by a professional team and paid an excellent salary. He was a bit flamboyant on the field, but he saw no problem with his antics. Whenever he was accused of a cheap shot, he just laughed it off.

His favorite incident had happened against Green Bay when he knocked a player unconscious after an interception. The man wasn't paying attention; but he should have been, so Sternway clocked him – clocked him good. The opposing coach took exception to it and legal or not, publicly declared that it was unnecessary. When questioned about it later, Sternway sniped, "I gave his boy an ass whoopin, and he didn't like it."

There were other incidents of bad behavior – on and off the field – but none of it ever bothered him, and whenever he had a brush with the law, he always managed to avoid any serious trouble. "That's why you have agents and why you have lawyers," he said in an interview. "I play hard – in football and in life – and if people get in my way, that's just too damn bad."

When Milo Sternway took a cheap shot with an unregistered weapon and paralyzed an innocent victim during the off-season of his fourth year, he couldn't laugh this one away; and his high priced agents and smooth talking lawyers couldn't help him either. Milo Sternway would spend the rest of his career in prison where the only football he played was a game of touch with some of the other local citizens.

His usual visitors were his mother and his aunt. The entourage, to which he had been so closely associated, no longer knew if he even existed; but he was still a big man to some of the less enlightened yet more impressionable youngsters at the resort.

"I can still kick just about anybody's ass," he said while waiting for his visitors to arrive. "That work out on the road. That ain't nothing. We used to work harder than that in training camp." The stories never changed, but there was always a new face to impress. Sternway still believed that he was important and still believed that he would get the chance to play again upon his release. "The league needs guys like me," he declared. "We bring excitement to the game, and the fans want excitement."

"Your uniform's the same color as mine," an older, less impressionable convict yelled from across the yard.

"Fuck you!" Sternway shot back.

The other inmate just laughed and kept walking. He knew that Sternway was finished because he had seen people like him before. Sternway tried to smile; but deep down inside, he knew it too.

Carl Freeman was given a six-year sentence for extortion. He had already served four, but his world was falling apart all around him. For two years, his wife paid him a visit every weekend, but eventually she stopped, divorced him, and ran away with another. The woman who had promised to wait forever could wait no more. He had aged considerably since the divorce, because now there was nothing waiting for him upon his release. His hair had turned white and was falling out in places. He was so depressed that he wanted to kill himself, but he didn't know how to do it. Weekends were the worst time for him because he was bored on the weekends, and with boredom, his depression increased. His face was blistered and red from too many days in the sun, and his back ached from too much heavy lifting. He wasn't sure if he could take it on the road anymore because he was a broken down man – old before his years.

"Move along," one of the guards said as Freeman stood and nonchalantly blocked one of the entrances to the visiting park.

"I'm not bothering anyone," he snapped.

"You watch your tone with me," the guard said harshly, "or you might be sitting in the box for a while."

If he thought it would kill him fast enough, he would have agreed to it, but Carl Freeman suffered from an ageless dilemma. He was tired of living but scared of dying. The lyrics from that old show tune rattled in his head till he was too feeble to stand. He sat on a hollow log and just watched the others. Four years ago, he was a human being, and he would not have suffered such humiliation – by anyone, let alone some punk correctional officer who hid behind his uniform. He took some pictures from his pocket and stared at them. The one of his wife was especially important to him. She was so beautiful, and she used to belong to him. The more he looked, the worst he felt; and he wanted to tear the picture up. He was a coward, however, and knew that he would regret it later. It was all he had. When he glanced over at the visitor's park, her image appeared but quickly faded. Like everything else, it was an illusion; and it just depressed him that much more.

At the age of forty-five, Fred Davenport was arrested for embezzlement. His indiscretion would cost him five years. His wife had been dead for a decade, and he was glad that she didn't see him like this. His son rarely missed a visit, and on this Sunday, he brought the grandchildren with him. Despite everything that went wrong, Fred Davenport was a happy man because he still had family; and not everybody could say that.

"So how's my little guy," Davenport sang as he threw his youngest grandson into the air. "And how's my favorite granddaughter?" he asked the six year old who stood so quietly next to her father. "We miss you, Grandpa."

"And I miss you guys, but as long I know that you're okay, then I'm okay."

"You've lost weight, Dad," the younger Davenport noticed.

"I'm not used to working on the road," the elder Davenport replied. "It's a little tougher than mowing the grass around the house."

"Aren't you too old for that kind of stuff?" his son asked disparagingly.

"Not according to the state," the father responded quickly. "It's not going to be forever, and think of the great shape I'll be in." He smiled and then whispered so it wouldn't bring attention to the children. "I did wrong, and I have to pay for it." He hugged his son and smiled, and for the rest of the visiting session, he told his grandchildren some funny stories.

Mark Kelso bought six years of prison life for attempted armed robbery. His younger brother was his only visitor; but since he lived so far away, he could only make it once a month. Mark was pleased when he saw him on this particular Sunday, and the two of them talked about anything and everything. Mark's only request was that his brother didn't make the same mistake he had, and so far, that request was being honored.

"You still in school?" Kelso asked more imperatively then interrogatively.

"Yes," his brother answered. "You always ask me that."

"And as long as the answer is yes, I'll be happy." He gave him a quick love tap to the shoulder. "So any girlfriends?" he asked in an attempt to lighten the conversation.

"You remember Carmen, don't you?"

"She's a fox," Kelso said approvingly.

"Well, we've been seeing each other for a few months."

"A few months!" Kelso shouted, "and you're just telling me now."

"I didn't want to jinx it," Kelso's brother said, a bit embarrassed.

"So is it serious?" Kelso asked with enthusiasm.

"I hope so," the younger brother declared. "I hope so."

"Me too, little brother," Kelso said with delight. "Me too."

Calvin Demerest was a product of a ghetto upbringing. He was a suppressed black man, who – at the age of nineteen – killed an equally suppressed black man simply because there was nothing better to do. His lawyer claimed that he was a product of his environment and as much a victim as the man he murdered. Prosecution saw otherwise, and the jury agreed. There was a certain level of controversy and some mild protest, but when several distinguished black authorities called the defense plea ludicrous, the public outburst disappeared.

Calvin had gotten religion since his incarceration, and the minister from his church was the only person to ever pay him a visit. The good reverend came on Saturdays when his schedule was lighter; and together, he and Calvin prayed. The pastor also took the time to perform some religious services for the other inmates as well. On Sundays, Calvin liked to sleep late but then spend the rest of the day in deep meditation. He was cordial to anyone who spoke to him but tried to keep himself ensconced in spiritual thought.

Irving Solter was arrested for drunk driving and fleeing the scene of an accident. His sentence wasn't a long one, but it would certainly cure him of both drinking and driving. He was a good-looking young man, aged twenty, and some heavy roadwork hadn't damaged his looks at all. He wouldn't allow it, and each day of work made him more determined to keep it that way. The sun had bleached his hair and tanned his skin, but he thought nothing of it. There were people who paid a great deal of money to go to some vacation resort to get the same results. Solter consoled himself with thoughts like these, but he could only fool himself so long.

His girlfriend was in the visiting area, and she looked good as always. He grabbed two cups of coffee and went to meet her. Her honey-blonde hair hung below her shoulders, and the outfit she was wearing should have been declared illegal. He put the coffees down and hugged her tightly. Her response was so favorable that he didn't want to let her go. His heart started to beat faster, and he swallowed hard before he kissed her. It was long and they pressed into each other seductively. "Do you have the money?" he asked. She smiled as she handed him a twenty-dollar bill. Together they walked to a special gate and spoke to the officer who stood before it. "You have my name on the list," he said, finding it difficult to contain his growing excitement.

"You have exactly one hour, Solter," the guard said flatly. "Use your time wisely." With that, Solter handed the officer the twenty-dollar bill. "Make it two," he amended, "but still use your time wisely."

It resembled a small motel with rooms that were no bigger than some oversized closets. Each came equipped with a small bed, a sink, a small-attached shower and toilet, and a very small chest of drawers.

"Do you feel strange doing it here?" he asked. She shook her head and then motioned for him to come closer. He removed his pants and obeyed her request. "I might be the only person in the whole joint who takes advantage of conjugal visits."

"Why is that?" she asked.

"I don't know," he replied. "They're barbarians in this place."

"Well the first hour is on the state," she said, "but the second hour is on me." She opened her arms wide. "Come here, you barbarian."

David Hailey was one of the best-liked men in the whole place. He was an accomplished guitarist, and the inmates – young and old – loved listening to him play. For the double murder of his wife and another man – after catching them in bed together – he was sentenced to life; and for doing what most of his jail mates thought was the right thing, he earned their universal respect. Hailey didn't talk about it much, and he was sorry for what he did; but he knew that he'd be spending his formidable years at the expense of the state. There were never any visitors, but it didn't bother him. On this Sunday, he was trying to cheer up those other guys who didn't have any visitors either. The first person he spoke to was Carl Freeman.

"I appreciate what you're trying to do, David, but I'm not in the mood for a psychoanalyst right now," Freeman said politely.

"I'm not trying to psychoanalyze you," Hailey said. "I just thought you could use someone to talk to."

"Go talk to the rookie," Freeman said. "He could probably use some advice."

"I *have* talked to the rookie," Hailey said. "He seems pretty well adjusted for someone who just got here a little while ago."

"You mean like you," Freeman retorted.

"I've been here for quite a while," Hailey countered.

"That's not what I mean," Freeman said and then sighed. "Go talk to the firebug. Nobody ever talks to him."

"Even I have my limits," Hailey said. "That guy is flat out crazy." After that remark, he slowly walked away.

Oscar Dole loved to make fires, and his passion for flames would cost him fifteen years. No one liked Oscar, and no one trusted him either; therefore, his weekends were spent alone, walking around trying to find someone who would talk to him. Each day Oscar had managed to sneak in a little more of what he needed. He had the time, and he made good use of it. He was also very good at what he did, and very careful not to be caught. The fourteen men in H Dorm were all convicted felons, but Oscar Dole was the most dangerous of them all.

***

"So what do you think?" the rookie asked, indicating that he was actually proud of the title.

"Why do they call you that?" she asked.

"Yea," her friend added. "You're no longer the most recent arrival at this place."

"They've modified the terminology," the rookie answered with authority. "They now refer to new entries as 'New Cock,' "

"That doesn't sound very flattering," she asserted.

Her friend smiled and then inquired, "Is it in reference to a rooster or a—?"

"Don't really know," the rookie interjected. "New correctional officers get the same calling card as well." He smiled and then leaned back as far as the rickety chair would allow before putting his hands behind his head. "As it turns out, I was the last person to be called 'rookie,' and I don't know why they stopped using it, but it makes me feel a little special to be the last." He dropped his hands and moved forward. "I'll take any accolades I can get."

"And how are things with your new students?" she asked while pantomiming the quotation signs around the word "students."

"They are a captive audience to say the least," he responded, trying hard not to laugh at his horrible pun. "They put forth a good effort, and they definitely want to improve themselves."

"And what about your recreational time?" his friend asked.

"The library keeps me pretty busy, but it also allows me first access to the daily paper and to several current magazines." The rookie shrugged and wrinkled the left side of his face. "But to answer your question, I read a whole lot; and I feel like I'm keeping up with things in the world. Hell, maybe I'll write a book."

They continued to joke about the situation with the hope that by laughing at the tragedy, which sat before them, they would forget that there was any tragedy at all. When it was time to go, he hugged them both; and it was at that moment when it became obvious to the two young visitors that the rookie wasn't so brave after all. "I love you guys," he said, "and I appreciate you being here."

"We'll try to get back in a couple of weeks," she said apologetically.

"Hey," the rookie chanted in a feeble attempt to mask his sorrow. "You've got your lives to live, and you've got important things to do." He nodded. "I'll try to call you during the week."

"I know," his friend concurred, "if the lines aren't too long."

"Don't worry about it," the rookie said. "Whenever you get the chance, it'll be fine. Like I keep saying, I'll be here."

Part Nine
The Student

It was cooler now, and her thoughts had returned to the present. She was relaxed and allowed the purity of her simple contemplation to take control. Although it was her favorite time of the day, she lamented that the day would soon be over. Once again that year had flashed before her eyes, and once again the benefit of a pleasant recollection was matched by the hurt that just wouldn't go away. She held Mac's latest letter tightly in her hand as if it contained some secret formula, which could reverse the clock. She wasn't ready to go back – not just yet, but the return was inevitable, so she gave in and replaced her soft meditation with another reflection about the past.

My remaining years at college proved to be the most rewarding. I was my own person, made my own decisions, and had become a responsible individual. There were still plenty of good times but nothing that frightened me or made me feel insecure. They were just that – good times. I made the Dean's List once as a sophomore, twice as a junior, and twice again as a senior. They were truly my biggest accomplishments, and I had every right to feel proud. Not even becoming the president of my sorority could equal them.

I attributed my success at college to hard work, determination, and confidence; and I attributed the attainment of those virtues to Steve Connolly. He gave me confidence when my spirit was broken and showed me that determination could be a good thing when expressed properly. As for hard work, I just assumed that he had done plenty of it in his life; and I found it to be beneficial.

I never stopped being idealistic, but I became a bit more grounded about accomplishing my goals – and those goals were achieved when they became an accessible reality instead of a pipe dream. I thanked Steve Connolly for that too. He helped me in many ways without even trying, and he would never realize just how much. I couldn't help but feel somewhat responsible for what happened to him, for it was I who convinced him to make that fateful trip. However, he would not stand for it and stopped me whenever I tried to bring it up. In time, it became a non-issue.

His case had provoked controversy right from the start. There were several who felt that it should never have gone to trial and even more who believed – after the outcome – that it was nothing short of character assassination. Then there were those who blamed the outcome on Steve himself, claiming that his refusal to let Dorothy MacIntyre hire a powerful lawyer instead of relying on a court appointed attorney, showed his extreme overconfidence and apparent naiveté.

The trial had all the ingredients of a three-ring circus and became a media spectacle before any real evidence was presented. Each side put forth a line of witnesses that could attest to Steve's personality. One group depicted him as an evil manipulator with a bad temper while the other rebuked those accusations and declared him nothing less than man of the year. When one faction called him smug and arrogant, the other countered with terms like humble and self-assured.

It was hard to pin point any one thing that worked against him the most. Steve had made threats, threats which had been documented; and he did appear to be hiding something with his use of an alias. He had motive; no one could deny that, but the proof of his actions was vague at best. I was tempted to perjure myself on his behalf and erase any doubt of his innocence by claiming that I had seen it all, but – not surprisingly – Steve was against it. Therefore, the question always remained. Had Steve Connolly been convicted because of what he *did* or because of what he *was*?

Further speculation arose when the verdict was announced. His absence of emotion was a sure sign of strength to his believers but a cold lack of remorse to his detractors. While many professed it was simply Steve's belief in a system which failed, too many found him callous and assumed his lack of demeanor as an admission of guilt. No one could read him, and soon people stopped trying. If he had some type of death wish, people stopped caring.

Steve never admitted to committing the crime, but he didn't exactly contest it either. When the question was posed to him in a post-trial interview, he said, "The court found me guilty, so it really doesn't matter." Steve carried this testimonial with him and told me that it was his stock answer if any of the other inmates pressed him for information.

When Mac and I saw him on that last Sunday, he looked a little older than he really was; and he definitely looked tired. I knew he wasn't happy, but he didn't want anyone to feel sorry for him. He accepted what had happened and tried to move on. After all, he had done that several times before.

Steve wasn't the only one who died in the fire, but he was the only one about whom I cared. I didn't know the others, and Steve never got the chance to tell me about them. However, I'm sure he would have. When I didn't hear from Steve by Thursday of that final week, I knew something was wrong; since those long lines he complained about would never have deterred him from getting in touch with one of us. I hadn't watched the news that night, so I found out about it when I saw the headlines in the morning paper. It was hard enough to believe that such a dangerous person could reside within the general population, but even harder to believe that he had stockpiled enough flammable material to firebomb the barracks with his Molotov cocktail. There was an immediate outcry for prison reform and even talk about a class action suit being sought by the relatives of the deceased. Since Steve had no family, there was no one to speak on his behalf. I requested that his remains be interred in a private cemetery, but my request was denied. It would always bother me, knowing that he lies in an unmarked grave in some prison boneyard.

There were no personal items to speak of, but before his incarceration, Steve gave me a portfolio that contained several of the things, which he had written over the years. It was gratifying to know that these too did not perish in the blaze. There were a number of short stories and several poems but, surprisingly, not one article that he had written while he worked for that New York newspaper. The poems reflected his love of nature and his attitude toward people in general; and the short stories – although fictional – in some way were autobiographical. As I went through each manuscript and dissected his poetry, I could sense the fuzzy parameters between reality and fantasy; and I often wondered if he actually knew the difference. Mac wanted me to make his writings a public matter, and Steve had never given me explicit directions to do anything with them at all. Therefore, it was entirely up to me, and I decided to keep them private. Someday, however, they might just surface for the world to appreciate.

Whenever the name, Steve Connolly, came up in conversation, people either knew him as the convicted murderer, who died in the prison fire; or they didn't recognize his name at all. Mac never stopped believing in Steve and often speculated that Steve had somehow escaped the blaze and was living a new life somewhere under a new name. In his own silly way, Mac was keeping Steve alive; and for that, I could never fault him; for in my own silly way, I was doing the same thing.

Made in the USA
Lexington, KY
12 May 2014